"You are our last hope to stay together," Bella said.

"What do you mean?" Philip ask[illegible]

She couldn't explain [illegible] their engagement. [illegible] end up in an orph[illegible]

Bella watched [illegible]ip's face. He was a hands[illegible] blue eyes and straw-colored ha[illegible]

So far she'd been timid with him, but her future and the future of her nephews depended on this man. She squared her shoulders and lifted her head high, then said, "Look, you placed the advertisement and I have arrived in answer to it. Are you going to marry me or not?"

Would he abandon her and the boys to their fate? She'd answered the advertisement expecting him to marry her. It'd never dawned on her that he might not have placed it.

She'd been wary of who might be at the end of the trail, but now that she'd met Philip, Bella knew God had a plan. If only Philip would see it, too, she'd be able to relax.

Rhonda Gibson lives in New Mexico with her husband, James. She has two children and three beautiful grandchildren. Reading is something she has enjoyed her whole life, and writing stemmed from that love. When she isn't writing or reading, she enjoys gardening, beading and playing with her dog, Sheba. You can visit her at rhondagibson.net. Rhonda hopes her writing will entertain, encourage and bring others closer to God.

Books by Rhonda Gibson

Love Inspired Historical

Saddles and Spurs

Pony Express Courtship
Pony Express Hero
Pony Express Christmas Bride
Pony Express Mail-Order Bride

The Marshal's Promise
Groom by Arrangement
Taming the Texas Rancher
His Chosen Bride
A Pony Express Christmas
The Texan's Twin Blessings
A Convenient Christmas Bride

Visit the Author Profile page at Harlequin.com.

RHONDA GIBSON

Pony Express Mail-Order Bride

HARLEQUIN® LOVE INSPIRED® HISTORICAL

Recycling programs for this product may not exist in your area.

ISBN-13: 978-0-373-42514-3

Pony Express Mail-Order Bride

This edition published by arrangement with Love Inspired Books.

www.Harlequin.com

Printed in U.S.A.

And the Lord, he it is that doth go before thee; he will be with thee, he will not fail thee, neither forsake thee: fear not, neither be dismayed.

—*Deuteronomy* 31:8

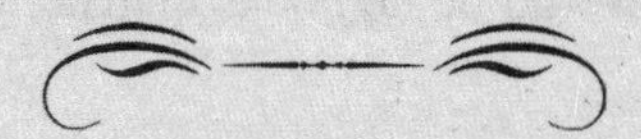

Thank you Michelle Matney for being such a great friend and critique partner. A special thanks to James Gibson for being my best friend and brainstormer, my books are not complete without you. Most importantly, I thank the Lord above. Without Him there would be no books by Rhonda Gibson.

Chapter One

Wyoming
January 1861

Philip Young's horse raced into the Turnstone Pony Express relay station. Extremely tired and chilled to the bone, Philip prepared himself to jump onto the cold saddle that awaited him. Relay stations were every ten to fifteen miles on the trail and this one had been fifteen. They were the places where Pony Express riders exchanged horses and continued on until they reached their home station.

Thankfully this was the last time he'd change horses before he would reach his family's farm and his home station. After a couple of days' rest at the home station, Philip would head on to the relay station he and his brother Thomas ran on the other side of Dove Creek.

He prepared to swing onto the saddle of the horse that the relay station manager, John Turnstone, held for him. "Glad to see you made it." John's grin spoke volumes of his pleasure and yet didn't tell him anything as to what he was getting pleasure from.

Philip paused with his foot in the stirrup. "What's going on?"

John's shoulders shook as he tried to hold back his laughter. He held the horse's head and said, "A special delivery arrived for you today by stage."

Philip dropped his foot back to the ground. "What kind of special delivery?" The need to get onto the waiting horse battled with his curiosity.

His job was to keep the mail going through, but then again John's curious behavior had him hesitating. Philip felt torn. John tossed him the reins to the horse Philip had just rode in on and then jumped on the back of the fresh mustang. "You best go inside and see. I'll finish your run. See you later."

Philip didn't take time to watch John and the horse speed away. He tied the spent horse to the hitching post by the barn and then hurried to the house. He took the steps two at a time.

The door banged against the wall as he called out to John's wife, Cara. "Cara, John says I have a package waiting and felt it was urgent enough to take the rest of my run."

His gaze fell on two little boys who sat side by side on the couch. Their big blue eyes stared at him in fear. He'd never seen them before and for a brief moment wondered as to their presence. Surely they weren't his special delivery.

"Cara isn't here. She went to check on Mrs. Brooks, their neighbor."

He looked to the kitchen, where a young woman with blond hair, blue eyes and a heart-shaped face stood in the doorway. He couldn't help but notice a dimple in her left cheek that came to life when she smiled. She motioned for him to join her. Hesitant, Philip moved into the warm kitchen.

John and Cara's house was small but comfortable. Most relay stations were manned by one man and consisted of a small shanty or barn for the man and Pony Express horses. This one wasn't like most; it held warmth and a sense of family.

He held out his hand. "I'm Philip Young."

She placed her smaller hand in his palm. Her fingers shook slightly. "Bella Wilson." Bella pulled her hand from his grasp.

Philip looked to the boys. They had stopped watching the adults and were playing with small wooden horses. His gaze returned to Bella. "Do you happen to know where the package is that the stage dropped off for me?"

A weak smile touched her lips. "I guess you're looking at it." At his frown, she pressed on. "I'm your mail-order bride."

"What?" Philip wished he could cover the shock in his voice, but he couldn't.

Bella twisted her hands in her skirt. "I answered your advertisement for a mail-order bride." Her cheeks flushed and her gaze darted to the little boys on the couch.

Philip didn't know what to think. She didn't appear to be lying, but he'd not placed an ad for marriage in any newspaper. He motioned for her to sit down at the small square table. When she did, he said, "I have no idea what you are talking about. I didn't place a mail-order-bride ad in any newspaper." Well, he had once—not for himself but for his brother Thomas.

She frowned and stood. "Hold on a moment." Her

skirt swished across the floor as she walked to where the boys sat playing. Bella dug around in the largest of the three bags that rested beside the couch and then she stood.

Dread filled him as she made her way back holding a small piece of newspaper. Bella handed it to him, still frowning. His gaze fell upon the writing.

> November 1860
> Wanted: Wife as soon as possible. Must be willing to live at a Pony Express relay station. Must be between the ages of eighteen and twenty-five. Looks are not important. Write to: Philip Young, Dove Creek, Wyoming, Pony Express relay station.

Philip looked up at her. He hadn't placed the ad but had a sinking feeling he knew who had. Just because he'd advertised for a mail-order bride for his brother, didn't give Thomas the right to do the same to him. "Did you send a letter to this address?"

Bella shook her head. "No, I didn't have the extra money to spare for postage. I just hoped I'd make it to Dove Creek before another woman." She ran her tongue over her lips. "I did, didn't I?"

He sighed. "Well, since this is the first I've heard of the advertisement—" he shook the paper in his hand "—I'd say your chances of being first are good. But this is dated back in November and it is now January, so I'm curious as to what took you so long to get here." He didn't add that he was also curious as to why he hadn't gotten letters from other ladies.

"Well, I didn't actually see the advertisement until a few weeks ago. My sister and her husband had recently passed and I was going through their belongings when I stumbled upon the paper. Your ad leaped out at me as if it was from God." Once more she looked to the two boys playing on the couch.

Philip's gaze moved to the boys, too. "Are they your boys?"

"They are now."

Sadness flooded her eyes. The family resemblance was too close for them not to be blood relatives. And since she'd just mentioned her sister's death, Philip didn't think it was too much of a stretch to assume that the boys had belonged to Bella's sister. "They are your nephews?"

"Yes. I'm all the family they have left. The older boy is Caleb Rhodes and the younger is Mark." Her soulful eyes met his. "And you are our last hope to stay together."

Philip didn't want that kind of responsibility. He wasn't the marrying kind. He didn't want or need a family. And from the sound of it, it was obvious that a family was something that Bella both wanted and needed.

Bitterness filled Philip. He couldn't get married. That would require him to love deeply and Philip couldn't bring himself to do that. His father had loved his mother so much that when she'd died in childbirth, he'd died, too.

The workers at the orphanage had whispered how sad it was when a man died of a broken heart from loving too hard. Even at the age of five, Philip had known that his father had hung himself in the barn. He'd seen him do it but had never told anyone.

Now here stood a stranger with two children who expected him to marry her. All women expected love to come with marriage eventually. He couldn't give her his heart. What if he carried his father's gene of weakness? Would he rather kill himself than live with the pain of knowing he'd never see his wife, the one who held his heart, again?

Bella Wilson watched the emotions rush across Philip's face. He was a handsome man with deep blue eyes and straw-colored hair. There was a small bump on the bridge of his nose, which had probably been broken sometime in the past. She thought the bump gave his face character.

Was Philip Young a take-charge man? Her ex-fiancé, Marlow Brooks, had been a take-charge man, but when she didn't want to follow his lead, he'd called off their engagement. The memory still stung. What had he expected her to do? Put the boys in an orphanage? There was no way Bella would allow Mary's children to be sent away. She had foolishly thought that she and Marlow would raise the boys and give them a happy home. Marlow had disagreed and broken their engagement.

Bella wanted to prove to Philip that she had a backbone. So far she'd been timid with him, but her future, and the future of her nephews, depended on this man. Exhaustion had about taken its toll, but Bella knew she had to be strong for the boys' sake. She squared her shoulders and lifted her head high, then said, "Look, you placed the advertisement and I have arrived in answer to it. Are you going to marry me or not?"

He swallowed. Philip ignored her question and asked one of his own. "What did you mean when you said that I'm your last hope to stay together?"

She wrapped her arms around her waist and looked to the little boys. "Mary and her husband, Jim, owed more than they owned. So there is no money to raise the boys. Before I knew that my sister's life had all been a lie, I quit my job and hurried to Denver, Colorado. Upon arriving I learned that they didn't have the money that she and her husband had led everyone to believe they did. So their debtors came and took everything Mary and Jim did have and then the bank froze their money to pay off their home mortgages. All I had left was what I brought with me and those two small boys with their small bags." Tears pricked the backs of her eyes. She fought to keep the moisture from falling. "Now I have no money, no way to feed them and no place for them to live."

"So why didn't you continue on to Dove Creek?"

"I ran out of money and the stage refused to take me any farther. Thanks to Cara and John I learned that you'd be arriving soon and they said we could stay with them until you did." Bella heard the desperation in her voice and swallowed hard. Would he abandon her and the boys to their fate? She'd answered an advertisement expecting him to marry her. It never dawned on her that he might not have placed it.

Bella gnawed at her bottom lip. Marrying Philip would assure the boys' security. She'd been wary of who might be at the end of the trail, but now that she'd met him, Bella knew God had a plan. If only Philip would see it, too—then she'd be able to relax.

His deep sigh drew her attention. "Where do we go from here?" he asked.

She shrugged. "I'm still waiting to see if we are getting married. If not, then I will have to decide what I will do and you can go on with your life." Bitterness laced her words and Bella wished she could take them back. Her life had changed so much in the last few months.

He nodded but didn't say anything.

What must he think? He'd just been told she was his mail-order bride. A bride he'd not sent for. He could go on with his life and Bella couldn't hold it against him. She'd gladly taken on her nephews because they were her family and she loved them. Philip didn't have such feelings and wasn't obligated to marry her.

Bella offered him what she knew was a weak smile. "It's all right, Philip, I understand. You didn't write the advertisement. I'm sorry I sounded resentful." She pushed away from the table. "God will provide a way." Were they empty words? Would the Lord really take care of her and the boys? Bella had to believe He would.

Philip pushed back his chair. "Give me time to think about this, Bella. It's sudden for me." His gaze moved past her to the two little boys. "And a lot of responsibility. But I'm willing to consider what is best for everyone."

That was all she could ask, and yet Bella wanted to ask so much more of him. Instead she nodded her understanding.

Chapter Two

The sadness on her face tugged at Philip's heart. He looked to the two boys, who were staring back at him. "Come on, boys, help me put the horse away."

They clambered down from the couch. The older boy looked up at him. He watched the younger one slip his small hand into his brother's. Philip assured them, "You don't have to come, if you don't want to."

The two looked at each other. Both seemed hesitant.

They were so small and unsure of what to do. Their little eyes were filled with a deep sorrow that could only be placed there by the loss of one's parents. How many children had he met in the orphanage, where he'd grown up, with that same lost, hurt stare?

Philip kneeled down in front of them. "Look, fellas. You don't have to go with me. I'm going to put the horse away and maybe find the old yellow cat that lives in the barn."

"There is a kitty in the barn?" Mark asked with new interest.

Philip stood. "Last time I was here there was. He's

old, so I like to check on him, and sometimes I sneak a little milk from the cow to give the old cat a treat."

Mischief replaced the look of loss in Mark's eyes. "Can I help you sneak the milk?"

Philip started to the door. "You sure can, and if we hurry, we can be back in the house before it gets dark."

Mark's little boots sounded on the wooden floor behind him. "What color is the cat?"

Philip stopped by the door and pulled down both little boys' coats. He held them out to the boys. Mark took his and thrust his arms into the sleeves while Philip answered, "He's yellow with white stripes all over."

Caleb looked to Bella one more time.

She smiled at him and motioned for him to go on. Her soft voice ordered, "Be good for Mr. Young and do as he says."

That was all the encouragement the little boy needed. "Does the cat have a name?" Caleb asked, taking his own coat and then following Philip and Mark outside.

Philip untied the horse and walked him into the barn. He rubbed the horse's velvety nose. "Cara calls him Sunny."

Mark ran deeper into the barn. Horses of all colors looked out over their stall doors at the little boy as he passed. "Here, kitty, kitty," he called in a soft voice.

"Caleb, take Mark up to the loft. That's where Sunny likes to hang out." Philip fluffed the older boy's soft blond hair. "Just be careful up there."

"Mark! Come on!" Caleb yelled. He hurried to the ladder that led up into the hayloft. "Mr. Young says the cat might be in the loft."

Philip chuckled. Both boys scrambled up the ladder. He listened as they searched the barn for the cat.

Tiredness weighed on him like a wet blanket as he rubbed down the horse and poured feed into the bucket in its stall. He picked up each of the horse's hooves and checked them for rocks.

As he worked, Philip listened to the boys rooting around in the hay above him. They seemed like nice little boys who needed a father figure. Just like he had at the age of twelve, six years ago, when John Young and his wife, Rebecca, had adopted him. John had been a good parent to him. Still, the thought of his own birth father troubled Philip.

"What are they doing up there?" Bella asked.

He'd been so deep in his work that he hadn't heard her come into the barn. Philip stood and stretched out his back. "Looking for the cat."

Her face was tilted upward as she tried to see the boys. Dark circles surrounded her heavily lashed blue eyes. She'd been through a lot over the last few weeks and Philip's heart went out to her.

Caleb called from above. "Mr. Young?"

He looked up, too. "Yes?"

The little boy's blond head popped through the railings. "We found a cat, but I'm not sure it's Sunny."

"What makes you think it isn't Sunny?" Bella eyed the loft warily.

Philip frowned. He realized that the old tomcat normally would have come out as soon as he heard voices. Why hadn't he been paying better attention to the boys? Philip just prayed that whatever kind of cat they found up there, it was a friendly one.

"Come see." Mischief filled the boy's smile.

Philip chuckled. Caleb reminded him of his younger self. He seemed like the adventurous, fun-loving type.

He looked back to where Bella still stood looking up into the hayloft. Her tan coat hugged her body and she crossed her arms about her middle. "Are you coming?" he asked.

She shook her head. "No, if it's all the same to you. I'll stay down here."

Philip nodded. Curiosity drove him up the ladder. Bent over at the waist, he gazed about. The loft was beginning to look like a storage shed. Tools, old furniture and wooden crates filled the space. "Where are you two?"

Caleb stepped out from behind a pile of furniture. "Over here." He disappeared again.

He walked toward the boy and stepped around the rubble of broken furniture. He found the boys crouched down staring into a pile of hay. He cleared his throat and caught their attention. "What are you two looking at?"

Mark ignored his question and asked one of his own. "I thought you said Sunny was a boy cat."

Philip grinned. "He is."

Caleb tried to muffle his laughter. "I don't think so, Mr. Young," he said.

Mark scooted back so that Philip could see what they'd discovered. A mama cat lay on her side nursing three kittens. She was yellow with big green eyes that didn't look happy to have her secret space invaded.

"Well, I guess you are right, boys. Daddy cats usually don't take care of their kittens. She can keep the name, though, don't you think?" He kneeled down beside Caleb.

Both little boys nodded. Mark reached out a hand to touch one of the kittens and the mama cat hissed up at him.

"Don't touch them, Mark. She don't want us to," Caleb said as he grabbed Mark's hand and pulled it back.

Philip agreed. He stood slowly. "Come on, boys, let's give the little family some privacy while Sunny feeds her young."

Mark's bottom lip shot out. "I want to stay and pet them."

Caleb shook his head. "Remember what Aunt Bella said, Mark. We better do as Mr. Young says." He tugged on his little brother's shirt.

Still not pleased at having to leave, Mark stood.

Philip looked down at them. "Boys, we best leave Sunny alone until the kittens get bigger. I'd hate for her to move them. Promise you'll stay out of the loft until I tell you that you can come back."

Caleb nodded and nudged his brother to do the same. Mark did so, but not with as much enthusiasm as his brother. The two boys descended the ladder first. Philip followed a little more slowly.

When he turned around, Bella was kneeling down in front of Mark. "What did you find up there?" she asked softly.

"A mama cat and kittens," Mark said, his bottom lip still pooched out. "Mr. Young told us to leave them alone. Do we have to, Aunt Bella?"

She looked up at him. Philip felt as if he could drown in her pretty blue eyes. To avoid them, he bent down and picked up a piece of straw. He chewed on the end of it, waiting for Bella to look away.

She turned her attention back to Mark and Caleb. "If he said so, then yes."

Mark kicked at a clump of wet hay. Disappointment filled his face. Tears filled his eyes.

Philip watched as Caleb placed an arm around his brother's shoulders, then looked to him. "Mr. Young? Are you still going to give the cat some milk?"

Philip looked up into the loft. "Not today. I don't think we should disturb the mama cat, but the cow still needs to be milked. Do you boys want to help?"

Mark seemed to brighten with the prospect of milking the cow and both boys nodded. Philip looked to Bella.

She stood slowly and said, "Before she left, Cara said we could warm up the pot of stew for our supper. While you men milk, I think I'll see if I can scrape together a pan of biscuits." Bella walked toward the barn door but then stopped. She turned slowly and studied them. "Are you sure you don't mind the boys helping you?" Her brow furrowed.

"I wouldn't have asked for their help if I didn't want it," he answered with a grin. Philip dropped a hand onto Caleb's shoulder.

Bella nodded and then left.

Philip turned his attention back to the boys. "Looks like we have chores to do."

"I've never milked a cow before." Caleb removed his arm from Mark's shoulders.

"Me, neither." Mark stooped down and picked up a piece of straw. He placed it between his teeth and chewed.

Philip tried not to smile as he realized Mark was imitating him. The boys needed a man in their lives. Could he follow in his adoptive father's footsteps and adopt the two boys as his own? Bella would have to be part of the package. He couldn't imagine her letting him raise the boys alone and, truth be told, Philip didn't want to. But he also didn't want to fall in love. Would Bella agree to a loveless marriage?

Bella missed her old job at the bakery. She even missed the early hours and found herself still rising long before the sun. If there was one thing Bella was good at, it was baking. The smell of biscuits filled the house. She loved mixing, kneading and baking bread.

Philip came through the door with both boys hot on his heels. "Woo-wee, something smells good in here."

Mark dashed around Philip. "I got to help milk the cow."

Caleb followed, carrying one of the milk buckets. "Me, too." He panted under its weight.

Bella couldn't help but smile. The boys were louder and more active than they had been since she'd taken them from their home a month ago. It appeared spending a little time with Philip had been a positive experience for the boys. She was thankful that Cara had suggested they spend the night with them so that they could all get to know each other better.

Philip put his bucket of milk on the kitchen counter and then helped Caleb with his. "You did a good job." He patted the boy on the shoulder and offered him a warm smile.

Caleb squared his body. He stood taller and nodded his thanks. Mark hurried to the settee, where they'd left their wooden horses. He carried them to Philip and Caleb. "This one is mine. His name is Brownie. Someday I'm going to have a horse like him."

Philip took the toy and examined it. "He looks good and sturdy. I think you have yourself a keeper there."

"While you men study the livestock, I'm going to butter this bread and get our supper on the table."

Bella continued to listen to Philip and the boys as she set the table for dinner. Cara had told her earlier that she wouldn't be back in time to eat, but for her and the boys to go ahead. It felt odd working in another woman's kitchen as Philip and the boys talked about horses, the Pony Express and the mama cat. She smiled at the way the boys responded to Philip. Caleb asked questions about the Pony Express and Mark talked about the mama cat and kittens.

She made sure to set a plate on the back of the stove for Cara and then called, "Time to eat, boys."

Philip pushed up from the couch. "Come on, boys, I'll show you where we men wash up."

"Do we need our coats again?" Caleb asked.

"Nope, we won't be outside. Cara talked John into making her a small pantry off the kitchen, where she made a place for him to wash up." He was already walking past Bella and into the pantry.

Bella smiled as the sound of the boys' laughter and chatter filled the small space.

"When I grow up, I want to fish, ride horses and hunt," Mark said.

Getting to know her nephews was a joy. Bella had the sense that Mark was more outdoorsy and that Caleb enjoyed being inside.

"Maybe someday you can work on my brother Thomas's ranch," Philip said, leading the boys back to the table, where they all sat down.

Bella frowned. That would never happen if Philip

wasn't going to marry her. It wouldn't do for Philip to fill the boys' hearts with dreams that weren't going to come true. After the boys were in bed, she'd talk to him.

"Aunt Bella, are you sick?" Mark studied her face.

She smiled. "No, sweetie. Why?"

"You aren't talking." He laid his spoon to the side.

"I'm tired, not sick."

Mark frowned. "Oh. All right." He picked up his spoon and tasted the stew. A big smile pulled at his mouth. "This is good."

Bella laughed. "I'm glad you like it. Now eat up and then we're going to get ready for bed. It's been a long day."

Both boys did as she said. They tucked into their supper as if it was their last meal.

She sighed. If Philip wasn't going to marry her, then how was she ever going to take care of the kids? Maybe she could see if Dove Creek needed a baker. But the short supply of money that she had wouldn't be enough to rent them a place to live. Worry ate at her insides like a gopher gnawing at the roots of a tree. What was she going to do?

Chapter Three

An hour later, Bella cleaned the kitchen. She'd put the boys down on a pallet beside the fireplace. Their soft snores filled the kitchen and sitting room. Philip sat at the table nursing a cup of coffee.

Drying the last dish, Bella eased into the chair across from him. "Thank you for being so patient with the boys today."

He nodded. "It was my pleasure."

Bella traced the wood pattern on the table with her finger. How did she bring up the subject of him not promising the boys things that he couldn't give them? She didn't want to offend him, but she also didn't want his empty promises hurting her nephews.

"Ma always says 'The best way to say something, is just to say it.'" Philip set the cup on the table and waited.

Had he read her mind? "Your mother says that?"

"Yes. She's my adoptive mother. She took me in when I was twelve years old," Philip answered. His gaze moved to the sleeping boys.

"Oh, all right. Philip, I like that you have made friends with the boys, and to be honest, they have been happier today than I've seen them in a long time." Bella stopped, once more wondering how to say what she felt needed to be said.

"But...?"

She sighed. "But please don't make promises you have no intention of keeping."

He frowned. "Like what?"

Bella met his gaze. "Like telling Mark that someday he could work on your brother's ranch. I've no idea where we'll be living."

"I see." Philip walked to the stove and refilled his cup. "What if I said I've been thinking about that?"

Did she dare hope he'd changed his mind about marrying her? Before her thoughts and worry overtook her, Bella asked, "Thinking about what?"

Philip returned, turned his chair around and sat down. He rested his arms against the wood. "Those boys need a father figure." He studied her face.

She couldn't argue with that, so Bella nodded. What was he saying? That he wanted to fill that position? And if so, what did that mean for her? The questions whirled in her mind like a Texas twister, but she held them inside, waiting for him to explain further.

He pressed on. "Seems to me that they've taken a cotton to me." Philip ran a hand through his hair. And looked at her, waiting.

Bella thought she knew where he was going with this conversation but wanted him to be the one to get there. She stared back at him.

He cleared his throat. "Um, I grew up an orphan."

She knew that. He'd mentioned it earlier. Bella continued to wait.

"And, well, I don't want to see those boys in an orphanage like I was." He paused again. "If you still want to get married, I'll adopt the boys as my own."

Bella wanted clarification. "You want to marry me?"

He sighed heavily and then answered. "Not really. But to keep those boys out of an orphanage, I'll do it."

So for the sake of the boys they were both willing to marry strangers. She sighed, too. "We are a pair, aren't we?"

Philip nodded. "I'm not the marrying kind."

"What does that mean?" Bella asked.

"My real mother died trying to give birth to my younger brother, who died with her. Then my pa simply gave up on life and grieved himself to death. When I was younger, I vowed not to marry or fall in love." He took a sip of the warm coffee. "I don't want to be married in the real sense of the word. I'm pretty sure my adoptive brother Thomas is the one who placed the advertisement that got you here. If it was up to me, I'd never marry, but since it's my brother's fault you are here, I will marry you and adopt the boys."

Bella's heart ached for the little boy whose parents both died, leaving him alone in the world at such a young age. It was obvious by the look on his face that Philip still hurt from his loss. She laid her hands on top of his folded arms. "I don't want to get married, either, but for the sake of my nephews I made the decision to do just that."

He cocked his head to the side. "Why don't you want to marry?"

She pulled her hands from his arms and tucked them into her lap. Swallowing the hurt that welled up in her, Bella said, "Up until a month ago, I was engaged. Then when my fiancé found out the boys came with me, he broke off the engagement. I don't want to get married or fall in love because I don't trust anyone but myself and God now. Men leave at the least bit of trouble." She turned her head so that he couldn't see the tears in her eyes. They weren't tears for the man who didn't love her, but for the loss of her own life. Now she lived and did things for the boys.

Philip reached out and turned her head so that she faced him once more. She tried to ignore the hurt and tears that threatened to spill from her eyes. "Are you saying you'd be happy with a marriage where I gave you my last name and adopted the boys?"

"I suppose so. As long as you understand I can never fall in love with you. Or anyone else for that matter. My only concern is for the boys."

Philip chuckled.

"What's so funny?"

"Thomas and his wife, Josephine, had what Thomas called a marriage of convenience. Sounds like we're agreeing to the same arrangement."

She frowned. "I still don't see the humor."

Philip explained, "I sent for a mail-order bride for Thomas, and Josephine answered his ad. Now he's done the same to me." He shrugged. "I don't know. All of a sudden, it struck me as funny."

Bella shook her head, still not seeing the humor in their situation. She didn't want to marry for love, but it saddened her that for the rest of her life she would be married to a man who didn't love her. Was she overly tired? Or had the stress of the last month addled her brain? For the sake of the boys, theirs was to be a marriage of convenience.

* * *

The next morning, Philip folded his blanket and laid it on the couch. His gaze moved to the two sleeping boys. Cara had returned shortly after supper and she and Bella now slept in the only other room in the house.

He quietly walked to the front door, pulled on his boots, coat and hat and then headed outside to feed the horses. John was due back later and Philip wanted the relay station to be in tip-top shape when he arrived.

Philip yawned as he slipped out the door. Cold air tugged at his hat. Even though he'd been bone-tired the night before, sleep had evaded him like fog on a new spring morning. His mind refused to shut down. How was he going to take care of a family? After praying during the early hours, sleep and a plan came to him.

If John returned early enough, Philip intended on packing Bella and the boys up and taking them to the Young farm, where his adoptive family and Pony Express home station was. He could only imagine what Ma was going to say when he arrived with his future wife and children in tow.

Philip hurried to the warmth of the barn. He hummed as he fed the horses and mucked out stalls. His ma would probably be surprised, but also proud of him for taking on the two little boys, he was sure of it.

It was a typical January morning and the trip to the creek would be cold. When it could be delayed no longer, Philip picked up two large buckets and pulled the barn door open. A cold wind hit him as he shut the door and then headed out to get the water. The wind had picked up and blew about him.

With his head down, he reached the edge of the creek in a matter of minutes. When Philip looked up, he was surprised to see Bella at the water's edge, scooping up a bucket of cold water.

Bella turned at his approach. "Good morning."

He walked to the bank. "Good morning. I should have thought to come get fresh water for the house before heading to the barn. Here, let me take that," Philip offered, setting one of his buckets down and reaching for hers.

She smiled and shook her head. "No, thank you. I've got it." Bella took a step up the bank, her eyes downcast.

Was she having second thoughts about marrying him? Or was she feeling shy this morning? Philip hurriedly filled both buckets and then hurried after her. "How are the boys this morning?" he asked for something to say.

Bella glanced at him. "They were still asleep when I left the house."

"Oh." He tried to think of something more to say. Philip cleared his throat. "If it's all the same to you, as soon as John gets home, I'd like to head for home."

"Home?"

Philip ducked his head against a cold blast of wind. "Yes. My family's home is the Young farm that is one of the Pony Express home stations. It's about ten miles from here. I'd like for you to meet my family before we get married and move to the relay station."

She nodded, also fighting against the wind. "That sounds nice. Do you have a large family?"

He grinned. "You could say that. Why don't you go on inside with the water and I'll be in as soon as I get the animals taken care of. We can talk then."

Bella shivered and clutched the front of her tan coat

tighter about her. "Sounds good." She walked to the house at a fast pace.

Philip hurried through the remainder of his chores. Once done, he returned to the house. His boots pounded on the steps of the porch. The wind continued to pull at him as he opened the door. Warmth washed over his flesh, sending prickles into his face.

"Breakfast is almost ready, Philip," Cara said, scraping scrambled eggs onto five plates.

His gaze sought out Bella's. Compared to Cara, Bella was tall. The two women were as different as night and day. Cara's hair was bright red, while Bella's was sunshine blond. Cara's green eyes were sharp and Bella's blue eyes were soft. Bella's voice was quiet with a gentleness that seemed to soothe, whereas Cara's held an Irish brogue that tickled the ear.

Yes, they were different. He hoped that physical appearance was the only difference. Cara was as kind as a kitten. So far, Bella seemed to have the same trait.

Bella smiled at him. A soft pink filled her cheeks, reminding Philip that he was staring. He grinned and winked at her. The pink in her face burst into flames and turned bloodred. Philip couldn't help but chuckle.

Cara laughed. "Hang your coat up, Philip, and stay awhile." She carried the plates to the table. How she balanced them so well, Philip had no idea.

He did as she said. "It sure smells good." Philip walked toward where the boys were seated at the table. "You men mind if I sit between you?" He pulled out the chair.

They both shook their heads. Their hair stuck up in all directions. They wore pajamas on their small bodies. "Bella usually sits between us," Mark said, playing with his fork.

"Does she now?" Philip arched his eyebrow at the boy.

Caleb scratched his head. "Yep."

He looked to Bella. She had moved to the stove and was pulling out a pan of fresh biscuits. "You can sit there. I'll sit on the other side of Mark." Once she'd placed the pan on the top of the stove, Bella motioned for him to sit.

Philip sat and waited for the women to join them at the table. Mark wiped at the sleep in his eyes, while Caleb yawned. When the women were seated, Cara asked him to bless the meal and he did.

The boys immediately began eating. They shoveled the food into their mouths as if they feared it would be their last meal. He remembered seeing other small children, half-starved, eating their first meal at the orphanage and his heart went out to the two small boys.

Bella softly said, "Slow down, boys. There is plenty of food."

Caleb swallowed hard. "For now."

Philip laid his hand on the boy's shoulder. Looking deep into Caleb's eyes, he vowed, "You boys will never go hungry again."

"They have never gone hungry," Bella said, her voice shaking. "I've always made sure they've had something to eat."

He turned to look at her. "I didn't mean to imply that you haven't done your best."

She lowered her head, but not before he saw that her eyelashes were damp. "And I didn't mean to snap."

Cara broke the silence that had formed around the table. “Philip, do you reckon John will be home today?”

“Probably. I’m sorry he took my ride.”

Cara laughed. “Not me. He needed a break from this place. Even if it is only for an overnight adventure.”

Philip nodded. He knew what she meant. A relay station was a place where the riders exchanged horses, unlike the home station, where they would stop and start their runs. A home station meant just that, home. John didn’t ride unless a rider couldn’t continue. He was pretty much stuck at the station, day in and day out. That was one of the reasons Philip and Thomas continued to ride for the Pony Express after they’d taken over the relay station on the other side of Dove Creek.

Bella looked from him to Cara. Confusion filled her eyes. Her forehead crinkled. “Why would he be glad to be gone?”

Philip answered. “Relay stations can be very lonely. I’m sure John is enjoying being at the Young home station. My brothers are probably telling him all kinds of stories.” Philip bit into the most delicious biscuit he’d ever tasted—and his adoptive ma’s were pretty good. Last night’s had been good, but this one seemed to melt in his mouth.

Understanding lit up Bella’s face, then remembrance. “Oh, you said you’d tell me about your family.” She smiled.

He savored the buttery bread for a moment longer before swallowing. “I did, didn’t I?”

She nodded her agreement.

Philip smiled. “Well, I was adopted when I turned twelve. John Young and his wife, Rebecca, not only adopted me, but also six other boys. Plus, they had a little girl of their own. So all together I have six brothers and a sister. Sadly, John passed away, but not before he signed all us boys, except Benjamin, up to be Pony Express riders."

"How come Benjamin didn't get to be a rider?" Mark asked around a mouthful of eggs.

"Don't talk with your mouth full, Mark," Bella scolded in a gentle voice.

The little boy ducked his head. "Sorry," he muttered.

"Because he's only eight years old. Oh, I take that back. He just had a birthday, so he's nine now."

"I'm sorry for your loss," Bella said. She stood.

Philip enjoyed the gentle swishing sound her skirt made as she walked to the washtub. "Thank you."

"I imagine that your adoptive father's death was hard on Rebecca," Cara said with a frown.

"It was, but then Seth Armstrong showed up at the farm as the Pony Express station manager and the two of them fell in love. They were married and now we are all a happy family again." He pushed his chair back and carried his plate to Bella.

She took it and slipped it into the hot, soapy water. "I'm glad she found a man who would take in all you boys."

Was that bitterness he heard in her voice?

She looked up at him with sadness in her eyes. Philip remembered her talking about her fiancé rejecting her after he discovered there would be children to raise that weren't his. His heart went out to the broken woman in front of him. What could he do to bring the smile back on her face?

Philip vowed that he'd make her smile again.

Chapter Four

"Do all these brothers and sister have names?" Bella asked as she wiped the food from the dishes.

"As a matter of fact, they do. I'll start with the oldest and work my way down to the youngest. Jacob, Andrew, Clayton, Thomas, Noah, Benjamin and, lastly, Joy."

Cara walked to them. "Bella, go sit down and enjoy your coffee. I'll do these dishes. After all, you did most of the cooking this morning and gathered the water." She held her plate and the boys'.

"I can help," Bella answered. "The job will get done faster with more hands and then we can all three enjoy another cup of coffee."

Philip went to the table and gathered the remaining dishes. He set them on the counter. She wondered if he would always be this helpful.

"Aunt Bella, can we be excused?" Caleb asked.

She glanced at her nephews. "Are your hands clean?"

Both boys looked down at their fingers and nodded.

"Then I suppose you can."

They scooted off their chairs and hurried into the sitting area, where their toy horses awaited them. Caleb rushed ahead and handed Mark his toy. Bella heard Philip chuckle and turned to face him.

At her inquisitive look, he said, "Caleb reminds me a lot of Benjamin." Philip shook his head.

"How so?" Cara asked. "If I remember right, they don't look anything alike."

Philip shook his head. "Not in looks but in actions. Ben is always looking out for Joy."

Bella had to admit that Caleb tried to look after Mark. Unfortunately, she'd learned really quickly that the little boy didn't care much for his older brother bossing him around. "Yes, but Mark doesn't always want his help."

They finished the dishes. Cara excused herself and left them sitting at the kitchen table nursing cups of warm coffee. Bella looked into the dark liquid and inhaled its rich fragrance.

"You are a very good cook," Philip said, complimenting her.

She looked up at him. "Thank you. I love to cook and bake." Bella twisted the cup in her hands. She'd always dreamed of someday owning her own café and serving fresh desserts. Her gaze moved to the boys. But now that dream was gone.

Philip chuckled, drawing her attention again. "Well, that's good, because I like to eat."

Bella smiled. "Most people do."

The door came open with a bang and John Turnstone entered the room. He pulled off his coat and looked around. Cara came from the bedroom with a bright smile on her face. "Did you have a good ride, dear?"

"I did." He walked across the room and hugged his wife tightly.

Bella pushed her chair back and walked to the stove.

She avoided watching the other couple's greeting. Instead she asked, "John, would you like a cup of coffee?"

"That sounds wonderful."

She poured the rich liquid from the pot and then turned. John had walked to the table. "So what do you think of your special delivery?" he asked Philip.

Philip grinned. "I like it."

Mark and Caleb came into the kitchen, too. "What's a special delivery?" Caleb asked, climbing into the nearest chair.

Bella felt her cheeks flame to life. She watched as Philip scooped up Mark and tickled him.

"You two are," he told the two boys.

Bella sat the mug in front of John.

Cara stood beside his chair, smiling at the boys and Philip. She patted her husband's shoulder. "Would you like something to eat?"

His gaze moved to the stove, where the pan of leftover bread sat. "I'd love a couple of those biscuits."

"With sausage?" Cara asked, heading to the stove.

"Yep, that sounds good." John picked up his cup and took a swig of the coffee. After he swallowed, John said, "That ride home was a cold one."

"I figured you'd get here later today." Philip grinned.

John shook his head. "Naw, I wanted to get back here." He grinned at Cara as she handed him his plate with two sausage biscuits.

Philip looked to Bella. "What do you think? Ready to head out?"

"Yes, but how are we going to get there? I mean, I didn't bring a horse or a buggy with me and you came in on a Pony Express horse." Bella couldn't imagine the boys having to walk in that cold wind. It might have calmed down, but ten or fifteen miles was a long way for the two little boys to have to walk.

"I've been thinking about that and was hoping John and Cara would allow us to borrow a wagon and horse." He looked to John. "I can have it back to you in a couple of days."

John had just taken a bite of the sausage biscuit. His eyes widened and he looked to Cara. He chewed with pleasure.

Cara laughed. "Nope, not my biscuits. Those are from this one." She pointed at Bella.

John swallowed. "You can borrow whatever you want as long as this little lady will give my wife the recipe for this bread." He held out the half-eaten biscuit, as if there was any question to which bread he meant.

"What do you say, Bella? Want to give away your recipe?" Philip grinned at her. Was that pride she saw in his eyes?

Bella turned her attention to Cara. "I'll be happy to give you the recipe." She whispered loud enough for everyone to hear, "The secret ingredient is lard."

John roared with laughter. "Best tastin' lard I ever had the pleasure of eating."

The little boys laughed along with the adults. Bella loved seeing them so happy. God had known what He was doing when He'd prompted her to answer the mail-order-bride ad. For that, she was thankful.

Still, she couldn't help but wonder what her new life would be like. Would the boys still be happy when the newness of their situation grew old? How were they going to feel the first time Philip reprimanded them? How was she going to react to that? So much was unsure in their lives.

* * *

Philip tried to focus on what John was saying, but his ears seemed only interested in what Bella and Cara were talking about. Her soft laughter and bright eyes continued to distract him.

"So, why don't you two at least stay tonight and that way you'll get an early start and not have to drive too long in the dark?" John asked.

He turned his attention back to John. "I think that's a good idea, if Bella is agreeable."

She turned her head and smiled at the two men. "That would give me time to write out a couple of recipes for Cara and in the morning she can make the biscuits."

John hit the table with the flat of his hand. His voice boomed. "It's settled, then." He pushed his chair back. "Philip, would you mind helping me fix one of the back stalls? I've been needing an extra pair of hands and yours look available."

Philip laughed. "Be glad to." From the corner of his eye he saw both of the boys scramble to their feet.

Bella must have noticed, too, because she said, "Boys, I need you to stay inside and help me mix up a batch of oatmeal cookies. I'm sure I'll need a couple of tasters."

They immediately ran to where Bella stood. "I'm good at stirring, Aunt Bella," Caleb offered, looking up at her.

"Me, too," Mark agreed.

John laughed. "Well, if I had known there would be cookies to sample, I wouldn't have mentioned the broken stall door." He started to sit back down. "That stall can wait another day or two."

Cara shook her head. "Oh, no, you don't. You go to

work. I don't want to have to help you later. You know how I hate being in that barn. Philip's here, so go." She pointed at the door with a stern look.

Philip saw Bella try to hide her grin. He pushed away from the table. "Come on, John. The sooner we get the stall fixed, the sooner we get to eat cookies."

John grumbled, "At times like these, I wish I was six again." He pulled his coat back on and headed out the door.

Philip pulled the door shut behind them, but not before he heard the women burst out into laughter. He buttoned his coat as he stepped off the porch, glad that the wind had died down.

His thoughts turned to the trip to his adoptive parents' farm. It would take between twelve and fifteen hours. Thankfully the road wasn't too bad. The wagon was light and, since they weren't taking much of anything with them, should be easy for a horse to pull.

Philip walked to the barn and could hear John singing a hymn inside. Since his real father's death, he never entered a barn when he knew someone was inside, until he heard them moving about or making some type of noise. The silence of the barn on the morning he'd found his father had taught him to be cautious before entering. The singing inside stopped and Philip pulled the barn door open and stepped inside.

"What were you doing out there? Woolgathering?" John asked, motioning for him to come farther into the barn.

"I suppose I was." Philip walked to where John waited.

John handed him a piece of wood. "Here, hold this."

Philip took it and held it in place while John hammered a nail.

"Were you thinking about that pretty lady inside? I imagine you were surprised when you saw her." He chuckled and continued working.

"No, I wasn't thinking about her, and yes, I was very surprised. You could have warned me." Philip picked up another board and handed it to John.

John nailed it into place. "Where would the fun be in that?" He swung the stall door back and forth.

Philip shook his head. He sat down on a barrel and looked at John, not bothering to answer him. Instead he said, "You didn't need my help with that. Why did you want to come out here?"

A grin split the other man's lips. "Well, for a couple of reasons. One, I wanted to thank you for taking care of the place while I was gone, and two, I was wondering what you are going to do about those boys."

"I didn't do anything special around here. As for the boys, I'm going to adopt them."

"That's what I figured." John rubbed his chin. "Why would you want to adopt two little boys that don't belong to ya?"

Philip frowned. What was the older man getting at? Why wouldn't he want to adopt Caleb and Mark? "I don't want them to go into an orphanage like I did."

"And there's no other reason?"

"Just say what it is you want to know, John." Philip locked eyes with his friend, not knowing what John would say next.

John shook his head. "Are you sure you're not taking the boys in so that their aunt will get feelings for you?"

Philip chuckled. "I'm sure. I don't intend to fall in

love with Bella. The boys need a father, and since my brother Thomas is responsible for bringing them into my life by placing that mail-order-bride ad, I'm going to be the one to take care of them." He stood. "Now that the door is fixed, we can mosey back inside and have a cookie or two."

"I vote for two." John slapped him on the back. "While we're at it, maybe you should take a good long look at the cook. She's a fine-looking woman."

Philip shook his head in mock defeat. How could he explain to John that he didn't want to fall in love? He didn't want to grieve for a woman, should something happen to her. And at the same time, Philip didn't want a woman grieving for him, either. Would he be able to maintain a friendship with Bella and not fall in love with her and the boys? Philip planned on guarding his heart and prayed Bella would do the same with hers.

Chapter Five

Philip rubbed at his shoulder as he drove the wagon. An ache had begun about midmorning and just hadn't stopped hurting. Probably from sleeping on the rough boards in the barn last night, he thought.

With John home, he and his wife had taken the bedroom, and Bella and the boys had slept in the sitting room, leaving Philip the barn as a sleeping place. He looked behind him at the boys huddled under the piles of blankets that Cara had insisted they take on the trip home.

Bella sat beside him on the wagon bench. They'd left a little after 6:00 a.m. She'd been quiet most of the morning. Since he really didn't know her, Philip wasn't sure if she was just being shy or if it was her personality to just be silent.

He pulled his hand away from his shoulder and focused on the scenery around them. The road was clear, making travel much easier. To the right he saw a large tree with dry ground under its branches and decided to pull the wagon over for a bit of lunch.

In a soft voice, Bella asked, "Is there anything I can do to ease the stress in your shoulder?"

He smiled. "Thanks, but I think all it needs is to stretch a little. I thought we'd stop here and have lunch, if that's all right with you." Philip set the brake on the wagon and slipped off the hard seat.

She nodded. "This is a perfect spot. The boys can play under the tree while I get lunch set out." Bella pulled a picnic basket out from under the seat.

The boys continued to sleep as she dug out sandwiches, pickles and a jug of apple cider. Philip walked about, swinging his arms and stretching his muscles. Sitting on a wagon all day wasn't something he was accustomed to. Now, riding a horse all day, that was a different story. He grinned. In a few days he'd be back in the saddle, riding for the Pony Express.

His gaze moved to Bella as she worked. Would they be married before he had another run? He walked to the tailgate of the wagon, where she had set out the food on a blanket.

"We should tell the boys we're getting married, before we get to your folks' house." Bella handed him a sandwich.

He looked to the two lumps under the blankets. "I suppose you're right." Although he thought they probably already knew, since they'd talked openly about it with John and Cara Turnstone.

She grinned at him and motioned for him to watch the blankets that covered the boys. Bella raised her voice slightly. "Would you like a cookie after you finish your sandwich, Philip?"

Two blond heads popped out from under the covers.

"I want a cookie," Mark exclaimed, shoving the blankets away and pushing his way toward the back of the wagon, where Bella and Philip were.

Philip brushed the hair on the little boy's head with his hand. "Sandwich first, cookies last."

"Aw, why do we have to eat the icky food first?" Mark protested, frowning down at the bread and meat Bella had just thrust into his small hand.

Caleb sat down beside his brother and yawned out the answer. "Because the icky food is the best for your body." He grinned at Bella when he took the sandwich she offered. "But Aunt Bella's food is never icky."

Philip laughed. "Already a charmer, aren't you, Caleb?"

He smiled at Philip but didn't answer. Pretty smart little boy, Philip thought. The sandwich was good but a little dry. That was what one could expect from trail food.

"Boys, I have something I want to tell you."

Wariness filled the children's eyes at Bella's words. Both lowered their half-eaten sandwiches.

Bella smiled at them. "This is good news, not bad."

Philip half expected the boys to relax but was disappointed. Mark's eyes began to fill with mist. He rubbed them in an attempt to fight off the tears.

Philip laid his hand on the little boy's shoulder. In a gentle voice he said, "Buck up, little man. You might like what she has to say." He nodded to Bella to continue.

She pushed a strand of hair from her face. "Philip has asked me to marry him and I've agreed."

They continued to look at her, waiting. He grinned. "That means you get to live with me at the relay station."

Caleb frowned. "We know that. Is that the news?"

Bella chuckled. "Well, yes. I thought you'd be surprised."

Both boys gave her another look of exasperation and then continued eating.

With disbelief filling her voice, Bella asked, "You really aren't surprised?"

"Nope, you told us we were coming out here so you could marry Philip. So since we found him and haven't moved on, we figured you two were getting married." Caleb stared at her as if she'd grown two heads.

"Plus, we heard you talking to John and Cara about it." Mark shook his head. "We aren't babies, Aunt Bella." Then he finished off his sandwich. With the last morsel still in his mouth, he asked, "Can I have my cookie now?"

Philip laughed. The boys were proving to be very smart. Bella would need to stay on her toes with these two. He wiped the last crumb from his own mouth and said, "Yeah, can we?"

She shook her head and handed over the cookies. Her fingers brushed his and Bella looked up at him. Had she felt a small spark, too? Or just been surprised at his touch? He'd never expected to feel anything for her, so what was this attraction? Perhaps it was nothing. Perhaps it was static electricity in the air. Or perhaps… No, Philip refused to even think that it could be more than just a small spark of electricity.

After riding for over fourteen hours, Philip pulled the wagon into the Young family farm's front yard. The sound of cows lowing and chickens settling in for the night were a comfort to his tired mind.

Andrew was the first to greet them. "Better move that wagon next to the porch. I have a rider coming in any minute now."

Philip nodded and grinned. "Nice to see you, too, big brother." He did as Andrew said and guided the horse to the porch, where his mother and her close friend, Fay, sat rocking.

His mother, Rebecca, stood and pulled her shawl closer. A smile graced her face. "'Bout time you got home, son. We've been waiting for days."

He set the brake on the wagon, then jumped down and hurried up the porch steps. Philip picked up his adoptive mother and swung her around. Her squeal was the reward he'd been looking for.

"Put me down." She playfully slapped his shoulder.

Philip hugged her close and then did as she ordered. He stepped back and grinned. "You'll never believe this, Ma, but I'm getting married." Not the most graceful way to announce his future plans, but no one had ever claimed he was graceful.

She looked at him with an open mouth. Her big blue eyes had grown even bigger. "You're what?"

"Getting married."

Rebecca looked to the wagon, where Andrew was talking to Bella. The little boys stood behind her in the bed of the wagon looking about. "I see."

Fay stepped up beside Rebecca. She grinned at Philip. "Why don't you all come inside? I'll put a fresh pot of coffee on and get those young'uns a glass of milk." She turned and entered the house before he had a chance to answer or respond.

He was grateful that Fay was taking the matter into her own hands. She had entered their lives at the same time that Seth had. Her husband had recently passed away and her landlord had kicked her out of her home. Rebecca, seeing a need, had invited her out to the farm. Fay was a part of their family now and Philip was grateful for her kind ways.

He hurried back to the wagon. First Philip helped Bella down, then he turned to swing both boys to the ground also. Then he led them up the stairs, where Rebecca still stood. He understood his mother's shock. How many times in the past had he sworn he wasn't the marrying kind? "Ma, I'd like you to meet Bella, Caleb and Mark."

Rebecca nodded. "Please call me Rebecca." She opened the screen door. "Come on in."

Bella smiled. "Thank you. I know this is probably a shock to you. But I hope we can be friends as well as in-laws." She entered the house. "Come along, boys," Bella called over her shoulder.

Caleb and Mark both grinned up at Rebecca. "Are you going to be our new grandma?" Mark asked.

Rebecca kneeled down in front of him. She wiped the blond hair from his eyes. "It looks that way." She stood and then asked, "Do you young men like cookies?"

"I do!" Mark grabbed Rebecca's hand and began pulling her into the house.

Philip caught the door and watched in amusement as Mark chattered. "My favorite kind of cookie is oatmeal. Caleb likes sugar. I'll eat them both. What kind do you have?"

Rebecca laughed. "I'm not sure. We'll have to ask my daughter, Joy. She's the one who bakes the cookies."

Bella frowned at the little boy. "Mark, stop pulling on Rebecca," she ordered.

He dropped Rebecca's hand. "Sorry." Mark bowed his head.

Rebecca looked at Bella. "Maybe we should have our snack in the kitchen. Is that all right with you?"

Philip watched as the two women walked to the

kitchen with the boys between them. He wondered how long it would be before Rebecca started asking questions.

The sound of horse's hooves pounding the ground drew his attention back to the yard. His brother Noah practically jumped from the horse. He tossed the mailbag to another of his brothers, Clayton, with a grin. Clayton was already in the saddle and halfway down the trail when Noah turned toward the house at something Andrew had said.

Noah was the smaller of the boys. Only thirteen years old, the boy could outfish, outhunt and outride all of them. He was darker-skinned and quieter than most of them. Noah raised a hand and waved.

Philip waved back as he watched the younger boy head to the bunkhouse. A yawn escaped Philip. He turned to the kitchen, knowing he'd not be allowed to stand in the doorway much longer.

Rebecca stuck her head through the kitchen door. "Come on, you have some explaining to do."

Yep, he'd been right. His ma wasn't going to wait much longer to find out what had happened in the last few days to change his mind on marriage. As he walked the short distance to the kitchen, Philip wondered if he should tell his family this marriage was a marriage of convenience.

He entered to find Caleb and Mark sitting at the table with a plate of cookies in front of them. Joy ran to meet him.

"I've missed you," she practically whispered. Joy loved to talk to family members but was always shy around strangers.

He grabbed his little sister up into a bear hug. "I missed you, too."

She pulled back and put her hands on both sides of his face. "Are you really getting married?"

"I am."

"Why?" She lowered her hands to his shoulders.

"Joy!" Rebecca scolded.

Philip laughed. "It's an honest question, Ma." He lowered Joy to the ground, grabbed her hand and then joined the others at the kitchen table. Philip sat down and pulled Joy up onto his lap. "We're getting married because Thomas sent for me a mail-order bride."

Rebecca frowned. "I thought he wrote all those girls and told them that you'd changed your mind."

"How could I change my mind? I didn't even know I'd advertised for a bride until Bella showed up." Philip reached for one of the cookies. So, Rebecca had known about the ad and made Thomas respond to the letters that had arrived. He bit into the gingersnap cookie and smiled. Served Thomas right for placing the ad in the first place. He could just imagine his brother having to answer each and every letter.

Rebecca asked, "Bella, would you like to take a quick walk with me?" She pushed her chair back and waited for an answer.

Philip held his breath. What would the two women talk about? What would his adoptive mother say? Would she try to talk Bella out of the marriage? If so, how would Philip feel? He'd already made peace with the idea of getting married. He looked to the two little boys, who were playing with his little brother Benjamin. What would become of them if Bella changed her mind?

Chapter Six

Bella slipped into her tan coat. What did Philip's mother want to talk to her about? Had she guessed their intentions of making this a marriage in name only? Would Rebecca try to talk her out of marrying Philip? She followed the other woman out into the cool evening air.

Rebecca stepped out onto the porch. "I thought maybe we could walk to the river and back." She waited for Bella to catch up with her.

"All right," Bella agreed.

When they were several yards from the house, Rebecca spoke again. "Bella, tell me about yourself."

Bella glanced sideways at her future mother-in-law. "What would you like to know?"

"Anything, everything. I want to get to know you. Find out who my son is marrying." Rebecca pulled her cloak tighter about her tiny waist.

Bella nodded. The best place to start would be close to the beginning. "I grew up in the city of Douglas City, California. My parents only had two children who lived to adulthood. Myself and my sister. My sister married and moved to Denver, Colorado. Both our parents caught a fever last winter and died. I chose to stay in California. When my sister died, I was working at a bakery and planning on opening my own shop someday. But now my goal is to raise her boys." Bella stopped talking. She wasn't sure exactly what Rebecca wanted to hear, but she felt that should pacify the woman.

They walked on for a few minutes. Finally, Rebecca said, "I'm sorry for your losses."

Bella swallowed. "Thank you."

"So you have no other family?"

"No, it's just me and the boys now." Bella had heard the water long before she saw it. It rushed over the rocky river bottom at a fast pace.

Rebecca stopped and sat down on a large boulder. "Are you sure you want to marry Philip?" She tucked her hands deep into the cloak.

The best answer was a truthful answer. Bella sat down beside her. "No, but I have no other choice."

"There are always other choices," Rebecca said, searching Bella's face.

She shook her head. "Not for me. My sister and brother-in-law left their children nothing. I quit my job unaware that my sister had lied about their wealth. If things had been as she'd indicated, I would have had the finances to raise the boys and used my savings to invest in a bakery of my own. As it turned out, I had to use most of my savings to get here." Her voice caught in her throat. Bella fought back the tears of frustration at the turn her life had taken. She would do it all again for the love of her nephews, but she didn't have to like it.

"What about love?" Rebecca asked.

Bella shook her head. "I thought someone loved me once, but it turned out he didn't love me enough. I doubt any man can truly love a woman the way she deserves. So I don't expect Philip to love me." She looked out at the rushing water. Darkness began to cut the beauty of the running water off from her view, much like her ex-fiancé had done with love.

Rebecca's soft voice penetrated Bella's thoughts. "Don't you think Philip deserves love?"

She stood. "Rebecca, we've talked about this. He is in no rush to fall in love any more than I am."

"Everyone wants to fall in love, Bella." Rebecca stood also. She dusted the back of her skirt before retracing their steps.

Bella felt a harsh laugh bubble up as she fell into step beside her future mother-in-law. "Only those who have never tasted love or who have gotten away unscathed by its cruelty."

Rebecca stopped and turned to face Bella. "It's obvious you've been hurt, but as far as I know, Philip has never been in love. He's never been hurt by it. Will you be the first by not returning his love, should he fall in love with you someday? I only want what is best for my son, so please just think about it before you actually get married." She searched Bella's eyes, then turned away.

Bella fell behind her. Was it possible Philip would fall in love with her? If he did, would her not returning his affections hurt him? He'd been the one to suggest a marriage of convenience. Was she doing the wrong thing by marrying him?

The next morning, Bella still didn't have any answers. She knew she had to consider Caleb and Mark, but she also worried that she'd be doing Philip an injustice by marrying him.

All day, she worried about what to do. Rebecca had said there were always choices, but Bella couldn't see them.

She felt Philip watching her and looked up. He studied her face as if he was trying to read her mind across the kitchen table. The Young and Armstrong families were eating dinner. They were a noisy bunch and none of them seemed to be paying attention to Bella and Philip.

They'd said less than ten words to each other during the day. Bella had been busy with the women, cooking, cleaning and planning their wedding. Philip had been with his brothers and his stepfather, Seth.

This wasn't the first time she'd felt his eyes upon her after her talk with Rebecca. Had he known what his mother was going to say to her? Did he read the doubt on her face regarding their upcoming wedding?

She lowered her head and continued eating. Pot roast and potatoes left a dry taste in her mouth. Bella made the decision to talk to Philip again about getting married.

If he had changed his mind, she wanted to give him the option of calling it off. Would he? And if he did, where would that leave her and the boys? Bella silently prayed that God would take control because at this moment she felt as if she had none.

During the few days that Philip had known Bella, he'd learned that she was quiet. But he sensed there was more to her quietness today than before. She'd seemed upset when she and Rebecca had returned from their walk last night.

Now that tonight's meal was complete and the dishes were cleaned, he searched out his future bride. Philip found her in the kitchen standing by the stove. He walked to her and laced his fingers around hers. "Bella, I'd like to have a private word with you."

She nodded and laid the towel in her other hand on the counter.

Philip looked to Fay. She rocked in her rocker by the fireplace. The younger children all played at her feet. "Would you mind keeping an eye on the boys for a few minutes? We won't be gone long."

"I'd be happy to watch them," Fay replied.

He smiled his thanks and then pulled Bella toward the front door. Philip noticed the frown on his mother's face. She'd been quiet since her and Bella's walk also. What was wrong with her? Rebecca had always been warm and loving to the strays who crossed her doorway. Why was she acting so different with Bella?

After putting on their coats, they stepped out onto the porch. Philip indicated Bella sit down in one of the chairs that faced the front yard.

Bella did as he indicated.

He leaned against the porch rail and studied her, then asked, "What is bothering you? Is it something Ma said?"

Soft words burst from her lips. "I'm not sure we should get married."

Philip had half expected her to say just that. "Why not?"

Bella stood to face him. Her blue eyes looked deep into his. "Look, I've been in love. You haven't. I don't want to be the cause of you not finding true love."

He took her hand in his once more and pulled her closer to him. "We've been through this. I've explained that I have no intention of falling in love and why."

"I know, but…"

Philip pulled her even closer. "No buts. I don't want to fall in love, you said you don't want to fall in love. Have you changed your mind about that?"

She shook her head.

"Then there is no problem. We are getting married for the boys' sake. Just because we aren't going to fall in love doesn't mean we can't be friends and talk about things. Especially when it is of this importance. Agreed?"

She took a step even closer. "Agreed."

The sweet scent of vanilla wafted toward him and he grinned. Impulsively, Philip bent his head and smelled the side of her neck. He murmured against her neck, "Did you let Joy dab you with vanilla?"

Bella nodded. Her hair tickled his face.

Philip pulled away. What was he doing? He grinned down at her. "I thought so." His little sister loved the scent of vanilla and used it like perfume.

They were standing so close that Philip felt her shiver. "I suppose we should go back inside." He looked deep into her eyes. "Do you still want to marry me, Bella?"

"As long as you are sure this is what you want," she answered.

He kissed her forehead. "I do."

She shivered again.

A giggle sounded to his right. He looked up and saw four small faces in the window. Then he heard his little sister announce to the room, "They're kissing."

Philip groaned. "We'd best get back inside." As he followed her in, Philip admitted to himself that he'd like to have stayed outside a little longer with Bella. He tried to convince himself that it was to assure her that he wanted to marry her, but the truth was, he enjoyed holding her in his arms and watching her cheeks turn a pretty pink.

Chapter Seven

The next day, he was still thinking about Bella's pink cheeks when he pulled his horse to a stop in front of the relay station he shared with Thomas and his new wife, Josephine. He dismounted but left the horse tied to the porch.

Josephine and their closest neighbor, Hazel, were sitting at the kitchen table peeling potatoes. They looked up as he came through the door.

His sister-in-law's mouth pulled into a big smile. "It's about time you got home. I was beginning to really worry about you."

Philip shut the door and hung his coat on a peg. "I was delayed by my future bride." He'd walked halfway across the room when the door opened again and Thomas entered.

Hazel demanded, "What future bride?"

Over the past year, Hazel had become motherly toward the two young men. Then when Josephine had arrived a few months earlier, Hazel had treated her as family, too. Hazel didn't hesitate to ask her question.

Philip turned and stared at his brother. "It seems

I've posted a mail-order-bride ad in Colorado and Bella Wilson felt the need to answer it by arriving by stage out at the Turnstone relay station." He had the satisfaction of watching Thomas's face pale.

"Um, Bella Wilson?" Thomas ran his hand through his hair and looked over Philip's shoulder at Josephine.

Philip turned in time to see her shrug her shoulders.

"Don't look at me. I've never heard of her," Josephine said before studying the wood pattern on the table.

Hazel frowned. "I thought I told you two to answer each and every letter and apologize for misleading those young ladies." She looked between Thomas and Josephine.

Thomas walked around Philip. He headed to the coffeepot. "We did."

Philip followed him. "Well, Bella didn't write a letter. She simply came, much like Josephine did."

Shock filled Josephine's voice. "She's a Pony Express rider, too?"

Hazel laughed. "Here I thought you were the only woman gutsy enough to pull a stunt like that." She held out her cup for Thomas to refill.

"No, she arrived by stage but didn't have enough money to continue on to Dove Creek. John got a kick out of sending me into the house for my special delivery packages."

The other three people in the room stared at him with open mouths. Finally, Josephine spoke. "Did you say packages? As in more than one?"

Philip took a cup down from the cupboard. "Oh, did I forget to mention that she has two children in her care, too?"

Thomas raked his hand through his hair. His face looked miserable.

Josephine's eyes grew big in her heart-shaped face.

Hazel whistled low and muttered, "Two children."

Philip took a sip from his warm coffee. It felt good to make them squirm a little. Josephine's gaze sought out her husband's.

Thomas finally found his voice. "How old are they?"

"Four and six," Philip answered.

Josephine gasped. "I can't imagine being all alone with a four-year-old and a six-year-old. The trip out here must have been so hard." Regret filled her voice.

Hazel shook her head. "Boys or girls?"

Philip walked over to the table and sat down. "Boys. Caleb and Mark. They are nice enough little boys. I believe I'll adopt them after the wedding."

Thomas pulled out a chair. "So you are going to marry her?"

"She has no other place to go and I can't let those young'uns go into an orphanage because their aunt can't take care of them." Philip palmed the cup in his hand, rolling it back and forth as he looked at each person sitting at the table.

Hazel finally snapped. "Philip Young, you stop feeding us a smidgen at a time and tell the whole story. Is Bella their mother or aunt?" she demanded.

He laughed and then told them everything that he knew about Bella and the boys. He finished with "They are staying out at Ma's until the wedding day."

Thomas nodded. "And when is the big day?"

"Day after tomorrow. I'm going to sleep now and head back sometime tomorrow. By now, Bella is overwhelmed with our rather large family." He pushed back his chair and yawned.

"Can just anybody come to this wedding?" Hazel asked with a grump. "Or do they have to have a special invitation?"

Philip walked around the table and gave her a big kiss on the cheek. "It wouldn't be the perfect wedding without you there, Hazel. I expect you to come with me."

A flush filled her cheeks. "Well, if you insist."

Josephine laughed and shook her head. "Go to bed, Philip. Hazel and I have to decide what we're going to wear."

"If we all go, who's going to man the relay station?" Thomas asked.

"Looks like you are going to miss the wedding of the season." Philip turned toward his bedroom. "Serves you right, too."

"You don't like shindigs anyway," Hazel reminded Thomas, picking up her cup and heading to the washtub with it.

"No, but I love Ma's cakes."

Philip laughed. "I'll eat an extra piece for you. If the boys don't eat it all up." He closed the door to his bedroom and leaned against it.

Would this be the wedding of the season like he'd told Thomas? Or was it all just a mockery of what a marriage should be? He walked to the bed and sat down.

His worn Bible lay on the side table. Philip picked it up. *Lord, I hope I'm doing the right thing by Bella and the boys.* He leaned back on the pillows and opened it up. Maybe he'd find the answer between the pages.

* * *

Bella put her face in her hands. She wasn't sure how much more pampering she could take. The outhouse probably wasn't the best place to get her thoughts together, but it was the only place she could be alone, away from all the questions and prying eyes.

Philip had been gone since early yesterday and during that time she'd met most of his brothers and his stepfather, and had been bombarded with wedding plans. Rebecca, Fay and their close friend Emma, who had come to the family as a slave to another couple, thankfully the Young men had made it possible for her to have freedom now. Each lady had their idea of what Bella's wedding should look like. The barn was decorated with white streamers and wooden planks stretched across barrels for seating. Pine branches hung from the rafters and the scent of their needles filled the barn, covering up the animal smells that normally lingered there. The added greenery and yellow ribbons tied to them gave the barn a fresh look.

What Bella had thought would be a simple wedding with family had turned into a town wedding. People from all over had been invited. Rebecca had sent Seth and Andrew into the general store with an open invitation flyer that was hung by the register. Already neighboring wives had arrived asking what foods they could bring. It was going to be a spectacle.

She raised her head. Well, it was more for show than actually a love commitment. What difference did it make if everyone showed up and had fun? Bella shook her head. To her it meant mingling with folks she didn't know. She'd never liked large crowds and now here she was stuck with the biggest event of her life.

"Bella? Are you all right?" Emma asked through the door.

She lied. "Fine." Bella liked Emma, even more so after she heard how Emma had been kept as a slave by an older couple and then the Young family saved her by purchasing her from her masters. They'd given Emma her freedom, but she'd stayed with them and become a part of the family. Bella suspected that the main reason Emma stayed was because she was in love with Andrew.

Emma's shadow blocked out a little of the sunshine as she leaned against the door. "The Youngs can be a little overwhelming. I guess we all can." She sighed heavily. "I hope you understand that we are trying to help and that we are excited to have you become a part of the Young family." The last part was said wistfully.

Bella straightened. "I know. I just needed some fresh air."

Emma giggled. "So you chose the outhouse?" She moved away from the door. "I think I could have found a better place."

Bella opened the door with a grin. "Yeah, probably not my best choice of the day."

"No, maybe not. Come with me." Emma headed down a small path away from the outhouse.

"Where are we going?"

"To a quiet place where you can think." Emma stopped in a small grove of trees.

Bella was surprised to see a small wooden bench sitting under one of the trees. "I didn't expect this," she said in awe.

Emma smiled. "Have you always been shy?"

She could deny it, but seeing how she already had

one lie to repent for, Bella chose to nod. "It's worse when there are lots of people around."

Emma smiled. "And you are going to marry the prankster of the family. Not a shy bone in his body."

"Afraid so." Bella sat down.

Emma nodded. "I thought so. When we get back, I'll speak to Rebecca and Fay. Between the three of us, we'll help you get through this wedding."

A bird landed on a branch over their heads. He sang for a moment and then took flight once more. Bella wished she could fly away like the little bird, but she knew that she had to get through this. The boys were depending on her. "Thank you. I think I'm better now. We can go back."

Emma stood. "I'm glad you feel better. This spot always makes me feel good." She glanced around with love in her eyes.

"Did Andrew put the bench here for you?" Bella asked, standing also.

"He did."

Bella smiled. "I thought so."

Emma looked everywhere but at Bella. "What made you think that? It could have been any of the boys."

It was Bella's turn to giggle. "Yes, but Andrew is the one who is sweet on you. So it made sense he would do something special like this for you."

Emma grinned. "I don't know that he is sweet on me, but he is very kind and understanding." She started walking back up the path that led to the house. "We'd better hurry. Fay and Rebecca are waiting to fit your wedding dress."

Bella groaned. The thought of spending more time

being stuck with pins and told to stand up tall made her want to run back to the outhouse.

As if she could read her mind, Emma teased, "Don't even think about going back to the outhouse."

Bella discovered that the afternoon hadn't been so bad after all. The three women worked on her dress while the children played outside. The men went about their chores and things seemed to settle down a bit. Perhaps it was because Emma had pulled the other two ladies aside and explained Bella's feelings.

As soon as the dress was complete, the four women began to make dinner. The beans had been on the stove most of the day and the roast in the oven, so all they had to do was make the potatoes and other vegetables. Joy loved making cookies. She and Emma had made a fresh batch that morning, so even dessert was prepared.

Bella found herself looking up the road for Philip's return. He'd gone to tell his brother and sister-in-law that they were getting married. If he didn't hurry back, he was going to miss his own wedding.

Anxiety hit her like a punch in the stomach. Had he left for good? Was he planning on coming back? Bella told herself she was being ridiculous, but the sudden fear was very real. She hated being this dependent on another person. Maybe she should talk to Philip about getting a job in town, once they were married. Would he go for such a thing? Or would he want his wife to stay home and pretend that theirs was a real marriage?

Chapter Eight

Philip, Josephine and Hazel arrived at the Young farm a little before dusk. He was thankful that the women had agreed to ride their own horses instead of bringing a wagon. It would have taken much longer to get back if they had brought the wagon.

Caleb spotted him and came running. "Philip! You came back!"

He dropped from the horse. "Of course I came back."

Caleb stubbed his toe against a small rock and sent it sailing across the yard. "Well, I wasn't so sure you'd be back."

Philip kneeled down in front of the little boy. Mark ran up to stand beside his brother. "As long as the Lord will allow me to live and breathe, I will never leave you." He pulled both boys into a hug.

"I told you he'd come back," Benjamin said, coming to a halt beside them. "Hi, Aunt Josephine, Aunt Hazel."

Both women slid off the backs of their horses. "Hello, Benjamin." Josephine gave him a hug.

When she released him, Hazel grabbed the boy. "Benny Young. You have got to stop growing." His head came to her chest. She released him, then turned her attention to the other two boys. “You must be Caleb and Mark.”

At their nods, Philip made the introductions. “Boys, this is your aunt Josephine and aunt Hazel.”

“Oh, Philip, they are adorable.” Josephine smiled down at them.

“Now, Josephine, don’t embarrass the boys. I want you to meet Bella, so let’s head to the house.” Philip handed the horses’ reins to Benjamin. “Do you mind taking care of the horses for us, Benny?”

“Naw, we’ll take care of them. Won’t we, fellas?”

Caleb and Mark nodded eagerly. Philip watched them lead the horses into the barn. It broke his heart that the boys hadn’t thought he’d come back. Had the same thought crossed Bella’s mind? He hoped not.

Philip opened the door for the ladies and then followed them inside. The smell of roast and potatoes greeted his hungry belly and it growled its approval.

Bella came through the kitchen door with a wide grin. Her hair looked a little mussed and her checks red. Was that joy he saw in her eyes? Had she missed him?

Don’t kid yourself, Phil. Your family is overwhelming and she’s simply happy to see a familiar face, he told himself.

He stepped around Josephine and Hazel. “Bella, I’d like you to meet my sister in-law, Josephine, and our next-door neighbor Hazel. Ladies, this beautiful young woman is my future wife, Bella.”

Bella stepped up beside him and grabbed his hand. She held on as if she was drowning.

Philip looked down at her, puzzled. Her eyes had gone from joy to wariness in the few moments it had taken him to make the introductions. He gave her hand a gentle squeeze.

"Oh, we are so happy to meet you," Josephine said as she offered Bella a quick hug.

Hazel stood back and eyed the younger woman. She gently pulled Josephine back. "Josie, give the girl some breathing room. She looks like she might just pass out from all this attention."

Bella squared her shoulders and smiled tightly. "It's nice to meet you both."

Josephine's expression said she didn't understand why there was so much tension in the room. Philip didn't really understand it, either. What was wrong with Bella?

She squeezed his hand tighter. "I'm sorry. I guess I should have warned Philip that I'm not very good around a lot of people. The last couple of days have been a little stressful for me. It's not you. I just..."

Hazel smiled. "Girl, there is no reason to explain. There's nothing wrong with you. I don't care much for crowds myself. That's why I live on the outskirts instead of in town."

"Is that Hazel's voice I hear out here?" Rebecca asked, coming through the kitchen door. She wiped her hands on her apron and hurried into the room for hugs.

Philip watched Bella's face. He noted the tightness around her mouth and the paleness of her skin. Gently he tugged on her hand. In a soft voice he asked, "Would you like to go with me to the barn to check on the boys?"

"That would be lovely." She sighed. Relief washed away a little of the tightness on her face.

The other women were busy catching up as they hugged each other and oohed over new hairstyles and dresses. "If you ladies will excuse us, Bella and I are going to go check on the boys."

"You kids go on," Hazel said, smiling at them with understanding.

Rebecca called over her shoulder, "Hurry back. Philip, we still need to make sure that your suit will fit."

"Ma, I'm not wearing a suit." Philip propelled Bella from the house.

Bella giggled. "Do you really think you are going to get out of wearing a suit to your wedding?"

"Yep. I hate being trussed up in layers of clothes. I'm going to wear my jeans, boots and a new shirt. It's blue. I got it while we were in Dove Creek." He winked at her and headed away from the barn and toward the creek.

"I thought we were going to the barn."

"We were, but now that I know she wants me to hurry back, I think I'll go somewhere else." Philip grabbed her hand and made a run for the tree line.

Bella laughed as they cleared the yard. "You are a mess, Philip Young."

He slowed down but continued to hold on to her hand. "How were things while I was gone?" Philip realized that he'd taken Bella from the house so fast that she didn't have time to get her coat. He released her hand, slipped out of his coat and draped it around her shoulders.

"Thanks." She snuggled into the warm jacket. "It was all right. I just hadn't expected there to be so many people about. Your mother invited the whole town to our wedding."

Philip wasn't surprised. "And I'm guessing she plans on using the barn for the ceremony and party afterward?"

Bella nodded. “People have been arriving to ask what they can bring.”

He led her to the water’s edge. “Or came to see the new bride.” He kneeled down and picked up a rock. The water was frozen, so his thought of skipping rocks vanished as quickly as it had formed.

“Maybe. I’ve met more ladies in the last two days than I have in two months.”

He frowned. “Really?”

She smiled. “When I say met, I mean spoken to and exchanged names.”

“Oh.” He tossed the rock across the frozen surface. “I’m sorry about that. We probably should have talked about the wedding more before we arrived.”

Bella sat down on an old log. “Yeah, I would have preferred a small wedding with just your family present.”

“I understand. I’m sorry Ma has gone all out.” He stood and walked back to her. “She means well.”

She nodded. “I know. And after tomorrow this will be behind us.” Bella stood. “We probably should head back.”

Philip chuckled. “You’re probably right. She’ll send a search party after us if we stay gone much longer.” Even though he laughed, Philip couldn’t help but feel bad that Bella was anticipating the wedding being over. It wasn’t that he wanted the wedding to be special for him. After all, he didn’t even want to get married. But he felt that Bella should have the wedding day she wanted.

They started walking back to the house. “Have you always been quiet?” Philip asked, tucking his hands deep into his front pockets.

“I don’t think I’m quiet when I’m with only two or three people, but I suppose I have been.” She looked off into the distance. "That's one of the reasons I love baking so much."

He didn't understand what baking had to do with being quiet.

His confusion must have shown on his face, because Bella explained. "When I worked at the bakery, I stayed in the kitchen and baked. Most of the time there were only two people besides me at the bakery and they were up front." She looked up at him and then continued with a shrug. "My day started early, so going to work there weren't many people about. Then when I was done, I'd go back to my home and read or sleep."

"I see. So you really aren't used to being around others." He almost felt sorry for her. Philip liked being with other people and talking, joking and laughing.

Bella shook her head. "No, until I got the boys, I didn't have to worry about anyone else and I enjoyed my own company."

He pulled his hand from his pocket and grasped hers. "Well, after our wedding we'll head back to the relay station. Thomas and Josephine are the only two other people that live there."

"So, we'll be living with them?"

Philip frowned. They really hadn't talked much about life after marriage. "Yes, the house has two bedrooms, so we'll have one and Thomas and Josephine will have the other. My room is small, but the four of us will be fine until we can make other arrangements. I'm sure the boys and I can make pallets."

She scowled but nodded. Bella remained silent the rest of the way to the house. Philip hadn't thought that she wouldn't want to live with his brother and sister-in-law once they were married. "Let's check on the boys before heading inside," he suggested when they came to the yard.

They went to the barn. When he pulled the door open, Philip gasped. Everything had been cleared in the center, looking much like it had at Christmas. Only now white streamers hung from the rafters and big yellow bows made from fabric decorated the stall doors. The horses had all been moved to the very back of the barn. Several tables stood off to the right—Philip assumed this was for the food that the neighbors and his mother planned on cooking up.

The boys were nowhere in sight and Philip realized it was suppertime as the triangle rang out. "Those little rascals are already in the house, probably at the table." He smiled at Bella.

"Probably. My nephews love to eat." She turned and walked out the door.

Philip followed. He pulled the barn door closed and watched as his brothers arrived from all directions. They laughed and pushed at each other. Thankfully there were only three of them at home now.

Seth rounded the barn beside him. He put his arm around Philip's shoulders. "Are you ready for the big day tomorrow?"

Bella looked over her shoulder and grinned but continued walking. Philip wasn't sure if she could hear them, or if she'd picked up her pace because she wanted to give them privacy.

"Hey, Bella. Can I have a quiet word with you?" Andrew asked, hurrying to her side.

Philip wondered what Andrew wanted with Bella but knew he needed to respond to Seth's question. "I'm ready for it all to be over and just to start a simple life with her."

Seth nodded. "I understand, son. That's how I felt when I married your mother. But truth is married life isn't always simple." He stopped with his arm still around Philip's shoulders.

Philip stopped also and turned his head to look at his stepfather. "Is there something you want to say, Seth?"

"As a matter of fact, there is. Your mother is worried about you."

"I can't imagine why." Philip shook his head. "Bella is a nice girl. The boys have been well behaved. What gives her cause to worry?"

Seth laughed. "It's not Bella that worries her, it's you."

"Me?"

"Aren't you the one who has always said you're not the marrying kind?"

Philip nodded. "Yep, and it's true."

"Then why are you getting married?"

He rubbed his chin with the back of his hand. "Because those boys need a father figure." Philip repeated what he'd said earlier, knowing it was true.

"Let someone else marry her and give them boys a pa. Why does it have to be you?" Seth crossed his arms over his chest and waited.

Philip watched Bella and Andrew talking with their heads together. Why did it have to be him? He wasn't attached to Bella romantically. Was Andrew interested in her? No, everyone knew Andrew had feelings for Emma.

"Because I'm the one she wants to marry. And I

want to make sure those boys are treated fairly," Philip answered.

"So you love her?"

Philip jerked back as if he'd been slapped. "No. You know I can't fall in love with her or any other woman for that matter."

Seth frowned. "Refresh my memory, why is that?"

Frustrated, Philip started to walk away, but respect for his stepfather held him in place. Seth knew about his past. Well, he knew the truth as the ladies at the orphanage had told it. They'd said his father died of a broken heart when his mother died. But Philip knew his father was weak and had killed himself.

He had no intention of falling in love or expecting someone to fall in love with him so deeply that should either of them die the other would kill themselves and leave behind small children. "You know the reason. Besides, Bella and I have no intention of falling in love. We have agreed to raise the boys together as friends."

Seth nodded. "I see. Son, love may creep up on you and then what? Will Bella only want friendship then or will she change her mind and love you back? Or what if *she* falls in love with you?"

Philip shook his head. "That isn't going to happen."

His stepfather shook his head. "We'll see. Come on. Time for supper."

Was he being naive to think they could just be friends? Hadn't people with arranged marriages gotten married and remained friends and never fallen in love?

His gaze moved to Bella and Andrew. Andrew nodded his head with a smile, gave Bella a quick hug and then bounded up the porch steps. She turned and smiled at him. It was a sweet smile. Bella was a beautiful young woman, with dreams.

Philip assured himself that those dreams didn't include falling in love again. But what if he was wrong?

Chapter Nine

The next morning, Bella fussed with her hair. Rebecca had insisted that since the preacher was there they should have Sunday morning services before the wedding. It seemed as if her future mother-in-law was trying to postpone the wedding for as long as possible.

Bella really didn't understand why. Rebecca claimed to like her, claimed to be all right with them marrying due to her answering a mail-order-bride advertisement, but she found all sorts of reasons to put off the actual event.

Church services, lunch and then the wedding. Didn't Rebecca know how nerve-racking this was for her? She smoothed down her calico dress while looking at the pretty pink wedding dress that she'd wear later. Her hands shook. If only there weren't so many people watching. Maybe then she'd be less nervous.

A soft knock sounded on the bedroom door. She was sharing the room with Joy, but the little girl had already dressed and gone down to play, so it was up to Bella to answer it. She took a deep breath, dreading to see who waited on the other side, and pulled the door open.

Philip stood before her. As he'd vowed, he wore a blue shirt, black jeans and black boots. His sandy-brown hair was combed into place and his blue eyes sparkled. "Can I come in?"

"I'm not sure if that is appropriate," she answered uneasily. The last thing she needed was for her future mother-in-law to find them alone in a bedroom before the ceremony.

Philip nodded. "Then can you come out?"

Bella realized that she was as ready as she'd ever be to face today's crowd. She'd heard wagons arriving all morning and knew there would be more introductions today than she'd ever experienced. "All right." She pulled the door closed behind her.

He grabbed her hand and headed down the hall, then quickly darted into the kitchen. Fay, Rebecca, Josephine, Hazel and Emma were finding places for covered dishes. Bella felt she should stay and help, but Philip tugged her hand and continued through the kitchen.

Several of the ladies, with big grins on their faces, wished her good morning.

Her answer sounded weak in her ears as she allowed Philip to pull her onward. "Good morning. Evidently I'm in a hurry."

The sound of laughter met her ears as the kitchen door slammed behind them. "Where are we going, Philip?"

"To the river to talk."

Would they forever be heading to the river to "talk"? Bella followed along as fast as she could. Several people called out to Philip with congratulations and he responded in kind as they passed. He continued at a fast clip even after they were out of the yard and into the woods. What could he possibly want to talk to her about that was this important?

As soon as they were at the water's edge Philip stopped and turned to her. "You don't want this large wedding, do you?" he asked.

Bella shook her head. "It terrifies me to think I have to stand in front of all those people and say anything, let alone 'I do.'"

"What if I told you I know how we can get out of a big wedding and still get married today?"

"I'd say you are insane. There is no way your mother is going to let us cancel this wedding." She shook her head. "No way."

Philip laughed. "Yes, there is. I'm going to convince Seth to help us and talk to the preacher about doing a small ceremony, after all the guests have gone home."

Bella couldn't believe that Philip could pull off such a feat. She gaped at him. "How?"

"Well, last night after everyone had gone to bed, I heard Ma say that she's always dreamed of the wedding she is giving us. Then I remembered her wedding to Seth was a small ceremony. So, I'm going to explain to Seth how you feel. At the last minute, I'm going to ask Ma to come to the back with me and then I'm going to walk her down the aisle to Seth. They can get married again and then he can whisper to her that as soon as all the guests leave, you will get the small wedding you want."

Bella clapped her hands together. "Are you sure she won't get angry?"

"No, she'll be so overwhelmed by the attention she's getting that she'll just agree and then we can have a quiet wedding with family. Ma will get to see me married and she'll be thrilled that Seth is so romantic." Philip grinned down at her.

"So, are you ready to help me put this together?" he asked.

She didn't know. It all sounded sneaky to her. What if Rebecca got angry? Told her to get herself down to that altar right then and there? Then what? Her embarrassment would be triple what it was now.

But if it worked as Philip thought it would, Rebecca would be happy, she would be happy and the preacher would get paid for two weddings instead of one and he'd be happy. She nodded. "What do I do?"

Everything was going according to plan. Sunday services and lunch were complete. Now everyone was headed into the barn. Bella held her breath as Seth made his way to the front. She allowed Rebecca to fuss over her dress one last time and then watched as Philip approached.

He stood tall and confident as he said, "Ma, I'll escort you to your place of honor."

She nodded, gave a teary-eyed look to Bella and then placed her small hand in the crook of her son's arm. Rebecca stood tall as she walked down the aisle. All eyes were upon mother and son as they went.

Bella saw Philip lower his head and whisper in Rebecca's ear. Her head shot up and she searched his face. Then she looked to the front, where Seth and Andrew stood. Rebecca quickly turned to look at Bella, who offered what she hoped looked like a happy smile and nodded.

Rebecca allowed herself to be escorted to the front, where her husband waited. With a sigh, Bella slipped into the back row. She couldn't believe how easily Rebecca had allowed herself to be moved into the position of the bride.

Murmuring among the guests began. Confusion laced their faces. Bella felt sure they were speculating on what had become of her and Philip's wedding.

Bella continued to watch Philip and his mother, refusing to meet anyone's gaze. Rebecca hugged her son before turning to face her husband.

As soon as Rebecca and Seth faced forward, the preacher cleared his throat and said, "Dearly beloved, today we are all in for a nice surprise. Philip and Bella have decided to give Rebecca and Seth the wedding they have always dreamed of. The young couple will be married at a later time. So today we are here to reunite this man and this woman in holy matrimony..." His voice continued on.

Bella focused on Philip's back.

He stood ramrod straight and was soon asked, "Who gives this woman?"

Then he said, "I do." He turned around and walked back to where Bella sat.

When all eyes were on the couple being married, Philip leaned over and whispered, "See? I told you it would work. Look how happy she is."

Bella shook her head. "We can't see her face. She might be ready to wring both our necks when this is over," she hissed back.

"No. She's happy. She even thanked me." He sat back with a look of satisfaction on his handsome face.

Bella thought about how easy it was for Philip to make things go the way he wanted them to. Did he do that with everyone? Would he manipulate her in the future?

She pushed the worrisome thought away and focused on Caleb and Mark. The two little boys stood behind Andrew making funny faces at the crowd.

Unlike her, the two boys loved all the attention they were getting. Joy stood on the other side behind Rebecca trying to get them to stop, which made the guests chuckle softly.

As soon as the ceremony was complete, the guests all rose to wish the happy couple well. The Young family, both men and women, began to clear away the seating. They scooted the homemade benches and chairs against the walls and stalls of the barn.

Soon the fiddle players took their spots and began to play a soft tune. Seth and Rebecca were the first couple on the dance floor. Everyone watched for several moments before joining them.

Philip came back and held his hand out to Bella. "Just one dance." He grinned.

How could she refuse? He'd made it possible for her to avoid the big wedding. His blue eyes shone down on Bella as he led her into the flowing dance steps. He twirled her about the dance floor, leaving her feeling breathless.

As soon as the music stopped, Philip walked with her to the refreshment table. "Where did you learn to dance like that?" Bella asked as she picked up a prepoured punch glass.

"Ma taught me. She taught us all." He grabbed a cup and took a big drink.

Bella looked to where Rebecca and Seth stood. Several people surrounded them. She assumed congratulations were being offered. She looked around the room, where the other brothers were dancing with young ladies. Not seeing Andrew or Emma, her gaze began to search the barn. Andrew had told Bella that he intended to ask Emma to marry him. Was he doing that now?

After several long moments, she spotted them standing beside the door talking to the preacher. Bella smiled as she watched as the three of them left the building.

"Now, isn't that interesting?" Philip said close to her ear.

She glanced sideways at him. "What?"

"Big brother Andrew and his sweetheart just left with the preacher." He grinned at her, then set down his cup. "Let's follow them."

"Why?" Bella put her cup in the tub for dirty dishes.

He grabbed her hand and tugged at it. "Why not?"

She allowed him to guide her across the barn floor and out the door. Andrew and Emma were nowhere to be seen. Bella thought she knew where they had gone, but she wasn't sure.

Philip asked, "Where could they have gone?"

Bella looked toward the hidden path that ran behind the outhouse. She grinned.

His gaze followed hers. "Not behind the outhouse." He shook his head. "The preacher was with them."

Philip looked so downhearted at having lost his brother and Emma that Bella giggled. "Oh, come on, nosy britches." This time she was the one doing the tugging. "But be quiet. I don't want to get caught."

Together they followed the little trail Emma had taken Bella down before. Just before entering the clearing where Andrew had created Emma a special place, they heard the preacher's voice.

"I'm sorry, folks, but you don't have any witnesses."

Philip whispered, "Witnesses?"

Bella nodded.

Philip stepped out into the clearing. "What do they need witnesses for?" he asked.

Emma turned with a gasp.

Bella wanted to throttle him. Why couldn't he just be still for once and wait to see what was going on? She followed him into the clearing.

Andrew looked at his brother and scowled. "What are you two doing here?"

"Following you," Philip answered. "What are you two doing here?"

The preacher looked from brother to brother. He seemed to have forgotten that Philip had asked him a question.

Emma looked at Bella, then a smile broke across her lips. She tugged on Andrew's arm. "Andy, they can be our witnesses."

The preacher finally found his voice. "Would you two be willing to stand in as their witnesses so that Andrew and Emma can get married?"

Philip smiled broadly. He searched his brother's face. "You do know Ma will have your hide for getting married without her."

Andrew nodded.

"And everyone says I'm the rebel." Philip looked to the minister. "I'll be a witness."

All three of them turned to Bella. "I don't know. What about Rebecca? She's going to be so angry at us all."

Emma separated herself from Andrew. "She might for a little while. But we really want to get married and Preacher Pruitt isn't going to be back for at least six months."

"Well, instead of making Rebecca angry, why don't we have a double wedding?" Bella turned to the preacher. "Would you mind marrying them at the same time you marry us?"

A smile lit up his face. "That sounds excellent."

Bella turned to Emma. "Do you mind?"

Emma looked to Andrew. "I don't, if Andy doesn't."

Andrew walked over to them. He put his arm around Emma's waist and gently pulled her to his side. "I don't care how we get married. I just want to marry you."

Philip was the only one who didn't look happy at the prospect of a double wedding. Bella frowned. "Philip?"

"What's the matter, little brother? 'Fraid I'll steal your moment?" Andrew asked, punching his brother in the shoulder.

Philip frowned at him. "No."

Bella placed her hand in his. "Then what is it?"

He pouted. "I was looking forward to watching Andrew tell Ma that he'd up and got hitched without her." Philip looked up and laughed, letting her know he was teasing. This time Bella hit him in the arm.

"Well, if all that's settled. We'd all better get back to the party before we're missed." The preacher walked away, shaking his head.

Bella thought she heard him mutter "Kids."

Were they all just kids? She looked at Andrew and Philip. She'd never asked Philip how old he was, just assumed he was the same age as her, eighteen. According to popular belief she should have been married two years ago. She followed the preacher back. He was short and round, and his hair was gray. So he probably did see them as a bunch of kids.

As they reentered the yard, Bella saw a couple of wagons driving away. Other families were gathering up their children and leaving. With their departure, Bella knew that soon she'd be standing in front of Philip's family and her nephews agreeing to be Philip's wife. Her hands and heart trembled at the thought of marrying a man she'd met only a few days before.

Chapter Ten

Philip sighed with relief when the preacher said, "I now pronounce you husbands and wives. You may kiss your brides." He bent down and lightly brushed Bella's lips with his own. They quivered beneath his.

She opened her eyes when he pulled back. He placed his forehead on hers and breathed. "We did it."

"Yes, we did."

The family cheered around them. Philip lifted his head and looked to Andrew. His brother only had eyes for Emma. Emma's smile spoke volumes as to her love for his brother.

Philip prayed they would be happy forever. He didn't want to open his heart to his new bride because he didn't want to be hurt. He also didn't want her to be hurt.

His gaze moved back to Bella. She'd moved away from him and was hugging Caleb and Mark. They'd agreed to be friends and thankfully she felt the same way about love as he did.

Caleb pulled away. "Are we going to Philip's house to live now?"

Bella smiled. "In a little while."

Mark tucked his small hand into hers. "I want to stay with you, Aunt Bella."

She picked him up. "I'm going, too, you little rascal." Bella tickled him and held on while he squirmed in her arms.

Philip didn't miss that his parents and other brothers were crowded around Andrew and Emma. They knew his and Bella's marriage wasn't a love match. He walked over to his new family.

Seth and Rebecca finished hugging Andrew and Emma and walked over to them. Rebecca hugged them both and touched the little boys' faces. Seth slapped him on the back and said, "Congratulations."

Philip smiled. "Thanks."

The rest of the family hurried over and offered their congratulations, as well. Hazel and Fay began cleaning up and chattering about the sounds of pitter-pattering feet in the near future.

Seth put the other boys to work and soon the barn was back to its original state. They all headed back into the house. The women went to the kitchen and the men into the sitting room. Philip watched Bella join his mother and the others. Did she feel as uncomfortable as he did right now?

Caleb and Mark looked lost. Benjamin had gone to his room to change out of his Sunday clothes. Philip called the boys to him. "Why don't you young men stay in here with the rest of us?" He smiled at them.

Caleb moved to his side, but Mark looked longingly toward where Bella had disappeared into the kitchen. Philip assumed the little boy was feeling unsure about his future. He walked to Mark and rested his hand on the little boy's head, drawing his attention.

Mark looked up. "Will Aunt Bella come back?"

Philip kneeled in front of him. "Sure she will. She's just going to help the women clean up." He felt Caleb move closer to his brother.

Tears filled Mark's eyes. "But she got married today. What will happen to Caleb and me?" he asked, with a crack in his young voice.

Aware of the other men in the room, Philip pulled Mark into his arms. "Your aunt Bella loves you very much and will never leave you." He lifted Mark's chin to look him in the eye. "And she married me. I'm now your uncle Philip. I'll take care of you, too. You're going home with us and we want you to live with us for as long as you want to."

Mark sniffled. "Really?"

"Yes, really." He smiled. "You're family now. All these people are your family." Philip indicated all the men who had gathered around them.

Seth laid a hand on Philip's shoulder. "That's right. You can call me Grandpa Seth, if you want to."

Andrew nodded. "And we're all your uncles."

Philip felt a lump in his throat. He swallowed and stood. His family were accepting Caleb and Mark.

Mark looked up and he smiled. "I have a big family now, huh?"

Clayton laughed. "Yes, you do, and you might not like it all the time."

Benjamin grinned. "I'm your uncle, too."

Caleb frowned. "But you aren't big yet."

"Don't have to be big," Benjamin insisted.

Seth put a stop to the arguing. "All right, boys, let's play a game of checkers while we wait for the ladies to join us."

Philip watched Seth lead the boys to the game board. He realized at that moment that his times of silliness and freedom were over. Would he be a good stepfather for the boys? The seriousness of his circumstances hit him hard. Could he handle all the trials that were coming his way?

Bella joined the women in the kitchen. They were a bustle of activity. Unsure what she should do, Bella walked to her mother-in-law.

"What can I do to help?" she asked.

"Would you mind putting a kettle of water on for tea? We have coffee made, but I'd like a spot of tea." She smiled at Bella as she set a pile of plates at Fay's elbow.

"I'll be happy to. I could use some tea myself." Bella picked up the teakettle and headed to the back door, where the well stood a few feet away.

She sighed as the bucket clattered down the well. What a day. Thankfully it would soon be over and in the morning she, Philip and the boys would be headed to the relay station. To their normal life. She poured water into the kettle. Would life ever be normal for her again?

Bella went back into the kitchen. Women's laughter filled the warm air. Maybe this was her new normal. She squared her shoulders and joined the others.

Within a matter of minutes, they had the kitchen clean and were sitting around the table sipping hot tea. Rebecca looked from Bella to Emma. "I truly am blessed. I have two new daughters."

Bella felt heat fill her cheeks. She'd not thought of herself as being Rebecca's daughter. The way her mother-in-law said it made it seem as if she was pleased.

Emma smiled. "We're the ones who are blessed. I never dreamed I'd really be a part of your family."

Fay smiled. "We are all blessed to be a part of each other's lives." She smiled at them all over her cup of tea.

Hazel raised her teacup. "I'll drink to that."

Giggles sounded around the table.

Little Joy watched as if fascinated at the activities around her. "I have two new sisters?" she asked.

"Yes, you do." Rebecca hugged her youngest close to her side.

Bella grinned. It would be nice to have a mother again. Rebecca would never replace her real mother, but to have someone to talk to when the boys did things that she didn't understand might be a good thing. Plus, sharing recipes and housekeeping tips might be nice. "I'm happy to be a part of the family, too," she said.

Emma leaned over and put her arm around Bella's shoulders. "You'll get used to us soon."

Bella leaned into her embrace. "I'm sure I will. It just takes me a little longer to get used to lots of people being around."

Her mother-in-law nodded. "Would you mind telling us a little about yourself, Bella? That might make you feel more comfortable around us."

Emma tightened her hand on Bella's shoulder, offering a form of comfort.

"Um, all right." She paused. What should she tell them?

Josephine spoke for the first time. She reached across the table and laid her hand on Bella's. "When I first joined the family, I felt a little like you, Bella. I came from a loving home, but when my ma died, I felt alone in the world. My papa was busy trying to make a living and then he disappeared, leaving me in the care of my uncle. He had a gambling problem and thought I was a pawn he could sell to pay for his debts. To get away from him and his gambling partner, I answered Philip's mail-order-bride ad to marry Thomas. That's part of how I came into the family. I'll tell you more once we get back to the house, but for now I hope knowing a little more about me will help you to share."

Bella nodded. "It does."

Fay set down her cup. "After my husband died, my landlord kicked me out of my home. He sold the house and it is being turned into a telegraph office. Thankfully Rebecca came by and rescued me. She moved me here with her family and has treated me like family ever since." She smiled at her friend.

Rebecca returned her smile. "You are family."

Fay nodded.

Hazel shook her head. "You folks sure are sappy." She took a drink of her tea and tried to hide behind the cup.

Josephine laughed. "Don't let her fool you. She's a part of the family, too. Hazel here started taking care of Thomas and Philip the day they moved out to the relay station. They love her and so do I." She removed her hand from Bella's.

Emma sat up straighter. "When I first arrived here, I was a slave to a couple who treated me well but used me to take care of their basic needs. Thankfully Rebecca and Fay, with the help of the rest, purchased me from them and then gave me my freedom."

Bella realized her story wasn't nearly as bad as theirs. "I'm sorry that happened to you all." She took a deep breath. "My story isn't quite that bad. My parents died when I was fifteen. My sister was already married and living in Denver. I didn't want to move to a big city, so stayed in the small town of Douglas City, California, where I got a job as a baker. My sister would send me news from time to time. She had a good life and two little boys. A couple of months ago, I got news that she and her husband had died in a train crash. I quit my job and hurried to claim my nephews. Only, when I got there, things weren't as I expected. The nanny had to be paid, my sister and her husband owed more than they owned and the bank had taken over all their assets. I wasn't allowed to take anything from the house other than Caleb and Mark." Tears had filled her eyes and were clogging her throat. Bella stopped and took a drink of the sweet tea.

Josephine shook her head. "How did you come across the ad that Thomas had placed? It had been months since he'd done that. I didn't think any more letters would be coming."

"The newspaper was beside the fireplace. I saw the ad and tore it out. With the boys, I used the last of my money to get to the Turnstone station." She set down her cup. "The rest you know."

Joy came to Bella and leaned against her side. "I'm glad you married Philip."

She smiled down at the little girl. "You are?"

"Yep. I always wanted a sister who was quiet like me. I'm glad God sent you." She wrapped her little arms around Bella's waist and hugged her tight.

Bella hugged her back. She looked up to find the other women wiping at their eyes. These women really did care about her. The thought was sobering. If only she and Philip could learn to love, this would be the perfect situation.

But Bella knew she'd never trust her heart to him. She'd been hurt before and he'd lost faith in himself to love without being hurt. No, she had to remind herself that theirs was a marriage of convenience.

Chapter Eleven

Philip guided the borrowed horse along the rutted road. Caleb sat in front of him, while Bella and Mark rode beside them. Josephine and Hazel were bringing up the rear. The two women were in deep conversation and not paying any attention to the newlyweds.

"Do you have to take the wagon back to Mr. Turnstone?" Bella asked.

"No, Noah said he'd take it back for us."

She nodded. "Good."

He wondered if she'd expected him to deposit them at the relay station and then take off again. Before he could ask her why she'd asked, Hazel rode her horse up between theirs.

"I've been thinking," she blurted.

Philip grinned. "When are you not thinking?"

"Hush up. Or I might just take my gift back." She slowed her mare so that she could remain even with them.

Bella started to drop back to join Josephine, but Hazel stopped her.

"Hold up, Bella. This concerns you, too." Hazel waited for Bella to come even again.

"Phil, I'm going to give you an acre of my land and the old homestead for a wedding present." She nodded her head as if in agreement with herself.

He pulled his horse to a stop. "Hazel, that's a mighty fine gift. I'm not sure we can accept."

They all stopped.

"'Course you can." She patted her mare's neck. "I still have acreage and the new house my man built before his passing. I want you to have it."

Josephine joined them. "It's a wonderful gift, Hazel. If Philip was any kind of gentleman, he'd thank you for it." She raised a brow at her brother-in-law.

Philip looked to Bella. Living at the relay station was going to be crowded. He wasn't sure Hazel's old homestead was any more comfortable, but it would be a place Bella could call her own.

Hazel turned her attention to Bella, too. "What do you think, Bella? You going to accept my gift?"

"I think it is wonderful, Hazel. Thank you."

Philip knew when he was outvoted. He laughed. "Then it's settled. Thank you, Hazel."

Hazel dug into her saddlebag and pulled out a slip of paper. "I was hoping you'd accept. Here's the deed to the land and homestead." She handed the paper to him.

He stared down at the deed. "When did you get this?"

"When we stopped in Dove Creek the other day." She grinned. "You aren't the only one who is tricky."

Josephine laughed. "Well, looks like we'll be stopping in Dove Creek again."

Philip frowned. He didn't want to stop. Thomas had been alone for too long. "Why?"

"We'll need fabric for curtains," Josephine answered.

"And cleaning supplies," Hazel added. "That old homestead is going to need a lot of cleaning before it's fit for living."

Philip groaned. "We can't be in town long," he told them.

Caleb tilted his head back and looked up at Philip. "Can we have some lemon drops?"

Mark protested, "No, I want a peppermint stick." He twisted to face Bella. "Can I get peppermint? Please?"

Philip saw the sad look on her face and realized she didn't have the money to pay for either of them to have candy. He cleared his throat. It had the effect he expected. Bella looked up at him. He gave her a quick nod.

"If Philip says so, then yes."

He laughed, leave it to her to turn it back to him. "We'll see what we can do."

The women quickly changed the subject back to cleaning, sewing and cooking, leaving him and the little boys to discuss horses, candy and new chores.

"We have to do chores?" Caleb asked, as if the idea of working was foreign to him.

"Sure you do. I expect you to help out," Philip answered.

Mark looked across at him with a frown on his small face. "Me, too?"

"Yep, you, too."

Caleb asked, "What kind of chores?"

Philip really hadn't given that much thought but now felt inclined to answer. "Well, it will depend on our new place. But I'll expect one of you to take care of the chickens—"

"We have chickens?" Mark interrupted.

"Not yet, but we'll get some."

Caleb asked, "What else?"

"Well, we'll need to get a milk cow and maybe a couple of hogs to butcher in the fall." He thought about all the things his young family was going to need. "But first we'll need to gather wood for the fireplace. It's still cold here."

Mark pulled his coat closer around his small body. "It is," he agreed. "What about fishing? Is that a chore? I want to do that."

Philip laughed. "Well, I like to think of fishing as a fun thing to do. So we'll all share in the fishing."

"Even Aunt Bella?" Caleb asked.

He looked to his new wife. She looked pretty. Her blond hair shone in the sun—he could see the highlights shimmer against her back even with a bonnet on. "If she wants to fish, she can."

Bella didn't seem to be paying any attention to them, so Philip turned back to the boys. "Do either of you know how to clean fish?"

They both shook their heads.

"Well, that's something we'll have to remedy."

Mark looked across at him. "What's *remedy* mean?"

Philip thought he saw Bella's lips twitch. She seemed in deep conversation with Josephine and Hazel, but he suspected her of listening in on his and the boys' conversation.

"Fix. We have to teach you how to clean fish." He tested out his theory that Bella was eavesdropping. "Your aunt will have to learn, too."

Just as he suspected, Bella reacted to his words by crinkling up her nose. Philip laughed at the expression.

"What's the matter, Bella? Don't like the idea of cleaning fish?" he asked.

She turned to him. "No, and with three healthy men living with me I don't see me ever learning, either." Bella looked back to the other ladies.

"Now, Bella. Cleaning fish is a good skill to have. Especially if you find yourself living alone in your old age," Hazel said knowingly.

Philip laughed harder. The boys joined in, not really sure why they were laughing, but following Philip's lead.

He loved having the little boys as companions. They were going to make life fun. His gaze moved to Bella. He might just enjoy teasing her on a regular basis, too.

Exhaustion weighed on Bella's shoulders like a wet blanket. The small side trip into town had been fun, but now that they were at the relay station, she felt the effects of her long journey. So much had happened during the last few days.

Dusk was settling over the yard at an alarming pace. Mark's small body was getting heavier and heavier. He wasn't asleep, but his full weight rested upon Bella.

A man and two small dogs stepped out of the barn. Josephine had already taken the lead and was the first to dismount. She hurried into the arms of the man. Bella grinned. So that was Thomas Young. From this distance and with the fading sun and shadows, Bella couldn't see him very well but knew Josephine would only run to her husband like that.

Bella followed Philip to the barn, where the happy couple stood. He pulled his horse to a stop and carefully lowered Caleb to the ground. Then he dismounted and came to help Mark down. The two little boys stood side by side, looking around.

Thomas bent down and picked up one of the dogs. He and Josephine walked toward them. Thomas handed the dog to Hazel and then smiled at his brother. "Glad you made it home."

Philip waited for Bella's feet to touch solid ground and then answered, "Thanks." He took Bella's hand and with a dramatic flair said, "Bella, I'd like you to meet my brother Thomas. He's the reason you are here."

She held out her hand. "It's nice to meet you."

Josephine stooped down and picked up the smaller dog. She cuddled it in her arms like a baby. Bella grinned at the sweet scene. If the boys had been more alert, they would have been begging to pet the dog.

"I'm heading home," Hazel said from atop her horse.

"Hold up, Hazel. I'll ride with you." Philip released Bella's hand and turned to get back on his horse.

"No reason for you to do that. I've been taking myself home for years," she grumbled.

Josephine set the dog down, walked back to her horse and climbed into the saddle. "Thomas and I will ride back to Hazel's place with her, Philip. Why don't you show Bella and the boys the house?"

It wasn't a request. It was more like a command. Josephine looked at Hazel. "And don't you complain. I'd like a few minutes alone with my husband on the way home, so we're not taking no for an answer. Not that I asked you." She motioned for Thomas to get on Philip's horse.

Which he did.

"Hazel, let's take the cleaning supplies and fabric to

your house," Josephine added, repositioning the flour bag that hung over her saddle horn.

"Might as well," she said with a nod of her head.

Philip laughed as Thomas took the reins from his hands and followed the two women. The little dog followed the horses, its tail wagging from side to side.

"You two come on over in the morning and I'll show you the homestead," Hazel called over her shoulder.

"Will do," Philip answered and then turned to face Bella. His gaze moved to the little boys, who were leaning against her legs. "I'll tie the horse up and then we'll get these young'uns to bed."

Bella nodded. She pulled their bags off of the saddle horn, their weight feeling heavier than ever before. She covered her mouth to stifle a yawn. Weariness eased into her bones as thoughts of where she and Philip would be sleeping crept into her head. He'd said they had a small room, but did he expect to sleep in the same bed as her?

As soon as he'd tied the horse up, Philip picked up Mark and headed to the house. "Our room is small, but we'll all fit."

Bella took Caleb's small hand and followed him into the house. Warmth greeted her. Her gaze moved over the large settee and the rocking chairs. She didn't have time to see much else as Philip led the short distance to a door.

"This is our room." He opened the door and stepped back so that Bella could enter first.

It was a small room, just as he'd said. A large bed with a beautiful log cabin quilt rested against the back wall. The wooden bedposts and footboard were exquisite. Two small pallets had been spread out on the floor at the foot of the bed, and she assumed they were for the boys.

Bella put their bags on the bed and dug inside the boys' bag. She handed each of them a change of clothes. "Do you need to go outside before bed?" she asked.

Mark nodded. "Come along," Philip said. He took Mark's hand and motioned for Caleb to follow. "You might as well come, too. Might save us a trip in the middle of the night."

Bella sat down on the edge of the bed. She watched the boys hurry after Philip. Looking around, she noted that there wasn't much more in the room as far as furniture went. A small chest sat in the far corner. She assumed Philip's clothes were in that. A little table held a washbasin and a small mirror hung over that.

The thought of checking out the remainder of the house entered her tired mind and fled just as quickly. All she wanted to do was go to sleep. Bella shut the bedroom door and quickly put on her white gown. Thankfully she'd brought a nice robe to cover the thin nightclothes.

Once dressed, Bella opened the door and returned to the side of the bed. A few minutes later, the boys returned looking even more tired than when they'd left.

Philip excused himself, saying that he needed to take care of the horse.

She helped Caleb and Mark change into their nightclothes, said their prayers with them and then tucked the boys between the sheets. "I'll be just outside the door if you need anything." Bella kissed both of them on the forehead and then stood.

Philip had returned and now sat at the kitchen table

waiting for her. He held out a cup of coffee. "Sorry, Thomas isn't the best coffee maker, but it's not too bad."

She took the cup and a small sip. "How is it possible that coffee can taste thick?"

He shook his head. "I'm not sure how he does it."

Bella laughed. "That wasn't meant as a compliment."

His lips split in a handsome grin. "I didn't think it was." He lowered his cup and stared at her.

Bella felt a flush fill her face and neck. She lowered her eyes to the coffee.

"We need to talk about sleeping arrangements before the others get back," Philip said, setting down his cup.

Bella focused on the cups on the table. "You said this was a marriage of convenience."

"And it is. I was thinking that we can pull the bed out to the middle of the room. I'll make a pallet on the floor by the back wall. No one has to know what our sleeping arrangement is." He ran his finger around the rim of his cup. "What do you think about that?"

She looked up and met his gaze. "That might work, but what about the boys? They'll know."

He shook his head. "I'll go to bed after them and get up before they wake up."

Bella nodded. "That might work. They both like to sleep late."

Philip pushed his chair back. "Good. Let's go move the bed before Thomas and Josephine get home."

She nodded and followed him into the bedroom. A glance at the boys told her they were both sound asleep. They looked so sweet and young.

He moved to the end of the bed and lifted it. His muscles strained against the weight.

She whispered, "Wait, I'll help you."

Together they lifted the bed and moved it to the side. Then they moved to the headboard and did the same until they had the bed away from the wall. Bella's arm muscles were on fire.

"That should do it," Philip groaned.

They looked at their handiwork and both of them sighed at the same time. Bella dropped to the edge of the bed and whispered, "Whoever built this bed planned on it never being moved."

"Well, I wouldn't say that. I'd planned on taking it with me when I left."

She stared at him. "You built it?" Bella looked at the carving on the headboard.

Philip leaned against the doorjamb and nodded. "Yep."

"Why is it so heavy?"

He shrugged. "Well, I made it out of the same wood I made the couch in the sitting room. Since I'd already paid for the wood, I didn't want to waste it. So I made the bed."

She stood and ran her hand over the vine pattern on the headboard. "Did you do this, too?"

Philip pushed away from the wall and opened the chest that sat in the far corner. "That wasn't too hard to do. I used the branding iron." He returned with a thick quilt and a blanket.

Bella frowned. "I thought branding irons had a bigger tip than this. I've seen a few brands and they aren't like this." She watched as he spread out the quilt and then laid the blanket on top of it.

He pulled one of the pillows off the bed and placed it at the top. "That should do it." His gaze met hers.

"Philip, how did you get a branding iron to do this detail?" She blew a strand of hair off her forehead.

He grinned. "I broke the end off it. Sharpened it into a point and then used it like a piece of chalk on a slate."

Bella yawned. "That is really good drawing."

Philip walked around the bed and smiled. "Thank you. I'm going to get out of here and let you get some rest." He left the room and shut the door behind him.

She smiled at his thoughtfulness. Bella pulled the quilt and spread down. Leaning over the lantern, she blew out the light and crawled between the covers.

Bella looked forward to tomorrow and starting her real life. She knew that she'd wake up long before the sun rose, so she closed her eyes. Questions began to swirl in her tired mind, keeping her from sleep.

What would the homestead be like? Would Philip insist on sleeping in the same room? Would the boys have their own room? Would the homestead be a one-room building? What was life going to be like from here?

Chapter Twelve

The next morning, Philip rose to find the bed empty. His gaze moved to the window. It was still dark outside. Was Bella having trouble sleeping? He rose from his pallet and went in search of her.

The hearty smell of fresh bread baking filled his nostrils as soon as he opened the bedroom door. He made his way to the kitchen, where Bella stood mixing dough. She hummed softly as she worked.

The little dog sat on the floor beside her. When the dog saw him, she walked over to him to get a head rub. Philip obliged and then eased into one of the kitchen chairs and watched Bella work.

She kneaded the dough with strong hands. He'd been surprised the night before when she'd lifted the bed with him to move it. He hadn't expected her to have that much strength.

She covered the bread and then moved on to her next project. Bella picked up a large knife and began hacking off ham onto a hot skillet. The sweet fragrance joined the baking bread.

His stomach growled hungrily. Philip put his hand over it.

Without turning around, she asked, "When did you sneak in here?" Bella moved to the coffeepot and poured a fresh cup.

Philip grinned. "Just a few moments ago. I didn't want to interrupt that beautiful humming."

She set a cup in front of him and smiled. "Well, at least you didn't scare the daylights out of me." Bella returned to the sizzling skillet.

Philip took a sip of the coffee. Its richness coated his tongue and he sighed with contentment. "Now, that's good coffee," he said, complimenting her.

"I'm glad you like it." She took the slices of ham from the skillet and added more.

While he drank his coffee, Bella continued to cook. He heard her humming once more and grinned. She truly seemed happiest in the kitchen.

Josephine stepped out of her bedroom. "Oh, my. I can't remember the last time someone else cooked breakfast." She walked over to the coffeepot and poured herself a cup.

Philip looked to the bedroom Josephine had just left. "Is Thomas sleeping in?"

She grinned in his direction. "No, he's probably out in the barn doing morning chores." Josephine raised an eyebrow at him.

"Oh, I suppose I should go help." He pushed away from the table and headed back to his and Bella's room.

As soon as he got inside, Philip glanced in the boys' direction and was assured they were still sleeping. Poor little tykes were tuckered out. He tossed his pillow from the night before onto the bed and scooped up his bedding. Then he quickly put on his socks and boots before leaving the room once more.

At the front door, he stopped long enough to put on his coat and hat. When he opened it, Bella called to him. "Please tell Thomas breakfast will be ready in about fifteen minutes."

Philip smiled at her and then hurried to the barn. Cold air nipped at him as he pulled the big doors open. He cast a quick look about and then headed to the back stall, where he heard Thomas working.

"The ladies say breakfast will be ready in about fifteen minutes," he announced, picking up a pitchfork.

Thomas grunted. "Good, I'm as hungry as an ant at a picnic."

Together they cleaned out the remainder of the stall and then made sure all the horses were fed and watered. As they were walking back to the house, Thomas asked, "Did you tell Bella your run starts tomorrow?"

"Has it been a week already?" Philip groaned.

"Afraid so," Thomas answered. He walked around to the rain barrel and poured out a bit of water into the basin that was sitting on a nearby table.

"No, I guess I'll do that on the way to Hazel's place."

"Josephine tells me that Hazel gave you two the old homestead as a wedding present." Thomas dried his hands off on a small towel and stepped to the side to make room for Philip to wash his hands.

"She did. I guess we'll have to wait to move in until I get back." He sighed.

Thomas slapped him on the back. "Are you in that big of a hurry to get your own place?"

"Wouldn't you be?" Philip asked. He didn't tell his

brother that sleeping on the cold floor, no matter how thick the quilt, was still sleeping on the cold, hard floor.

"I reckon so," Thomas answered. He handed Philip the towel.

"I was kind of hoping that Josephine and I could get away for a few days, after you get back. We would like to go look at some property not too far from here."

Philip nodded. "I don't know why you can't. I'll be here to take care of the place." He hung the damp towel back on the nail beside the table.

Together they hurried back inside for a hot breakfast. Philip noticed immediately that Bella had changed into a pretty yellow day dress with little blue flowers on it. Her hair was pulled up into a ponytail much like the one that Josephine wore.

He dreaded telling her he'd have to leave the next morning. It would have been nice to be able to move into the homestead. Philip frowned. Was it still livable? And if not, how much longer would they need to stay with Thomas and Josephine?

Bella wiped her hands on the dishcloth and turned to face the sitting room, where Philip and Thomas sat talking about the ranch Thomas and Josephine hoped to visit. "I'm ready." She hung the cloth on the nail beside the washbasin.

Josephine handed Mark a slate and piece of chalk. "Do you want to practice drawing on this?"

He grinned up at her. "No, I want to go with Aunt Bella."

Josephine slipped into the chair beside him. "Well, I understand. But Bella and I have talked and we decided that you and your brother will stay here and help me around the house."

At his frown and the puckering of his lips, Josephine continued. "So, you can either draw me a pretty picture or sweep the whole house."

Caleb sat on the floor between the men's chairs. He rubbed the puppy's ears. In a low voice he grumbled, "That's women's work."

Bella gasped. Where had her nephew heard that? She opened her mouth to scold him for the tone he had used with Josephine, but Philip raised his hand.

He dropped it onto Caleb's shoulder. "Not around here it isn't."

Surprised blue eyes turned to him. "It's not?"

Philip shook his head. "No, here we all do the same chores."

Caleb's expression went from surprise to horror. "Even dishes?"

"Yep. I'm a mean dishwasher. And since you brought it up—" he grinned at Bella over Caleb's head "—you and I will do supper dishes for the ladies."

Mark asked, "And she and Aunt Josephine are going to go feed the horses?"

Thomas laughed. "Nope, that's our job tonight."

The little boy tilted his head to the side and studied Thomas. "You and me?"

"Uh-huh."

Mark swung his head back around to Josephine. "So what are you going to do?" He no longer sounded disrespectful.

Josephine smiled at him. "Well, that depends on you." At his confused look she continued. "Are you going to sweep? Cook supper? Or draw a nice picture?"

He tapped the piece of chalk against his chin. "I suppose I'll draw the picture."

Philip got up and walked to the door, where Bella now stood. He held her coat out for her and she slipped her arms inside. "That sounds like a good idea to me. I'd hate to have to eat your cooking."

Caleb laughed. "Me, too."

Thomas stood. "Well, Caleb, since everyone now has chores, you can help me chop some wood."

Philip placed his hand on Bella's back and gently propelled her to the door. He closed it softly behind them. At her worried expression, he said, "They'll be fine for a couple of hours."

Bella nodded, knowing he was right. She buttoned her coat, thankful the wind wasn't blowing. Philip helped her up on the horse that waited by the porch. "Thank you."

He pulled himself into his saddle and smiled over at her. "My pleasure."

Together they rode out of the yard. "I can't believe it will be a week tomorrow that we met," Philip said. He glanced her way. "I'll be riding out tomorrow morning for my run. I should be back in a couple of days. Do you mind staying at the relay station?"

Bella shook her head. "No, Josephine has been nothing but kind to me, but if the homestead isn't too bad, I'd like to move there as soon as possible."

He nodded. "I can understand, but we don't have provisions for you to move."

Bella frowned and asked, "Meaning?"

"Food and wood for the fireplace." He looked at her as if she was still wet behind the ears.

"I've already worked that out with Josephine. She's

going to loan us flour, sugar, salt and a few canned goods until we can get to town. Then we'll pay her back." Bella felt pleased with herself. She might have been living in town, but that didn't mean she was ignorant in the ways of country life.

Philip nodded. "And Thomas and Caleb are cutting your wood now, aren't they?"

She couldn't stop the grin from forming on her lips. "They are." Bella pulled her horse to a stop in front of Hazel's house. At least she thought it was Hazel's, since Philip stopped there.

Hazel stepped out on the porch and pulled the door shut behind her. The mama dog followed close on her heels. "I thought you two would never get here. I have my old mare saddled in the barn. We can leave now, if you want to."

Bella smiled. "Good morning, Hazel."

Hazel frowned up at her. "Good morning."

Philip laughed, then said, "We'd love to see the house now."

The older woman stomped off the porch. "Well, that's what I figured."

Hazel shooed the dog into the barn, pulled the little mare out into the yard and then climbed into the saddle of the waiting horse. "Well, after you see the house, you might change your mind about it," she said, leaning over the horse's back and shutting the barn door.

What kind of house was this? Bella wondered. Surely Hazel wouldn't give them a run-down shack for a wedding gift. She found herself trying to see around the older woman as they rode through what Bella thought was an apple orchard.

They came out of the fruit trees and saw a small

building sitting about four hundred and fifty yards away on a small hill. What looked like an old barn sat a few feet away. Bella couldn't really see what the house looked like from this distance and wished Hazel would go a little faster. She chanced a look across at Philip.

He, too, was straining to see the house.

Hazel explained, "Now mind you, it's not that great to look at, but I think it's still pretty sturdy." She noticed their animated looks and laughed. "You two look as excited as two puppies seeing a kitten for the first time."

Philip grinned. "We're just excited to see it."

"Then go on. I'll follow at my own pace."

"Race you!" Philip yelled, setting his mount into a run.

Bella laughed. She also prompted her horse to run. "That's not fair. You're used to racing across the countryside." Still she laughed as her hair flew from its confines and slipped down her back.

Philip was already standing by the door when she arrived. He grinned up at her. "Beat you."

"I can see that." She laughed.

The house was small and weatherworn. There were no windows, so they'd have to enter it to see the inside.

He helped her slide off her horse. His hand caught in the tangles of her hair. Philip looked deeply into her eyes. "Our first house."

Bella felt his fingers in her hair. She ducked her head. "We should probably get inside and look at it."

Philip pulled his hand from her hair and nodded. "That would be good." He opened the door and stepped inside.

For a few moments she stood still. What had he been thinking, holding her like that? And why had his hands in her hair caused her scalp to tingle? It had been like the kiss they'd shared on their wedding day. The emotions rose and the intensity of them scared her a little. She couldn't be falling in love with her husband. Falling in love was not in her plans.

Bella shook her head to clear her thoughts. Maybe it was a good thing he had to leave in the morning for his Pony Express run. It would give her time to get her emotions under control.

Chapter Thirteen

Philip held his breath. Her hair had felt like corn silk in his hands. He'd never felt anything like it and reckoned that was the reason for the weird feeling in his gut.

"Oh, look how cute it is," Bella exclaimed as she came into the room behind him.

Cute? He looked at the dirt-covered floor. Kittens were cute. Baby colts were cute. Even the way Bella wrinkled her nose was cute. This house wasn't cute. Cobwebs filled the corners, dirt covered every surface and the fireplace was filthy.

"I love it, don't you?" she asked, twirling around in the center of the floor.

Philip laughed. "*Love* is such a strong word."

"I know, but look. We will be able to see the boys no matter where we are." She indicated the kitchen. "I can cook and you and the boys can relax on this side of the room."

He nodded. "Yes, but where will we all sleep?"

Hazel stepped through the door. "In the bedrooms, of course."

Philip glanced around. "I don't see any bedrooms."

To his way of thinking, they were standing in one large room, with front and back doors.

Hazel huffed. “Open your eyes, boy.” She headed to the back door.

They looked at each other, baffled. Neither spoke as they followed Hazel. She’d gone through the door. Philip allowed Bella to go first. Her gasp had him hurrying after her.

Bella stood just inside the door looking down. The back door wasn’t a door to the outside at all. It went into a large pantry. At the back of the storeroom was an open door in the floor. She stared into the hole.

Hazel appeared at the bottom of the stairs with a lantern. “Come on down.”

Philip narrowed his eyes. “Are you telling me our bedrooms are down there?”

“Didn’t say that, but yep.” Hazel laughed. She set the lantern on a small side table and then moved out of their sight.

Bella shrugged and then walked down the narrow steps. Philip followed. He gasped. “Hazel, there is a whole house down here.” The large room he stood in was circular.

She nodded. “Yes, and it was mine and my husband’s secret. No one else knows about these rooms but us.”

Bella had moved into the room. One side held shelves lined with jars of canned foods. Several barrels stood under the shelves. She read their labels out loud. “Potatoes, onions, carrots, apples and beets.” She turned to face Hazel. “Are those vegetables and fruits still here?”

“Not as much as there used to be, but yes. There is a large garden spot behind the house. I’ll show it to you tomorrow,” Hazel answered. She held a candlestick in her hand. "Come with me and I'll show you the bedrooms."

Philip stopped in the middle of the room to look at a fire pit. His gaze moved upward, where a small hole had been cut out of the floor above. Had Hazel's husband built the house over an old Pawnee home?

He shook his head and then followed Hazel and Bella to the other side of the large room. Large canvas-type fabric hung across logs and it created two rooms. She pushed back the fabric from the first room. "This is the bigger of the two. I suspect it's where you two will sleep." She moved on down and pulled back the second. "I think this will be big enough for the boys."

Philip noticed a small table by the door with another candlestick on it. He lit the candle and stepped into the bigger room. Light bounced off the cloth walls. Like the rest of the house it was empty, but from the looks of things, his big bed would fit in here with plenty of space left over for other furniture. He turned to see Bella standing beside him.

"This is amazing," she said, looking around the room. Her big blue eyes shone in the candlelight.

"If you two are done gawking at the walls in that room, come look at this one," Hazel called from inside the smaller room.

He smiled at Bella. "She's a little bossy today."

Bella giggled. "Just today?" she said over her shoulder as she made her way to Hazel.

Hazel stood in the smaller of the two rooms. To Philip it looked almost as big as the first room. "This isn't that much smaller than the other one," he said.

"I didn't say it was a lot smaller, I just said it was

smaller." Hazel grinned, taking the sting out of her words.

Bella looked at the older woman. "Hazel, are you sure you want to give this to us?"

Hazel nodded. "Yes, I love the other house my husband made for me. Besides, this house is too big for just one person and those stairs are hard on an old woman's knees."

Philip watched as the two women hugged.

"Thank you. This is a wonderful gift," Bella said as they separated.

Hazel nodded. "It needs a lot of cleaning." She made a mark with the toe of her boot on the dirt floor.

Bella put her arm around Hazel's shoulders. "I love it and don't mind cleaning. It will be fun and will feel like home when I'm all done."

Philip marveled at the difference in Bella when she talked to people one-on-one and when she was in a group. Her face shone with thanksgiving and her eyes with excitement at the prospect of what she could do with her new home.

Bella sighed. "This will be a great room for the boys and they can play down here, as well."

Philip shivered. "I'm not sure this will be the best place for them to play." He turned around and looked about. "It's pretty cold down here."

Hazel nodded. "It is. But the fire pit still works. I'll show you where the smoke comes up. Let's head back upstairs."

Together the three climbed the stairs. Philip couldn't help but wonder about the area downstairs. It wasn't any bigger than the top of the stairs, but he'd never seen anything like it. He shook his head as he shut the door.

Had his first instincts been correct? Was the house over another home from years gone by?

The old woman walked to the fireplace. She waited for Philip to join her. "See that hole in the back?"

He nodded.

"That's where the smoke rises from below and then goes on up through the chimney." She straightened and rubbed her back.

"Are you two ready to head back to my house? I have hot coffee and sweetbread."

Philip grinned. "You know I can't resist your sweetbread." He headed to the front door. Bella followed slowly. She seemed deep in thought as they walked outside and to their horses.

Hazel grunted as she climbed into the saddle. "Maybe I should just move to town," she groaned.

"How long have you lived out here?" Bella asked. She rode her horse up beside Hazel's.

"Longer than most." Hazel kneed her horse and sent her into a gallop.

Startled, Bella looked to him as Hazel shot ahead of them. The older woman's braid swayed against her back as she entered the orchard. "That was strange."

Philip nodded. "Yep, even for Hazel."

"What do you know about her?" Bella patted the horse's neck.

"Not much. When Thomas and I took over the relay station, Hazel came for a visit. We knew she was lonely because she came over every day, usually with food. Since it's pretty isolated out here, we sort of just started taking care of each other. She cooked us food and we helped her with chores. But we never asked her personal questions, so other than she was married and her husband died, we don't know any more." He wasn't sure he liked the look of determination in Bella's eyes. "Bella, leave it be. She's old and has a right to her privacy."

Bella glanced his way. "And we have two small boys to take care of. We need to know more about our nearest neighbor." She set her jaw.

Philip thought he was a pretty good judge of character and didn't think Hazel would ever hurt the boys. "Hazel is also our friend." Well, she was his and Thomas's friend. Over the last year, she'd begun to feel like family.

They entered the orchard. Philip couldn't help but think about the house. How old was it? Was the lower half a Pawnee home? Why was Hazel really living in the other farmhouse?

Bella entered Hazel's house. She loved it immediately. A plush settee and large chair sat in the center of the main room. The hardwood floor was covered by a gorgeous rug. Her gaze moved up the walls, which were covered with colorful paintings. "Oh, Hazel. Your home is beautiful."

The older woman walked into the room carrying a tray with a coffeepot, cups and a plate on it. "Thank you, Bella." She stopped and looked about the room. "It is cozy, isn't it?"

Bella looked toward Philip while Hazel busied herself putting out the midmorning snack.

Philip held Bella's gaze and said, "I'll unsaddle your horse, Hazel." He moved to Bella and whispered, "Behave yourself."

What did he expect her to do? Bella frowned at him and motioned for him to leave.

He winked at her, then left.

Hazel chuckled behind her. "Now, what naughty thing is he expecting you to do?"

Bella turned to face the other woman and shook her head. "I have no idea."

"Sure you do. Think about it." She poured coffee into one of the smaller cups and then handed it to Bella.

She took the cup. "Well, Philip mentioned that he doesn't know you very well and then said I'm not to ask you any questions about your past."

"That sounds about right."

"What? You don't want me asking questions? Or the fact that Philip doesn't want me asking questions?"

Hazel shook her head. "Girl, if you want answers, ask." She sat down with her own cup of coffee.

Bella studied the older woman closely. "All right. I'm curious about the room under our house."

The other woman picked up a slice of the sweetbread and looked at it. "What would you like to know?"

"It's not your typical house. Is it?" Bella waited. When Hazel didn't immediately answer, she pressed on. "I mean, I've never seen a house with a circular room under it like that one. Do you know its history?"

Hazel nodded.

At that moment, Philip came in. "You two didn't eat all the bread, did you?" He hung his coat by the door.

Bella shook her head. "No, but Hazel is going to tell us the history of our house. So come sit down."

Hazel waited until Philip was sitting on the overstuffed chair and then handed him a cup of coffee. He took the cup but looked expectantly at the bread. She laughed, then gave him a small plate with a slice of the bread.

Philip reminded Bella of Mark when he sat in a chair

that was too big for him—out of place but content to eat his bread. She grinned and then turned her attention back to Hazel.

"Well, about twenty years ago my family was traveling through the Nebraska territory. Our wagon broke down a few miles from here. Back then there weren't many white people in the area. My whole family got sick. Pa died first, then my older brother. My other brother and sister got very sick, too. Ma and I tried to keep them alive, but soon they, too, died." She paused and looked off into the distance as if the story was taking her miles away.

Bella looked to Philip, who also looked as if he hadn't expected Hazel to go so far into the past. She took a sip of her coffee and felt her heart ache for the young woman who'd lost her family.

Hazel shook her head as if to clear it and then continued. "Ma died last, but before she did, she said, 'Hazie, do whatever it takes to stay alive.'" She took a sip of her coffee. "So, when the Pawnee warrior arrived, I stood up and waited to see what fate had in store for me." She swallowed as if reliving that moment. "One young man jumped from his horse and looked about at all the dead bodies. His friends all backed their horses away and told him to get back on his so they could leave."

Bella said, "I'm so sorry, Hazel."

"For what? You didn't make my family sick."

"You don't have to tell us this story, Hazel. What I think Bella is trying to say is, if it's too painful to remember, stop."

Hazel smiled. "Oh, Phil, I have long since stopped grieving for my family. They went when the good Lord called them home. I don't really know why He felt I should live, but He did."

Philip's jaw hardened. Bella wished she hadn't started this conversation. It looked as if she might have hurt two people with her curiosity. In the time she'd known Philip, he hadn't looked sad. What was he thinking? Was he regretting having married a nosy woman?

Chapter Fourteen

Philip couldn't help thinking about his parents. How he wished he could stop grieving and move on. But the circumstances were different. Hazel's family had gotten sick and died. His mother had died in childbirth and his father had killed himself to avoid the bitter pain of loss.

He was pretty sure God hadn't just called them home. Everyone at the orphanage had whispered his father had died too young and of a broken heart. He didn't think the Lord wanted anyone to kill themselves.

Hazel's voice pulled him from his reverie.

"To make a long story short, that young man married me and built the house in the hill. It took time, but soon I understood his language. Never was very good at speaking it, but I learned enough to know that he loved me. After five years, I finally found out that his tribe had left him here to die with me. They were afraid the fever would kill them all. Since he wouldn't leave me, they left him."

"That is so sweet," Bella said when Hazel paused.

"He was a good man," Hazel agreed.

Philip asked, "How did the top part of the house come about?"

"Well, in the winter I read the books I'd brought with me out here. One evening I showed him pictures of a white man's house. Come spring he started cutting down trees and dragging the logs home. Together we built the house on top of the hill. We were happy for another five years until one day a grizzly bear got him. He made it home to me but didn't recover from the wounds." A tear trickled down Hazel's wrinkled cheek.

Once more Bella said, "I'm sorry." She held her hand up to stop Hazel from saying it wasn't her fault. "I know I didn't tell the bear to attack him, but I can still feel bad for your loss."

Hazel wiped the moisture from her face. "I know, child. Anyway, for the next year I mourned my husband. It was a few months later that I met my second husband and he built this house for me. He was a good man and I loved him, too. Just differently."

Bella nodded. Doubt filled her eyes, but she didn't contradict what Hazel had said. She smiled. "So in the end, you did find happiness again."

Hazel nodded. "I did. Now, would anyone like a fresh cup of coffee?"

Philip held his cup out and grinned at her. He deliberately put a teasing tone into his voice when he said, "And I'd love more of that bread. I do believe you are the best baker around."

His words caught Bella's attention. She leaned forward, holding out her cup for Hazel to pour the coffee into. "I'd love to share recipes with you Hazel. Baking is something I really enjoy."

Joy filled Hazel's watery eyes. "I would like that,

too." She waved a hand at Philip. "This one is a flatterer, but from one baker to another, what do you think of my sweetbread?" She handed Philip another slice of bread.

"It's good. I love the flavor." She smiled at Hazel. "This is one of the recipes I want."

"I'll be happy to share it." Hazel stood, but Philip waved her back down.

"We need to be getting back to the relay station. I'm supposed to ride out tomorrow." Philip stood.

Bella stood also. "I can get it later, Hazel. Now that we are neighbors we'll be able to spend lots of time together."

Philip held Bella's coat out to her. She slipped her arms into the sleeves and said, "Thanks for giving us the house, Hazel. I love it."

"You're welcome, child. I hope you are as happy in it as I was." She picked up their dishes and added them to the tray. "You can start moving in whenever you are ready."

"We'll wait until I get back," Philip said as he opened the door. "I'll see you when I get back."

Bella waved. "'Bye."

Philip shut the door. The wind had picked up and blew coldly into their faces. He held Bella's elbow as they stepped off the porch.

When they were on their horses and headed out of the yard, Bella said, "Hazel is an interesting woman."

He nodded. "Yeah, I learned a lot today. I'd no idea she was married to a Pawnee or that she'd been married twice."

They rode in silence. Then Bella asked, "Do you think the Pawnee keep an eye on her?"

"You mean, like family?"

"I suppose." She looked around as if thinking that one of the tribe would step out of the woods at any moment.

He shrugged. Now was as good a time as any to warn her of the dangers in these parts. "I've seen them around, but they've been friendly enough. Never connected them to Hazel before." Philip glanced her way. "Promise you won't ride alone out here. It's dangerous and not just from the Pawnee. Like Hazel said, there are bears out here."

Bella nodded. "I promise. I've heard that there are also bandits that prey on single travelers. I'll be careful." She stroked the horse's mane.

"Good." He rocked with the movements of the horse. A light snow began to fall and he shivered. If it continued to snow, his ride tomorrow would be miserable. He hated riding the trail in the cold and snow.

His thoughts moved to the house. They would need a kitchen table, furniture for the sitting room, and the boys would need a bed. He dreaded sleeping on the cold floor. Maybe he should give Josephine and Thomas his bed and build two smaller ones. When would he have time for that? Was it time to give up riding the Pony Express trail? Apprehension crawled up his spine. If he did, would he be able to make a living selling his furniture?

Bella enjoyed the silent companionship that Philip offered. From the look on his face, she knew he was deep in thoughts and that they troubled him. Could it be he regretted marrying her and taking on a family? She asked, "Would you like to talk about it?"

Startled, he answered her question with a question. "Talk about what?"

"Whatever has your gut tied in a knot." She offered him a smile.

He sighed. "Am I that easy to read?"

Bella shrugged.

"I was thinking about quitting the Pony Express and opening a furniture business." He pulled up his collar to deflect the snow that was drifting down.

Bella pulled her own coat tighter about her waist. "Why do you want to quit?"

"Well, we need lots of furniture and there isn't really any place in town to buy it. I'll have to build beds, tables, chairs and chests for clothes." Philip looked at her. "Riding once a week doesn't leave a lot of time to build."

"We don't have to have it all at once. If you want to quit the Pony Express, that's one thing. If you feel like you have to quit to make us a comfortable home, that's another." She smiled to take the sting out of her words.

"You don't mind sleeping on the floor or eating standing up?"

"Not my first choices, no. But we'll figure out something. People have done without fancy furniture since the beginning of time. Besides, I'll help you and we'll get it done, one piece at a time."

He grinned. "You really are something, you know that?"

Bella laughed. "I'm something, all right." She gently kicked her mare. "I'll race you to the house."

Wind and snow whipped their faces as they raced to the barn. Bella heard his horse catching up with her and laughed. She lay low over the saddle and yelled to the horse. "Run! Run! Run!"

As if it understood, the Pony Express horse tore off.

She caught her breath as adrenaline raced through her veins. Never before had Bella ridden so fast. Exhilaration caused her to laugh with joy.

Philip raced beside her. His own face was filled with enjoyment. They raced into the yard. He pulled back on the reins and bellowed, “Whoa!” His horse stopped.

But no matter how many times Bella screamed “Whoa!” her horse kept on going. Her excitement turned to fear as the horse continued past the house and up the trail.

She heard horse’s hooves thundering behind her and, without turning around, knew Philip was giving chase. He raced up beside her horse, leaned over and grasped the reins from her hands. His strong voice called, “Whoa!” and both horses came to a slow stop.

Bella felt as if her heart was going to pound out of her chest. Uncontrollable tears began to slip down her cheeks. Shame filled her when she saw the expression on his face.

Philip moved his horse beside hers and climbed from his saddle behind her. His strong arms wrapped around her and she lowered her head. With gentle hands he pulled her deeper into his embrace and whispered words of comfort.

Bella leaned back into his hug and allowed herself to cry. Tears hadn’t fallen even at her sister’s funeral. She’d had to be strong for the boys’ sake. Now fear had brought all those emotions up to the surface.

Philip released her and slipped off the horse’s back. He reached up and pulled her down with him. Once her feet were on the ground, Philip pulled her into his embrace.

Snow fell around them. Bella knew they should get

out of the cold, but she couldn't stop the flow of tears. She pressed her face into the front of his jacket and wept for all she'd lost over the last few months. His hands rubbed her back and soothed her broken heart. Bella wished they could stay here always but knew that soon life would call them both away.

Chapter Fifteen

The next morning, Bella got up ready to face the day. Philip had slipped out of the bedroom sometime in the early morning hours. He'd carried his boots out to keep from waking her and the boys. She'd known the moment he'd sat up.

She pushed the covers back and quietly got dressed. The smell of ham cooking drew her to the kitchen, where Josephine stood beside the stove.

"Good morning, sleepyhead. How do you feel this morning?" She handed Bella a cup of hot tea.

"Better. Thanks." She sipped at the tea and smiled at its sweetness. "This is such a treat."

Josephine nodded. "I love tea, but the men always want coffee. I'm glad you are here to share the tea with."

"Me, too." She straightened her shoulders. "I'm sorry about yesterday." Bella had gone straight to her bedroom after they had returned from Hazel's house, claiming her head hurt. It wasn't a lie. After all her tears had been spent, her head had hurt.

Josephine waved the apology away with her spatula.

"I understand. I used to have days when my head hurt so bad I didn't get up."

"Really? What caused you to have headaches?"

She scraped scrambled eggs onto a plate. "I think it was stress. After Thomas and I married, the headaches stopped."

"I'm glad."

Josephine placed the plate in the center of the table. "Me, too. What are your plans for the day?"

"I'd like to go to our house and clean today, but I promised Philip I wouldn't go alone." She pushed her chair back. "What can I do to help you this morning?"

"You can do the dishes later." Josephine smiled as she set the teapot on the table.

"Deal." Bella sat back down.

Cold air swept through the house as Thomas entered. He hung up his coat. "Good morning, Bella."

She smiled. "Good morning."

"Did you finish what I asked you to do?" Josephine asked, handing him a cup of hot coffee.

"Sure did. When you ladies are ready, we'll head that way." Thomas sat down at the head of the table. "Breakfast smells wonderful."

"Where are we going?" Bella passed him the plate of eggs.

He scraped some out onto his plate. "Didn't Josephine tell you?" His blue eyes searched his wife's.

"Not yet." Josephine grinned mischievously.

Bella's gaze moved from Thomas to Josephine and then back again. "Will someone please tell me what you two are talking about?"

Josephine slipped into her chair. "Are you going to

get the boys up for breakfast?" She looked toward the closed bedroom door.

"No, I thought I'd let them sleep a little longer."

Thomas raised an eyebrow. "My ma would never have let us sleep and then eat whenever we got up."

Bella frowned. "Why not?"

"It instills laziness," Thomas answered. He bowed his head, indicating he was going to say grace.

Josephine and Bella followed his lead. Bella listened as he said the prayer and asked herself if he was right. Was she instilling laziness in the boys? She echoed Thomas's "Amen," then looked up.

"The boys are fine sleeping in today, Bella. Don't let it bother you," Josephine said, pouring more tea into her cup.

Bella nibbled at her bread. She'd grown up in a home in town. Her parents had let Bella and her sister sleep as long as they liked. She hadn't considered that country life would change that for the boys.

Thomas laid his fork down. "I'm sorry, Bella. I didn't mean to upset you." He looked to his wife's concerned face.

"I'm not upset. I was just thinking about how city life and country life are so different. Tomorrow I'll start getting the boys up earlier." She offered a smile to prove she wasn't angry with them.

Thomas winked at his wife. "At least now she's not bugging us to tell her our secret."

Bella's smile grew. "Oh, I'd forgotten. What secret?"

Josephine laughed. "I sent Thomas over to your house to get the fireplace going. It should be toasty warm in there when we go over to clean."

"Really? You're going with me?" Bella couldn't wait

to get started on cleaning their home. The sooner she got it cleaned up, the sooner they could move in. She dug in to her breakfast.

Thomas shook his head. "I've never seen a woman in that big of a hurry to clean." His statement was rewarded with a stern look from Josephine.

Bella swallowed. "I want to get moved in as soon as possible. Wouldn't it be great if I have everything in order when Philip gets back?" She pushed her chair back and started toward the bedroom. "I'll get the boys and we'll be ready to go in no time."

Mark and Caleb moved like two turtles. No matter how much she rushed them, they were in no hurry to get dressed or eat.

Caleb whined, "Why are we getting up so early?"

"I told you, we're going to go clean the new house today." Bella handed him a boot to slip on.

"I don't want to clean no old house," Mark grumbled as Bella buttoned his shirt for him.

She frowned. "Well, I do. Just think, boys. You'll have your own bedroom again."

Caleb yawned. Mark frowned.

"Don't you want your own room?" Bella asked, shoving them toward the door.

Caleb shrugged his shoulders. "I don't care."

Bella shook her head. How could they not care?

"Where's Philip?" Mark demanded when he didn't see Philip at the breakfast table.

Thomas answered, "He's riding the Pony Express trail."

Caleb slipped into one of the chairs. "Aw, I'd forgot. What are we going to do while you clean, Aunt Bella?"

Josephine had already filled the little boys' plates.

She set fresh milk in front of them. "You are going to do chores with Uncle Thomas."

"What kind of chores?" Mark grunted, pulling himself up into the chair beside Caleb.

Thomas leaned back in his chair. "Well, since the ladies want to go clean the other house, I was thinking we could help them by doing the dishes."

Both boys groaned. Bella had to hide her smile.

Thomas laid his napkin on the table and turned to look at Josephine. "If you are ready to go, I'll ride with you over there while the boys eat."

"Are you sure they will be all right?" Bella asked. She'd never left the boys alone before.

Josephine nodded. "Caleb is old enough to watch his little brother for a little bit. They can eat their breakfast and then make their beds. If Thomas isn't back by the time they get through making their beds, they can sit on the couch and look at picture books until he gets back."

Bella frowned. "I'm not sure."

Thomas stood. "They'll be fine. Won't you, boys?"

Caleb nodded. Mark yawned again.

Josephine headed for the door and her coat. "Boys, stay away from the stove and the fireplace." She put on her coat and then hurried into her bedroom.

Thomas put on his coat and motioned for Bella to come get hers. He held it out to her and whispered, "They'll be fine."

Bella nodded and put on her coat. She walked back to the boys and kissed each of them on the head. "Be good for Uncle Thomas while I'm gone and do what Josephine said. Eat, make your beds and then look at the books until Thomas gets back. All right?"

"All right," they said in unison.

Josephine returned with the books and put them on the settee. “There you go, boys. See you soon.”

Thomas opened the door. “I’ll be back in a few minutes. Caleb, you’re in charge. Take care of your little brother.”

Caleb sat up a little straighter in his chair. “All right, Uncle Thomas.”

“I love you, boys. Be good for your uncle Thomas while I’m gone.” Bella allowed herself to be hurried to the horses that were waiting.

“I don’t think they’ve ever been left alone,” she said once they were riding out of the yard.

“My parents left me alone all the time,” Josephine said. She patted her horse’s neck. “Trust me, Thomas will probably find them still sitting at the table with their breakfast only half-eaten.”

Bella gently pressed her knees into her horse’s sides. If she hurried, Thomas would be back with the boys and she would be cleaning their new home in a matter of minutes. “Let’s get going. I want to be moved in as soon as possible.”

Thomas and Josephine came along beside her. Thomas said, “I’ll bring the boys down with lunch.”

Josephine laughed. “You’re going to fix lunch, too?”

He sat up straighter in the saddle. “I know how to pack bread, ham and pickles.”

Bella and Josephine laughed harder. When Bella caught her breath, she said, “There you go, Josephine. You’ll never have to cook again.”

“Let’s don’t go that far,” Thomas answered.

They soon arrived in Hazel’s yard. Bella got down from her horse and headed to the front door, giving Josephine time to say goodbye to her husband. She sighed with relief when Thomas turned his horse and headed home.

Excitement filled her as her worry over the boys ebbed. What would Philip think when he got home and found out that she'd moved into their new home with the boys? Would he be pleased?

Philip was bone-tired. He yawned as he climbed the stairs to the house. Josephine met him at the door. "Hey, Philip, come on in and have a cup of coffee."

"I'd rather just go to bed, Josephine. But thanks anyway." He started to walk toward the bedroom. But then his tired mind registered that Bella and the boys should be in the house, too. "Where are Bella and the boys?"

Josephine grinned mischievously. "At your house."

He instantly became alert. "Alone?"

She closed the door and walked to the kitchen. "Yes. They've been there a couple of days now."

Philip closed his eyes. The woman had gone and done just what he'd asked her not to. "Do you mind if I sleep here for a couple of hours before heading home?" He should have slept at the home station, but he'd wanted to get back to his small family. Now he felt so tired he didn't think he could take another step.

"Not if you don't mind sleeping on the floor." She poured a cup of coffee and held it out to him. "You sure you don't want this?"

Philip ignored the offered cup and asked, "Why should I sleep on the floor when I have a perfectly good bed in there?" He hooked his thumb over his shoulder to indicate he meant the bedroom.

"Because Bella took the bed to your house."

Philip shook his head. How in the world did she move

that big bed all the way to the homestead? His wife had been busy while he was gone. He walked back to the door, put his coat on and slapped his hat onto his head. "Thanks, Josephine. I'll see you in a few days."

She toasted him with the coffee cup. "Tell Bella and the boys hello for me."

He closed the door and stomped down the porch stairs. It would have been nice if Thomas had told him that Bella and the boys had moved to the homestead. He looked around the barn for his brother. Not seeing him, Philip began to saddle his horse. Within a few minutes he was riding out to his place.

If he hadn't been so tired, Philip might have been angry, and for a brief moment he had been. Now he was simply weary. The horse made good time to the homestead. An old barn that looked as if it had seen better days stood a few feet away and Philip thought he'd need to repair the old building soon.

Thankfully the barn was blocked from the wind by the house. He didn't feel the gusts as he unsaddled the horse and settled him in for the night. Philip patted him and then said, "We'll get a new barn up as soon as possible, ol' boy."

The horse snorted a reply and continued eating from his oat bag. Philip brushed his hand over the horse's neck, then headed to the house. He climbed the short stairs and twisted the doorknob. It moved, but the door didn't.

"Bella, I'm home." The words sounded funny in his ears. He heard a bar being lifted and then the door swung open.

"I'm so glad you are back," Bella whispered as she moved back so he could enter.

Philip stood in the doorway. He couldn't believe the transformation of the house. It was clean from top to bottom. The fresh scent of baking bread filled the room. To the right of the fireplace a pile of quilts and pillows made a nest where the two little boys were curled up sleeping. That explained why she was whispering. A rocking chair sat on the left-hand side of the fireplace. A rope rug decorated the floor and two small pictures of mountains and streams hung on the walls.

"Could you come a little farther inside? I'd like to shut the door." Bella gently pushed his back.

Philip walked to the kitchen area. Two log sawhorses held a wooden plank in place for a table. Four logs surrounded the table as chairs. In a soft voice so as not to wake the boys, Philip said, "Nice furniture."

Bella grinned. "It isn't much, but you will be able to make us a much nicer table. The boys really like it."

He nodded and yawned. "I'm sure they do."

"Are you hungry?" she asked. "I have a pot of stew hanging in the fireplace."

Philip turned to look at the fireplace again. Sure enough, a pot hung suspended in the center. He turned his attention back to her. "No, I'm more tired than hungry."

Bella nodded. "It's cold in the bedroom, but I have lots of quilts on the bed." She rubbed her arms as if she could feel the cold.

"I'm sure it will be fine." Philip walked to the closet, where the hidden stairs were located. He turned and looked at Bella.

She stood in the same spot. Her blond hair was down in waves of soft curls around her shoulders. Twin pink circles graced her cheeks. The blue dress she wore was covered with an apron made from a flour sack. How had such a small woman done so much while he was gone? Her pretty blue eyes had a guarded look, as if she worried he might be angry with her.

Philip walked back to her, pulled her into his arms for a quick hug and then released her. "I'm glad I'm home, too. I missed you and the boys."

Her eyes softened, her shoulders relaxed and she smiled. It was a radiant smile that raced into her eyes and gave him a warm feeling in the pit of his stomach. He wanted to pull her into his arms again and kiss her smiling lips.

Philip turned away quickly. As tired as he was, he didn't trust himself not to act on those thoughts. As he climbed down the stairs and made his way to the bed, Philip told himself he needed sleep. There would be plenty of time later to ponder his thoughts and feelings.

Chapter Sixteen

Bella placed a bucket under the leak. Why did it have to rain tonight? Philip wasn't going to be happy when he awoke to a leaking roof. That was one of the many things she couldn't fix in this house. Well, she probably could, but climbing on the roof with just the two little boys home wasn't safe or smart.

She glanced to where the boys were playing by the fire. Downstairs had been much too cold to sleep at night. Bella marveled that Philip hadn't emerged yet, freezing.

Thankfully the rain had stopped for the moment. She glanced out the window to see that the sun was almost down and it was time to put the boys down for the night.

"Boys, it's time for bed."

"Already?" Caleb asked with a frown. "But we never got to see, Philip."

"I know. Philip is extremely tired. Riding for the Pony Express is hard work. He'll be awake in the morning when you get up."

Mark looked up. "Aunt Bella, I'm hungry."

Bella shook her head. The boy couldn't be hungry.

For supper they'd eaten ham, canned new potatoes, fresh bread with butter and canned apples. Hazel had stopped by before dark and brought both the boys gingersnap cookies. "No, you are looking for an excuse to stay up. Now, stop making excuses. Put your toys away and we'll go to the outhouse before we go to bed."

They put the toys in the box she'd supplied and went to get their coats from the hooks by the door. Bella grinned. She'd worked hard to bend the nails into hooks and hammer them low so the boys could reach them. Bella intended to leave the nails there and just add new ones above those as they grew. It would be fun in later years to see how small the boys were when they'd moved here.

Mark looked at her. "Aren't you coming, too?" He pulled his gloves out of the coat pockets and began putting them on.

Bella giggled. "Yes, I was just woolgathering." She walked to the hooks and pulled down her own coat. Bella put her gloves on, too.

This was their routine. Put away toys, go to the outhouse, come in, get drinks of water, then settle down for a story, prayers and sleep. For the first time since she'd taken custody of the boys, Bella felt as if she was doing the right thing.

She handed Caleb the candle to hold while she raised the bar from the door. As soon as it was open, he handed it back and then raced Mark across the yard to the outhouse. They jumped over the many puddles that had accumulated with the afternoon rain.

While Mark was inside, Caleb said, "I wanted to see Philip tonight."

She placed a hand on his shoulder. "I know you did,

sweetie, but he is very tired. Riding a horse for several days is hard work. We need to let him rest."

Mark flung the door open and announced, "I'm going to ride horses on Uncle Thomas's ranch someday."

Caleb hurried inside the dark latrine. "I don't want to ride horses all day."

"I do. Uncle Thomas said we were going to raise cows and that I'd get to help round up the babies."

"Calves," Caleb called from inside.

Mark nodded. "Yeah, calves." His small voice always filled with wonder when he spoke of the ranch that Thomas and Josephine hoped to own someday.

Bella enjoyed this time with the boys. Caleb came out of the outhouse with a little more dignity than Mark had. "What do you want to do?" she asked him.

"I don't know for sure, but whatever it is, I'll have fun, too." He looked at his little brother. "I'll race you back!"

And away they went.

"Don't get my floors muddy. Wipe your feet!" she called after them.

Bella followed, carrying the light. While they were outside the sun had sunk even farther and it was beginning to sprinkle again. She looked up into the heavens and allowed several drops to land on her face. "Thank You, Lord, for holding the rain back so the boys could come outside."

Her gaze returned to the porch, where the boys were wiping their feet. "Wait for me," she called, wanting to make sure that their boots were clean of mud before they entered the house.

Just as she stepped onto the porch, the rain began to fall steadily. "Let me see the bottoms of your boots, boys." Just as she suspected, they were covered in mud. "Take them off and set them beside the door.

Bella pulled off her gloves and began to unlace her own boots. The boys pulled theirs off quickly, but she had to work the buttons on hers.

"Can we go in, Aunt Bella? It's cold out here." Caleb rubbed his stocking feet one on top of the other.

"Yes, but don't run or make any noise. Remember Philip is trying to sleep downstairs."

Caleb nodded. "We'll be quiet." He pushed the door open and then yelled, "Philip!"

"Yay! Philip is awake!" Mark ran into the house behind his brother.

The sound of Philip's laughter floated out onto the porch. Bella smiled. She'd missed his laughter. Her fingers trembled as she continued unbuttoning her boots. Cold quickly seeped into her fingers and caused them to work slower.

"Where's Bella?" Philip asked.

"Outside. She's taking her boots off," Caleb answered.

It was nice that he'd thought to ask about her, Bella thought, pulling off the first boot. She bent down and began to work on the other boot. The sound of Philip and the boys talking drifted out the open door.

Bella focused on the buttons. Her fingers now felt as if sharp needles were going into them. She pressed on.

"Here, let me help." Philip's warm hand covered hers.

She looked up into his blue eyes. "Thank you." Bella moved her hands away, missing his warmth immediately.

Philip made quick work of the buttons. He slipped the boot from her foot. "If you walk on this wet porch, your stockings will get wet." Not giving her time to protest, he swept her up into his arms and carried her over the threshold.

Bella felt her face flush with embarrassment. He gently set her down and smiled. She looked to the boys, who had their nightclothes on and were sitting on their pallets.

Mark held his favorite book, *The Remarkable Story of Chicken Little*. His head was tilted sideways as if he was contemplating something important.

"Go hold your hands to the heat and I'll get you a cup of coffee to help warm you up," Philip instructed.

Bella walked to the fire and sat down on the quilt beside Mark. "How about we start your story while I wait for my drink?" she asked, trying to act as if everything was normal, even though her heart was pounding in her chest.

Both boys nodded their heads. Caleb laid back and put his arms under his head. Mark imitated his older brother.

Bella read the story aloud, pleased her voice didn't betray her inner emotions. Why did she feel so shaky inside? Philip carrying her inside shouldn't have caused these feelings. Mentally Bella tried to push them away. She was not going to fall in love with her husband. He didn't want anything except her friendship and she didn't want to be hurt again by giving her heart to a man.

Philip took his time getting the coffee. He listened to the sweet sound of Bella's voice as she read the story to the little boys. She knew when to read excitedly and when to lower her voice. Memories of his mother reading to him filled his mind. Philip missed his mother and father. Even though his father would rather have died than to stay with him and live, Philip loved the man he remembered before he'd seen him die.

He handed Bella her coffee. Philip nodded to the boys. "Good night, boys." He turned on his heels and headed back down to the cold bedroom.

There he sat in the middle of the bed with the quilt wrapped tightly around him. He forced himself to remember the whispers of the women at the orphanage. They said his dad had gone insane after his mother died. That his heart had broken so badly that he died, too. Philip refused to love that deeply. He and Bella were friends, only friends. That was what they'd agreed on. That was what he planned to stick with. He couldn't love so deeply that it would drive him insane if she died.

Several hours later, Philip crept back up the stairs. The house was quiet. Bella and the boys were sleeping beside the fireplace. They looked like a pile of puppies. He grinned, then tiptoed to the kitchen area.

His stomach growled loudly. Philip knew that Bella always had bread around. He searched the countertop and found a plate of food sitting there. His gaze moved back to Bella. She'd made sure that when he was ready there would be food for him to eat.

He carried the plate to the table and uncovered it. Bread, sliced ham and three small pickles were on the plate and a small bowl rested in the center. Philip picked up the bowl and sniffed. Apples and cinnamon greeted his nose.

His gaze moved to the pail Bella was using to catch rainwater. As he ate, his gaze moved around the house. He noticed several other pails that had caught rainwater.

That meant the roof needed repairing. He thanked the Lord that Bella hadn't tried to climb up and fix it.

After eating, he quietly emptied each bucket of rainwater out the back door. The cold rain continued to fall, causing him to shiver. Philip went back downstairs and grabbed the quilt and pillow off the bed. He hurried back up and closed the door to the lower part of the house.

He folded the quilt to make a cushioned bed for himself. Philip used the final fold as a cover. He snuggled down into his warm bed. For several long minutes Philip listened to the steady breathing of his new family. The responsibility of three people weighed heavily upon him. Would he be able to provide for them? Care for their basic needs and not grow to love them?

In a way, he knew it was silly to cling to old fears. People died every day. He'd even heard of several who had taken their own lives, like his father had. Philip didn't want to believe he'd be weak should he fall in love with his family, but still... It was crazy, but he didn't know how not to feel this way.

Angry, Philip turned his face to the fireplace and punched the pillow several times in frustration. Knowing something was silly and not knowing how to deal with it was enough to drive a sane man insane.

For the first time in many years, Philip wished he had someone to talk to about his fears and emotions. He closed his eyes and willed sleep to overtake him so that he could start tomorrow pretending that nothing bothered him. That he was perfectly normal and was leading a normal life.

Chapter Seventeen

Philip woke the next morning feeling as if he'd slept on rocks. The smell of bacon filled the little house. He looked around for the boys but didn't see them on their bed.

The sound of humming filled his ears. He turned toward the sound. Bella worked in the kitchen. She was placing bacon on four plates alongside flapjacks.

He pushed off his quilt. "Something sure smells good." Philip folded up the quilt and laid it on top of the bedding that had been hers and the boys' beds.

"I thought I'd make flapjacks, since you are home. Hazel brought maple syrup over the other day." She set the plates on the table. "Would you mind calling the boys in for breakfast?"

"Be happy to." He walked to the front door and pulled it open.

He was surprised to find the boys playing on the porch instead of out in the mud puddles. "Bella says breakfast is ready." Philip stepped to the side and let them run past.

"Hold up." She held her hand up to stop them from climbing up on the logs. "Hands washed first."

It was an order, not a request. Both boys looked at their hands. Mark grumbled, "Mine are clean."

"Uh-uh. You were picking your nose outside," Caleb said as he started walking toward the washbasin.

Mark stuck his tongue out at Caleb's back but followed. "I bet my nose is cleaner than yours."

Philip shook his head. The boys were a lot like Benjamin. Was he ever that ornery? He walked to the table.

Bella said, "You, too."

He grinned. "Yes, ma'am." Philip followed the bickering boys.

Caleb was drying his hands. He looked to Philip and grinned. "She's making you wash your hands, too?"

"Yep, and my ma always says never argue with the person who is cooking your meals." He waited for Mark to move over and then dipped his hands into the warm water. Amazed, he said, "The water's warm."

"Aunt Bella heats it for us," Mark said, taking the drying cloth from his brother.

"Nice." Philip grinned at them. "Makes washing your hands much better."

Caleb crossed his arms over his chest. "Philip, have you noticed the roof needs to be fixed?"

Philip looked at the boy's serious face. "Yep, I did."

"We gonna fix it?" Mark asked.

Philip took the offered drying cloth. As he dried his hands, he answered, "I reckon we have to."

"How are we going to do it?" Caleb asked. He leaned against the wall. His blue eyes were very serious. Was he trying to be the man of the house?

He decided to see where the boy was going with his

line of questions and thinking. "What did you have in mind?" Philip asked. He hung the cloth on a nail and waited.

"Well, I've never fixed a roof before. Have you?"

"Are you guys going to stand out there talking all morning? Breakfast is getting cold," Bella called from the kitchen.

Philip walked to the table. He wasn't about to let his breakfast get cold. "I've fixed a barn roof before, so I imagine I'll be able to figure out something." He sat down on the log at the head of the table.

Caleb and Mark crawled up onto their log seats. He waited for Bella to join them and then said a quick prayer over their food.

After everyone had said amen, Philip answered Caleb. "We'll need to make some shakes to cover the damaged ones."

Bella looked at him with a frown. "What are shakes?"

"The pieces of wood on the roof that overlap each other to keep us dry in here," he answered. The bacon was crisp, just the way he liked it.

Caleb nodded as if he understood exactly what Philip was saying. Mark was more interested in the maple syrup that Bella was pouring over his flapjacks. He realized that his little family had distracted him from his chores. "As soon as breakfast is over we need to go feed the horses and then head over to the relay station and help Thomas with the chores there," he said.

The two boys were deep into their breakfast, focusing on the pancakes in front of them. Philip wasn't sure they heard him. He decided to try the flapjacks. His eyes widened at the buttery flavor.

Bella grinned at him. "What do you think?"

It was obvious that she knew what he thought, but he recognized that women like to hear they did a good job. "They are so buttery."

"That's because I use a little more than other people and the trick is to start whisking as soon as you add the milk because the cold milk will cause the butter to set up if you don't." Bella took a bite of a flapjack.

"Well, it sure is good. Isn't it, boys?"

Both boys looked up with full mouths and nodded. Mark dipped his finger into the syrup and tucked it between his lips.

"Mark, don't use your fingers," Bella scolded. She handed him a cloth to wipe his sticky hands on.

They finished breakfast and Bella began to clean up the table. Philip stood and rubbed his stomach. "Thanks for making breakfast, Bella. That was some mighty fine eatin'."

Mark imitated him by poking out his tummy and rubbing it. "Yep, mighty fine eatin'," he repeated.

Bella laughed. "Glad you boys enjoyed it."

"Aunt Bella, do you want me to help you clean up the kitchen?" Caleb asked. He carried his plate to the washtub and slipped it into the water.

She gave him a big hug. "Not this morning, little man. I believe you and Mark are going to go help Philip and Thomas with the chores." Bella kissed the top of his blond head.

Caleb wiggled out of her grasp. "All right, you don't have to get mushy about it."

Mark laughed. Bella made a quick grab for him and soon had the little boy in a tight hug and was planting kisses on his face. She let him go and wiped her face. "Mark, you have a sticky face."

"Well, you have wet kisses," he returned, wiping at his face.

Philip laughed at their antics. Mark had been stunned that Bella had gotten ahold of him so quickly. He stopped laughing when he heard Mark's next words.

"Aunt Bella, aren't you going to kiss Philip all over? He laughed, too."

Bella's face turned red and she looked away quickly.

Philip decided to join in the fun. He raced across the room, snagged her around the waist and started planting kisses all over her face. She squealed and giggled. He let her go and grinned at the boys. "I'm faster than her." Philip raced to the coats as if afraid she was going to get him. "Hurry, boys, let's get out of here before she starts kissing us again," he called.

He tossed each of the boys their coats, then opened the door and let them run outside. Philip turned back to face Bella. "Let's do that every morning. That was fun." He hurried out the door before she could reply.

Bella stood in shock. She knew Philip was playful, but he'd just caused her heart to pitter-patter again. How was she going to stop him from doing that? If she told him to stop carrying her and kissing her, he'd know the effect he was having on her poor nervous system. Then what?

A knock sounded on the door. Bella approached with caution. Was that Philip playing tricks on her? Was he thinking it would be funny to kiss her again? She pulled the door open and jumped back.

Hazel looked at her with a quirked eyebrow. "Is that a new way to answer the door?"

Bella felt her cheeks burst into flame. "No, I thought

you were Philip." She opened the door wider to let Hazel inside.

"Does he usually knock?" Hazel grunted. She stooped over and picked up a medium-sized wooden box. "I'm so glad that the rain has finally stopped. A woman could catch her death of a cold, waiting on the porch to be let in."

"No. What's in the box?" She hoped her question would distract Hazel.

The older woman smiled. "A surprise for the boys."

Bella's interest was tweaked. "Can I see?"

Hazel gave her a mischievous grin. "Sure, but only after you tell me what you thought was going to happen when you opened the door for Phil."

So much for distracting her. Bella sighed. "He was teasing me earlier and I thought he was going to grab me again when I opened the door."

"Sounds fun." Hazel smiled.

"It was," Bella admitted. "Now, tell me. What's in the box?"

Hazel pulled the lid off the box. Inside were blocks, wooden wagons and a couple of stickmen, what looked like puzzle pieces and several books. "It's not a lot, but I thought the boys would like them."

"I'm sure they will love them." Bella pulled a small wooden house out of the box. "This is so cute."

"There's also a fence and barn in there," Hazel said, digging into the box. She held up the little barn. "See?"

Bella stood up. "I know they are going to love these. Are you sure you want to give them to the boys?"

"What am I going to do with them?" Hazel asked.

Bella wanted to answer her with a few questions of her own. Like what Hazel was doing with these toys?

Where did they come from? But she knew that would be rude, so instead she grinned. "I guess give them to the boys. Thank you."

Hazel dug in her apron pocket. "I brought something for you, too." She pulled out two pieces of paper folded together.

Bella took them and unfolded them. "Oh, these are cookie recipes. Thank you." She started walking to the table. "Let's sit down and have a cup of tea. How does that sound?"

"Wonderful. These old bones are tired and cold."

The dirty dishes were going to have to wait until she had visited with Hazel. Bella laid the papers on the table, put a pot of water on to heat and then took down her tea bin.

"That second paper has that sweetbread recipe you wanted and a few other breads I thought you might like." Hazel sat down. "I'll sure be glad when that man of yours builds you some decent chairs."

"Oh, I can't wait to try the sweetbread recipe." Bella decided not to comment on Hazel's thoughts on her chairs. She was proud of the fact that she and the boys had found the logs to use for chairs. The Lord had provided and she'd not complain.

Mark ran into the house. "Hi, Hazel!" He gave her a big hug.

"Where have you been?" she asked.

"Out helping Philip with the chores." He turned to Bella. "Philip asked if you'd mind packing us a box lunch."

"A lunch?" Bella didn't understand why they'd need a box lunch.

Hazel pulled the little boy up onto her lap.

"Uh-huh. We're going to go to Dove Creek for some wood after we finish our chores at Uncle Thomas's station." He pushed down. "I'm going to grab my horse."

"Oh, all right." Bella pulled a box from under the cabinet. She quickly sliced bread and ham for sandwiches.

"Can I do anything to help you?" Hazel asked.

Bella smiled. "No, thanks." She paused. If Philip was going to the store, then there were a few things she'd like. Should she send a list or just get ready and go with them? Her gaze moved to Hazel.

Hazel nodded. "Yep, I'd go, too."

"You would?"

"Beats staying out here. Unless you have a good book to read." Hazel stood to leave.

"Where are you going?"

"Home."

"I thought you said you'd go, too. Do you have a good book at home waiting for you?" She placed her hands on her hips and grinned at Hazel.

"Well, no. But I just thought you'd want to go as a family." Hazel put her hands in her pockets.

"You are family. Mark, tell Philip I'd like to speak to him before he goes to Thomas's place."

The little boy ran from the house again, this time with his horse in his hands and in a gallop instead of a dead run. Hazel followed. "I'm going to run back to the house and get my bag."

"Hurry back. I'd like to have tea before we go."

Hazel nodded and followed Mark. Just before she shut the door, Hazel said, "Thank you, Bella." Then she hurried out.

Bella finished making the sandwiches. She wrapped

them in a cloth, then added pickles and cookies to the box.

Just as she put the top on the box, Philip walked in. “Mark says you want to talk to me.”

She turned to face him. “Yes, Hazel and I would like to go to town also. We’ll come to Thomas’s in about an hour. That should give you plenty of time to get the chores done, shouldn’t it?”

He nodded. “I believe so.” A frown marred his features.

Bella frowned, too. “Do you not want us to go with you?” she asked, feeling a little hurt at the idea that he hadn’t wanted her to go.

He looked at her. “Why would you say that?”

“You’re frowning at me.” She crossed her arms over her chest.

Philip crossed the room and draped his arm over her shoulders. “Oh, I’m sorry. I was just thinking about space on the wagon. Of course I want you to come.”

She smiled up at him. “Well, that’s an easy fix. Hazel and I can ride our horses and you and the boys can ride in the wagon.” Bella didn’t tell him that she preferred riding on her horse. Wagons bumping along jarred her to the point of being sore the next day.

He gave her a hug and then nodded. “So, it’s settled. I’ll take the boys, lunch and the wagon now. We’ll meet at the relay station in about an hour.” Philip released her.

Bella grabbed the lunch box from the table and handed it to him. “Thank you.”

Philip took the box. “You and Hazel be careful coming over to Thomas’s.”

“We will,” she promised.

He turned and left. Bella smiled. Philip Young was

a good man. She wished she could have met him before she'd met her ex-fiancé. Her ex-fiancé had proven that no matter how good of a man he seemed it wasn't always the way they were. She couldn't trust her heart just because she felt Philip was a good man.

Chapter Eighteen

Philip arrived at the relay station and jumped down from the wagon. “Hey, Thomas!”

Thomas came out of the barn and waved. He walked to the wagon and helped Mark down. “What are you all doing this morning?”

“We came to help you with the chores,” Mark answered as his feet touched the ground.

“Oh, you have, have you?”

“Yep, Philip says you got two new hogs for us to feed.” Caleb jumped down from the wagon by himself. He looked up and grinned. “Can we see them, Uncle Thomas?”

Thomas nodded. “You sure can.” He started around the back of the barn. “I put them as far away from the house as I could. Josephine doesn’t care for their smell.”

Mark grabbed his little nose. “I don’t, either.”

Philip laughed. “They aren’t that bad. It’s the mud and muck that smells, not the pigs.”

Caleb looked up. Doubt filled his blue eyes. “I’m pretty sure it’s the pigs.” He motioned toward the two big hogs.

They were covered in mud. So much so that Philip couldn't tell what color they were. "Well, that mud would make them stink, I suppose."

Philip watched as Thomas showed the boys how to fill the pig trough full of feed and scraps. He then took them to the well and filled up two large buckets full of water and poured it into the round water barrel that sat in the corner of the pen. The boys asked lots of questions about pigs and even tried scratching one behind the ears.

"Are there any chores left for me to do?" Philip asked with a grin, knowing they were really late arriving and the answer would probably be no.

Thomas surprised him. "I saved the best for last. There are about four stalls that need mucking out. You are welcome to start on one of those."

Caleb laughed. "That's funny, Uncle Thomas. You saved it for Philip to do."

Philip grabbed Caleb around the waist and picked him up. He started walking to the barn with the struggling little boy. Philip called over his shoulder, "Caleb just volunteered to help me. You'll have to get Mark to help you finish up with the pigs."

Caleb slumped like a bag of potatoes. "Aw, that's not fair."

Thankfully Caleb couldn't see his grin when Philip said, "Not so funny now, is it?" He set Caleb on the ground.

The little boy wrinkled his nose. "Nope, not funny at all."

Philip and Caleb began mucking out the stalls. Caleb broke the silence after several long minutes of hard work. "When I grow up, I think I want to live in town."

"How come?" Philip pitched the old hay out into the center aisle.

Caleb leaned on his pitchfork. "I don't care much for tending animals." He grinned. "I don't mind riding horses, but I don't like cleaning up after them."

Philip nodded. "What would you do in town? As a job? You'd still have to work."

The little boy went back to work. "I don't know. I'm still young. I have time to learn. Maybe after I grow up some, I'll have a better idea." He used his pitchfork like a shovel and pushed hay out into the center passageway.

"True, but while you're growing, you'll get to do all kinds of jobs."

Thomas and Mark entered the barn. Philip could hear Mark talking about horses. With a grin, he thought he knew what Mark would be doing when he grew up.

"Have you heard that the telegraph wire is pushing its way here?" Thomas asked, grabbing a shovel.

Philip stopped working. "No, I really haven't been paying much attention to anything other than my new family. What have you heard?"

Thomas pushed the soiled hay toward the barn door. "Just that the telegraph lines are headed this way. There is a rumor that the Pony Express won't be needed much longer."

Philip went back to his work. What if the telegraph office did put the Pony Express out of business? What would he do? How would he feed his new family? He wasn't sure his furniture was good enough to sell, but he felt the need to work on it.

Bella knew something was on Philip's mind. Now that they were home from town, she intended to find out what. She looked to the boys, who were sleeping soundly on their mountain of quilts and blankets.

The fire crackled and created a soft light throughout the room that was soothing. "I've been thinking all day, Bella."

Their eyes met across the room and she waited for him to continue. Maybe she wouldn't have to ask. It had been obvious that he'd been thinking all day, but his silence now was putting her on edge.

"Thomas said this morning that the telegraph lines were coming this way and the men in town confirmed it." He paused again with a sigh. "I suppose I knew the Pony Express wouldn't last forever and I saw men surveying the land, but I didn't think it would end this soon." Worry laced his voice.

Bella spread out his quilt and then her own a few feet away and closer to the boys. "Yes, some of the women were talking about it in the dress store also." She spoke softly so as not to wake Caleb or Mark.

He nodded and chewed on his fingernail. "I bought extra wood from the lumberyard so that I can make a couple of items and see if they will sell in the general store."

At this point, Bella felt as if he was talking to himself more than to her. She sat down on her pallet. Her sewing basket wasn't far away, so she dug in it and found one of the boys' hole-filled socks. "I think that's a wonderful idea."

"You do?"

"Uh-huh. Once you sell a few pieces, you will know how nice your building is." She smiled happily at him. The bed he'd made downstairs was simply beautiful and

Bella hated to admit that she was envious of Josephine's couch, which Philip had made her for Christmas.

"It will take up a lot of my time. With building and the Pony Express, you and the boys might not see me much," he said, watching her face to see her reaction.

Bella laid the mended sock in her lap. "Why can't you do your furniture work in the house?"

He looked around. "Where would I do it at?"

She grinned. "Well, larger pieces would have to be outside in the barn, but smaller items, like rockers, cabinets and other things, could be made either here in the sitting room or downstairs. There is lots of room down there."

Still unsure, he said, "It will be noisy work."

"As long as the boys aren't sleeping, I don't think that will be a problem." She pulled out a shirt that was missing a button.

"I could work on larger items out in the barn while the boys are napping." Philip grinned. "I suppose you want me to make your furniture, too?"

"Of course. But as much as I love Josephine's settee, I'd like mine to be a little smaller and I want two rocking chairs in here. One for you and one for me." She giggled at the look on his face. "Oh, and the boys each need a bed."

"Woman, when am I going to have time to build furniture to sell?" He leaned forward as if waiting expectantly for her answer.

"Well, when you build my rocking chair, you can make a second one to sell." She dug in her button box for a button. Between Hazel and Josephine sharing their buttons plus the few she'd bought at the general store, Bella had a nice collection of buttons.

Philip made a "humph" noise, then said, "Well, that sounds good."

Bella sewed the little button into place. "Have you spoken to the owner of the general store about selling your furniture there? Or are you planning to?"

"I mentioned it. He said to bring a couple of things down and we'd discuss it." Philip lay down on his quilt and put his hands behind his head.

Bella knotted her thread close to the button and then bit off the remainder of the string. She folded the shirt and then laid her work to the side. "So when will you start working on something?" she asked, lying down on her pallet.

He yawned. "Maybe tomorrow afternoon. The boys and I will do our morning chores and then Thomas has offered to come over and help me repair the roof. If you don't mind, maybe you could make us all a hot lunch."

"I'll be happy to," Bella answered.

They lay there in comfortable silence for several long moments. Philip spoke in a soft voice. "Thank you, Bella, for helping me feel better about the furniture business."

"You're welcome. We'd better get some sleep. Morning will be here before we know it." She turned over on her side and tucked her hands under her head.

Philip answered, "Good night."

"'Night." Bella listened to his steady breathing that soon turned into soft snores.

Sleep should have come swiftly to her also, but her mind refused to shut down. Even though she'd been positive about Philip's furniture business while speaking with him, Bella couldn't help but worry. If Philip did well selling furniture, would he want to move to town? And if he was really successful, would he decide this ready-made family wasn't for him? As much as she didn't want to compare him to her ex-fiancé, Bella couldn't help it. Had he married her only to leave them when better things began to happen for him?

Bella prayed a simple prayer, asking God to help her learn to trust her new husband. Even after she'd said a silent amen, she didn't feel any better but knew she'd support Philip. He had the right to pursue his dreams.

Chapter Nineteen

Philip and Thomas stomped into the house just as lunch was being served. Mark and Caleb followed close behind. Mark's bottom lip was pooched out in a pout.

Josephine smiled at the little boy. "Mark, you are going to trip on that lip if you don't pull it back in."

Everyone laughed as he sucked his bottom lip into his mouth. Mark ignored their laughter and climbed up on one of the logs that served as dining table chairs. "Philip wouldn't let me help," he told Bella.

"He wouldn't?" she asked.

Mark shook his small head. "Nope, he said I'm too little."

"He is too little," Caleb said. "I'm not. I got to hand up the shakes to cover the holes."

Philip ruffled the little boy's hair as he walked past him. "He did a good job, too."

"That's good, Caleb. I'm proud of you." Bella grinned. She looked back to the pouting Mark. "You are still too little to hand up those heavy pieces of wood. Don't pout. You get to do lots of things."

Mark didn't look any happier, but honestly there

wasn't much Philip or Bella could do about it. The little boy was too small to be working on a roof.

Philip heard Bella try to distract Mark from his pouting. "You and Caleb get to have a picnic in the living room or on the front porch. Mark, where would you like to have it at?"

"I don't care."

"I want to sit by the fire, Aunt Bella. I'm a little cold," Caleb answered.

Thomas and Philip returned from washing their hands. "Your turn, boys. Go wash your hands," Philip ordered as he took his place at the table.

Bella looked from Philip to her nephews. Caleb ran to the washbasin in a hurry to do his bidding. Mark went also, but at a much slower pace. She turned questioning eyes on him. "Philip?"

He looked up at her. "Let it go for now, Bella."

She looked from Thomas to Josephine. He had to admire them. They both seemed busy filling plates with food, obviously not wanting to get into their family affairs.

"All right," Bella finally said as she walked into the living room and laid a blanket down for the boys to sit on while they ate. It was clear that she didn't like that Mark's feelings were hurt, but that she also knew now wasn't the time to talk to him about it. She sighed.

When the boys came back, Philip handed each of them a plate. "Thanks, Philip," they both said.

Bella returned to the table and sat down. She and Josephine had already set the table with coffee, tea and a full plate for the four adults. Philip said a quick prayer and they all began to eat.

"I think we did a pretty good job on your roof," Thomas said before taking a big bite of roast.

Philip nodded his agreement. "Hopefully we got all the holes and cracks covered."

Bella seemed to be listening as they discussed the roof. Philip watched as her gaze continued to move to Mark.

The little boy ate with Caleb and seemed to have forgotten his aggravation at being left out of the repairs. Philip wanted to include Mark, but the boy didn't want to do what they asked him to and so finally Philip had simply banned him from helping at all. He felt bad about it, but Mark had to learn to do as he was told even if it wasn't what he wanted to do.

"Bella?"

She turned back to Josephine. "I'm sorry. What?"

"I was telling you that Hazel and I have come up with a way to have fresh bread all the time without baking it ourselves." Josephine grinned across the table at her.

"You did?"

Philip marveled that Bella seemed to be dismayed at the thought of someone else baking bread for her and the other ladies. From the confused look on her face, she simply couldn't imagine someone else doing her baking. He knew she enjoyed it.

"Yes, do you want to know how?"

Bella nodded.

"It was really Hazel's idea."

"What was Hazel's idea?" Bella asked, sounding a little frustrated that Josephine wouldn't just tell her what their plans were.

"You will bake our bread!" Josephine giggled.

"What?" Shock filled his new wife's voice.

Josephine's giggle turned into a full belly laugh. The boys stopped talking to each other and turned their attention to the women's conversation.

Once she'd gotten control of her merriment, Josephine explained. "We thought you might like to trade us bread for milk and eggs. You could send my bread by Philip and the boys when they come to the relay station to help Thomas, and I could send back eggs."

"Well, I'll be. That makes perfect sense." Philip held up one of her rolls. "You make wonderful bread and we could use the milk and eggs, since we don't have our own cows or chickens yet."

Josephine nodded. "That's what we thought and we both love her bread. Hazel said that Bella's sweetbread was even better than hers and that Bella is using her recipe."

Thomas laughed. "Will you two let Bella get a word in edgewise?"

Bella smiled at him. "Thank you, Thomas." She turned her attention back to Josephine. "I think it's a great idea, too. I love baking, so it wouldn't be any trouble to make extra loaves for you two."

"Good, we'll need to let Hazel know you've agreed to our bargain." Josephine picked up her fork and began eating also.

Philip loved the way Bella's eyes lit up when she was talking about bread. The woman truly loved to bake. He knew she'd worked in a bakery before she'd taken on her nephews' raising. Had she dreamed of running the bakery someday? For the first time, he realized exactly what all Bella had given up to raise the boys and marry him.

His heart went out to her. She was willing to allow

him to follow his dream of furniture making but may have given up hers of owning or running a bakery someday. Could he help her fulfill her dreams? What were her dreams? Philip decided then and there to find out what they were.

Bella finished cleaning up the kitchen. Thomas and Josephine had left a few minutes earlier. Josephine had offered to stay and help her clean up, but Thomas was in a hurry to get back to the relay station. A Pony Express rider would be coming through soon and he had to be there to meet the rider with a fresh horse. Bella assured her new friend that she understood and to go on home.

The boys lay on their pallet. Mark was already asleep.

Caleb got up and walked over to her. He whispered, "Aunt Bella, I'm not sleepy. Can I go see what Philip is doing in the barn?"

She gave him a quick hug. "Yes, I think I'll go, too. I can use the fresh air."

Together they walked quietly to the door and put on their coats and gloves before heading outside. Bella inhaled the fresh, cold air. She supposed their warm spell had vanished. Wrapping her coat closer to her body, Bella followed Caleb to the barn.

It wasn't a whole lot warmer in the barn and she couldn't help but shiver. She heard hammering toward the back of the barn and followed the sound. Caleb hurried ahead of her.

"What are you making?" Caleb asked as soon as he saw Philip.

"A rocking chair for your aunt Bella."

She came around the corner. "Oh, good." Bella

looked forward to having furniture in her house. The kitchen table was nice, but she was tired of always sitting at it or on the floor.

"I didn't realize you were out here." Philip stood.

Bella shivered. "It's cold out here."

Philip agreed, "Yes, but with the boys napping I thought I'd work out here." He looked at Caleb. "Why aren't you napping?"

"I wasn't sleepy. Aunt Bella said I could come out here with you."

She rubbed her arms. "I didn't realize it had turned so cold outside."

"Why don't we all go back inside? I think I'll go downstairs and start the fire." Philip stepped out of the little room he'd been in and closed the door.

Bella didn't have to be asked twice. She walked at a swift pace back toward the house. Caleb and Philip hurried up the steps behind her. Just before opening the door she shushed them. "Mark is sleeping, so be as quiet as you can."

They nodded and she opened the door.

Mark sat in the middle of his pallet looking disheveled. "Where have you all been?"

"Oh, I'm sorry, Mark. We didn't mean to wake you," Bella said as she hung up her coat.

"We was in the barn with Philip," Caleb said, answering Mark's question.

"I thought we were supposed to take a nap," Mark accused, rubbing his eyes and yawning.

Caleb answered again, not giving the grown-ups time to respond. "Aunt Bella said I didn't have to nap. So I went to the barn. Philip is building a rocking chair for

Aunt Bella." He dropped down on the quilt beside his brother.

Hurt filled Mark's sleepy eyes. "Oh." He lay back down and turned his back on them.

Bella went to the kitchen and made a cup of hot tea. She looked to Philip, who had followed her. "Would you like a cup of coffee before you head down?"

"I'll take it with me, if you don't mind pouring me a cup."

She poured the rich brew into a large mug and handed it to him. Then Bella turned to her recipe box and brought it to the table.

Philip took a sip and sighed. "Thanks, that's just what I needed to warm up my insides."

"You're welcome."

"What are you doing?" he asked.

She smiled up at him. "I'm going to decide what kind of bread to make this week."

Philip shook his head. "Plain ol' white bread would be nice."

She'd really hoped to try something different, but if he wanted ordinary bread, she could make that, too. "I can make white bread."

"No, make whatever you want. I like it all."

Bella looked at her recipes. They were written on small pieces of paper, some in her handwriting and others in Hazel's. "I'll make white bread and maybe a sweetbread, too. As a treat."

"I like your sweetbread," Caleb said in a soft voice.

Philip looked to the boy and grinned. "Me, too."

Bella bent her head to the chore at hand. She wanted to start on the bread as soon as Mark got up. His even breathing told her he'd gone right back to sleep.

"I'm going downstairs now," Philip remarked.

"All right."

Thankfully Caleb followed him down. Bella wanted to study her recipes in peace. Sometimes she wondered if Caleb deliberately baited his brother, hoping for an argument. Or had he just been so happy to get out of taking a nap that he'd shared the information with Mark?

Her gaze lifted from the recipe in her hand. Was she doing a good job of raising the boys? What could she do that would be better?

Philip had the fire pit going downstairs in no time. He opened the curtains around the bedrooms so that the heat would fill them, as well. His gaze moved about the spacious room. "What do you think of it down here?" he asked Caleb.

The little boy looked around. "It's kind of scary but kind of fun."

The fire cast shadows on the wall. Philip laughed. "Yeah, I understand what you mean."

Caleb went to the room that was to be his and Mark's. "I wish we had real beds, like at home."

Philip had followed. He laid his hand on the boy's shoulder and said, "You will have. Would you like to help me make them?"

"Uh-huh."

He grinned. "Then you will. I hope you enjoy making stuff out of wood as much as I do."

An hour later, they climbed back up the stairs. Caleb had told Philip all about his parents' deaths and how he and Mark had been put into one of his pa's employee's homes before Bella had arrived to take them with her.

The little boy missed his papa and said that someday he wanted to grow up to be just like him.

When they walked into the main part of the house, they found it empty. Both Bella and Mark were gone.

Philip frowned.

"I wonder where they went," Caleb said, looking around the room. "And Mark didn't make up the pallet." He walked over to the blankets and began folding them.

Philip found that odd also. Bella insisted that the beds be put away as soon as everyone was up. Why would she and Mark have left the house before it was made? Then it dawned on him that they probably had gone to the outhouse.

He walked to the stove and poured himself another cup of coffee. Philip glanced around his warm home. Bella's feminine touch could be seen in each area. She'd made paper flowers and put them in clear jars about the sitting room. In the center of the table she'd placed a bowl and put colorful balls of yarn inside it to create a splash of color in the otherwise dull room.

The door opened and Bella hurried inside. She shut the door as fast as she could. "It's getting colder out there."

Philip pushed away from the counter he'd been leaning on. "Where's Mark?"

Her gaze moved to where Caleb stood, folding the last quilt and laying it on top of the others. She turned stricken eyes on Philip. "I left him sleeping. Isn't he here?"

"Evidently not." He started toward the door. "You stay here. I'll go search for him. He can't be far." Philip grabbed his coat off its hook, thrust his arms into the sleeves and then pulled his gloves out of the pocket.

His heart beat fast as he tried to imagine where the boy might have gone.

"He's probably in the barn," Caleb said.

Bella turned toward Philip. "I'll go with you."

Philip shook his head. "No, you stay with Caleb. If he comes back, you will need to come tell me. Caleb will need to stay with Mark. He's too young to be out on his own." Caleb was too young to be outside on his own also. The two boys would be better off in the house.

At her nod of understanding, he pulled the door open. "I'll find him. Don't worry."

Philip hurried to the barn. "Mark!" he called as he opened the door.

The horses stomped their feet, but Mark didn't answer.

He stood in the yard trying to think where the little boy could have gone. Had he gone to the outhouse and then, finding Bella there, ventured into the woods to do his business? Philip hurried to the outhouse.

"Mark!"

Still no answer. The wind had picked up and now carried Philip's voice back to him. He went around to the back of the small building and searched the ground for prints. Seeing none, he turned back to the house.

Would Mark go to Thomas's? Or Hazel's? Why hadn't Mark come down to where he and Caleb had been? Had the little boy run away from home?

Philip knew Mark had felt left out earlier, but that was no reason to run away. He decided to tell Bella Mark wasn't in the barn. The little boy may have thought he could go to Thomas's and help with the chores.

He entered the door and was immediately questioned by Bella.

"Did you find him?" Her lips trembled.

"No, I'm going to saddle up my horse and ride over to Thomas's. It's time to do chores over there. Mark might have thought to help." Philip walked over to Bella and pulled her into a tight hug. "You know how much he loves horses." He pulled back and looked deeply into her eyes. "We'll find him."

Her blue eyes filled with tears, but she raised her head and said, "I know we will. Hurry."

Philip didn't need any further prompting. He spun on his heels to leave. Then turned back to look at Caleb. "Take care of your aunt while I'm gone."

"I will."

He hurried back to the barn and began to saddle his horse. As he worked he prayed, asking God to watch out for Mark. The temperature was dropping with the sun. Philip fought down the panic that threatened to overwhelm him.

Chapter Twenty

Bella paced the sitting room. Where could Mark have gone? And why? She fought back tears, trying to be brave for Caleb.

Caleb sat looking at his favorite book. His gaze wandered to the door frequently.

A sharp knock sounded at the door. Both Bella and Caleb jumped. Bella hurried to answer the summons. She pulled it open, praying it was Mark but knowing he wouldn't knock if it was him. Bella was surprised to see Hazel, Mark and an Indian standing on the porch.

Hazel had her hand clamped tightly on Mark's shoulder. "See? I told you she'd be worried sick. You should be ashamed of yourself, young man." Hazel gently shoved him into the house.

Mark hurried to Caleb, where he buried his face in his brother's chest.

"Thank you for bringing him home. Won't you come in?" Bella invited, curious about the man standing behind Hazel. His dark skin and the way his long black hair was fixed let her know that he was a Pawnee Indian.

Hazel marched past her and the man followed. Bella

shut the door and then turned to look at Mark. His legs were wet from the knee down. "Where have you been?" she asked.

His cheeks were wet with tears. "I went to the river," he answered.

"To the river!"

Mark nodded.

Caleb placed his small arm around his brother's shoulders.

"Why didn't you tell me you were leaving?" Bella walked over to him. She passed Hazel, whose arms were crossed. She had an angry gaze focused on Mark.

"I wanted to go fishing," he sobbed.

"Mark, it's too cold to fish and you aren't ever supposed to leave this house without telling me or Philip." She stopped in front of the boys. Tempted to get down on their level, Bella made herself not be too soft on the boy. He could have drowned. "Wait, isn't the pond frozen over?"

Hazel snorted. "That wasn't going to stop him."

Bella turned to her friend. "What do you mean?"

"When Johnny found him, Mark had busted a hole in the ice and then his feet slipped out from under him. Johnny pulled him out." Hazel pointed to the Indian man beside her to indicate that he was Johnny.

"Thank you," Bella said, looking at the dark-eyed stranger.

He dipped his head in her direction.

She turned back to the boys. "Mark, take off your wet clothes and then sit down there by the fire. As soon as Philip gets back we'll decide what your punishment will be for leaving the house and worrying us to death."

In a quiet voice, Caleb asked, "Can I take him downstairs to change?"

Realizing the little boy didn't want to undress in front of strangers, Bella nodded. "But you two hurry up and get back here. I'll not have you playing down there when Mark is in trouble."

"Yes, ma'am." Caleb took Mark by the hand and led him out of the room.

Once more Bella turned to her visitors. "I can't thank you enough for bringing him home."

"He is young," the stranger said in a gruff voice.

Bella nodded. "Yes, and he should not have been out by the river."

Hazel's face softened and she turned loving eyes on the Indian. "Johnny, do you have time to stay for a cup of coffee?"

He wrinkled his nose. "I would have water."

Bella smiled. Johnny was the first man she'd ever met who didn't seem to care for coffee. But even more important was the fact that Hazel seemingly loved him. "Let's move to the table."

Hazel led the way with Johnny following her and Bella following them both. Johnny wasn't an Indian name; she was pretty sure of that fact. So, how had he acquired his name?

As soon as they were seated, Bella dipped fresh water from the water bucket into a cup and handed it to Johnny. She then turned to the stove and poured hot coffee for Hazel. "Would you and Johnny like a slice of peach pie?" she asked.

"I wondered what that smell was when we came in. Knew it was some kind of pie, just hadn't realized it was peach. I think we'd both like a slice, if it isn't too much trouble."

"No trouble at all." Bella was glad she'd made the pie earlier.

Once her guests were served, she sat down and asked, "So, how do you two know each other?"

Hazel answered, "Johnny is my son." She took a bite of her pie and grinned. "This crust is so flaky. Mine never turns out this nice."

Bella looked from mother to son. He didn't look anything like Hazel.

Johnny smiled at her. "My mother has surprised you with her words."

"Yes, she has. I had no idea that Hazel had a child." She looked to her friend. "Do you have other children?"

"No, Johnny is my only child who lived. He is my pride and joy." She reached across the table and touched his brown hand.

Bella looked to the wooden box of toys and realized now where they'd come from. "I'm glad you found Mark. I don't know what I'd do if anything happened to him." She pushed back her chair. It was time to go get Philip and tell him that Mark was home safe.

Philip leaped from his horse and hurried up the porch stairs. He opened the door. "Bella, he wasn't at Thomas's. Thomas and I are riding—" His words trailed off as he saw Bella sitting at the table with Hazel and an Indian.

"I'm so glad you are back." Bella walked over to him. "Hazel and her son, Johnny, just brought Mark home. He's downstairs changing into dry clothes."

Thomas entered behind his brother and shut the door.

"Why didn't you come tell me?" Philip demanded.

Hazel said, "We've only been here a few minutes, Phil. Come have a piece of this peach pie with us. You, too, Thomas." She waved them to the table with her fork.

He looked to Bella. "It's true. They haven't been here long. I was going to come get you," Bella said.

"Where was Mark?" Thomas asked, walking around his brother and joining Hazel and Johnny at the table.

Philip followed his brother. He wanted to know what happened, too.

Bella answered behind him. "Down by the river."

"What was he doing there?" Philip asked, sitting down on the last log stool.

"Fishing," Johnny answered. "He is smart for one so young."

Philip and Thomas accepted plates with pie on them. "What makes you say that?" Philip asked. He really wasn't in the mood for pie, so when Bella came back to the table with two cups of coffee, he laid down his fork.

"I watched him. He took a big rock and slammed it into the ice to make a fishing hole. Then he found a stick and tied string, like that, to it." He pointed to the balls of yarn on the table.

"I wonder what he was going to use as a hook," Thomas mused.

Johnny shook his head and laid down his fork. "No know. His feet slid out from under him and he was trapped in the hole he had created. That is when I pulled him out." He drained the water from his cup, then stood. "Mother, are you ready to go now?"

Hazel pushed back her chair. "Thank you for the pie and coffee, Bella."

"Yes, thank you. Mighty good," Johnny said.

Philip stood and extended his hand. "Thank you for saving the boy's life. We are in your debt."

Johnny shook Philip's hand. "I am glad Mother knew where he came from. I would not have been happy to take him back to camp with me."

"I wouldn't have been too happy about that myself," Philip agreed.

"No, my father's people are not as accepting of the white man as they once were. It would have been a hard life on the boy." Johnny walked to the door. Everyone followed except for Thomas. He remained at the table, eating.

Philip knew that Johnny spoke from personal experience. Why had Hazel given her son to the Pawnee tribe? It was obvious that she loved him very much. He also knew that the Pawnee were not happy about the white man crossing their hunting grounds. He nodded.

"Hazel, come over tomorrow. I'll bake in the morning. I'd love your company." Bella hugged her friend close. "Thank you for bringing Mark home. I can't thank you enough."

The older woman returned her hug. "I could only imagine how frightened you must have been. It was the least Johnny and I could do."

Philip followed Johnny out onto the porch. Seeing only his and Thomas's horses tied to the porch post, he asked, "Did you walk over?"

Johnny nodded. "Mother refused to ride my mustang and I would not ride while she and the boy walked. So we all walked."

"Would you two like a ride home? Hazel can bring the horses back in the morning," Philip offered.

Hazel joined them. "No, thanks, Phil. If we walk,

I'll have more time with my boy." She tucked her hand into the crook of Johnny's arm.

Philip watched them leave.

Bella came to stand beside him on the porch. "Is it just me? Or does that look strange?" She waved her hand in the direction of Hazel and Johnny.

He had to agree. Seeing a short white woman walking with her hand tucked into an Indian brave's arm did seem a little out of place. Even for this part of the country. Philip chuckled, then turned to reenter the house.

Thomas pushed away from the table. "I think I'll head home, too." He walked past his brother and sister-in-law.

Philip waited until the door shut behind Thomas before turning to his new wards.

Mark and Caleb stood in the center of the room waiting. He hated the idea of disciplining the little boy. His own father would have had no trouble taking him out to the woodshed, but John Young, his adoptive father, had never laid a hand on him. Truth be told, he'd never had to. Papa John had given him a stern talk, explained why he was disappointed in him, and that had been enough. Maybe that was the approach he should take with Mark.

Bella entered behind him and shut the door. She walked around Philip. "Let's go to the table."

He heard the concern in her voice and wondered if it was because she dreaded disciplining the boys. Or did she think he should be the one to do it and dreaded what he'd do? Philip nodded his head and the boys walked slowly to the table.

They both looked so small sitting on the logs. Mark's eyes were downcast. Caleb chewed on the tip of one of his fingers, a sure sign the boy was nervous.

Philip and Bella sat down. "As a family, what should

we decide is a good punishment for Mark? He knew better than to leave without telling one of us," he said, making eye contact with everyone at the table except Mark, who still studied the tabletop as if it could swallow him.

Bella shook her head. "I'm not sure. I do know I was worried almost sick. Anything could have happened to him."

He looked to Caleb. The little boy swallowed hard and said, "I don't think I should say. After all, he is my little brother."

Philip nodded. "You're probably right." He turned his gaze to Mark. "Mark, what do you think is a fitting punishment?"

"I don't know."

"What would your father have done if you had left the house without an adult?" Bella asked. She folded her hands on top of the table and waited.

Mark lifted moist eyes. "He would have whipped me." Tears began to stream down his face.

Caleb wrapped his arm around Mark's shoulders. Mark leaned into his brother and cried all the harder. Philip looked to Bella, who looked horrified at the little boy's reaction to her mention of his father.

Philip said the little boy's name in a soft voice. "Mark…"

Mark slowly turned to face Philip. He used his hands to try to stop the flow of tears.

His watery gaze tore at Philip's heart. "We aren't going to whip you. But we were very worried. There is a reason we asked you not to leave the house without one of us. Can you tell us what one of those reasons might be?"

"Because I might get eaten by a bear?" Mark sniffled.

"Come spring, yes. Right now they are sleeping," Bella said.

"Any other reasons?" Philip asked.

While Mark scrunched up his face and thought, Bella stood up and got the cookie jar. She set it in the center of the table and then turned to fill two glasses with water from the water bucket.

"I might run into a Injun?" he asked.

Philip nodded. "Yes, and not all Indians are nice like Johnny. Right now they aren't happy that we are in their hunting grounds. In other parts of the country they are killing Pony Express men. Mostly stock holders and station managers, but they are still murdering good men."

Mark's and Caleb's eyes grew round and their mouths formed perfect O's.

"I didn't know that," Caleb said, picking up a cookie that Bella had placed before him.

Philip nodded. "I know you didn't. But, to be fair, the Indians are not the only people out there that will hurt a small boy, if given the chance. Bad men come in all colors and sizes. The Indians are no worse or better than the white man. You need to use good judgment when dealing with both. That's the reason Bella and I want you to never leave the house without one of us."

"Forever?" Mark asked.

Bella set a cup of coffee in front of Philip. "Well, at least until you are older."

"We'll let you know when you are old enough," Philip added. The rich fragrance of the coffee teased his nose. He picked up the cup and took a sip. Was there anything that Bella fixed that didn't taste wonderful? If there was, he hadn't found it yet.

She looked sternly at her nephews. "Promise you will not leave this house or go anyplace without an adult with you."

"I promise," Caleb said immediately.

Mark took longer. It seemed as if he was arguing with himself. Finally, Mark looked up at his aunt. "I promise, too, Aunt Bella."

"Good. Then eat your cookie." She smiled sweetly at him.

Philip studied the little boy over his cup. Mark was strong-willed and this troubled Philip. Would the boy take off again? He prayed not and made a decision to keep a closer eye on his youngest charge.

Chapter Twenty-One

Over the next month, Bella baked bread and kept her little house in tip-top order. She was pleased that they were becoming a family. Philip and Caleb worked on furniture for the house. Mark loved the horses and helped Philip feed and water them daily.

Bella admired her new rocking chairs and small couch. She finished wiping off the table and then hurried to her bedroom to grab her sewing box and fabric. Today Josephine and Hazel were coming over to make pillows.

Philip had left that morning on the Pony Express trail, so the boys were playing checkers on the floor. She smiled. Neither of the boys really knew how to play, but they enjoyed pretending.

Box and fabric in hand, Bella hurried back upstairs. She heard a knock on the door. As she passed the kitchen table, Bella laid down the fabric and box, then hurried to open the door for her friends. Bella pulled the door open with a big smile, but it quickly faded.

Marlow Brooks, her ex-fiancé, stood in the doorway. "Are you going to invite me inside?"

How had he found her? Why had he arrived? Bella had no intention of inviting him into her home. "No. My husband, Philip, isn't home and it wouldn't be proper."

He laughed. "You're going to be proper, even out here in the sticks?"

Caleb and Mark came to stand beside her. Caleb asked, "Who is he?"

Marlow bent down and offered the little boy his hand to shake. When Caleb took it, he said, "I am Marlow Brooks, your aunt Bella's fiancé." He looked up at her and smiled. "If she will have me back."

Bella gently pushed Caleb away from Marlow. She turned to the boys. "Go back to playing your game. Mr. Brooks is leaving now."

Marlow stood slowly. He leaned against the door frame and stuck out his boot to stop her from shutting the door in his face. "Aw, Bella. I'm sorry I hurt you. I was wrong." He reached out and touched her cheek lightly with one manicured finger.

She jerked away from him. Why had she ever found him attractive? He was a handsome man, but his behavior appalled her.

"I don't know how you found me, Marlow, but now you know I'm already married. Go home, Marlow." She tried to shut the door.

He planted a hand on the door above her head. "You don't love him, Bella. I know. I can see it in your eyes."

"If you see anything, Marlow, it's anger." She heard a horse and wagon come into the yard. Bella sighed with relief.

Marlow turned to look over his shoulder at the newcomers. "Friends of yours?"

Bella looked under his arm. Thomas had pulled the

wagon up to the barn. "My brother-in-law and sister-in-law."

"Pretty wife." He dropped his hand from the door. "I'll be back. I have business to discuss with you." Marlow turned and walked down the steps. He waved at Thomas and Josephine as he climbed back on his horse and then spun away.

Thomas waved at her from the barn. Bella returned his wave and motioned for Josephine to come inside. She turned to find the boys standing in the doorway. "Boys, get in the house. It's too cold for you to be standing out here in your stocking feet."

She turned back and saw Josephine walking to the house. Bella decided she didn't want the other woman to know any more about Marlow than she intended to tell her. She smiled at Josephine and then walked back to where the boys were playing with the checkers and their wooden horses.

Bella leaned close to them and whispered, "Don't say anything about Mr. Brooks to Josephine, Thomas or even Philip. I want to tell them. Understood?"

"All right, Aunt Bella," Mark agreed. He used his horse to knock Caleb's over. "I got you!" he yelled.

Caleb shouted, "Did not! That wasn't fair. I was listening to Aunt Bella." He picked up his horse and pretended to trot it around the checkers.

Satisfied they'd already forgotten about her visitor, Bella stood. Josephine entered the house and quickly shut the door. "It is getting so cold out there. I feel bad about Philip being on the trail in this weather." She took her sewing box and fabric to the table. "Thomas talked to a rider this morning that said they are getting snow in the direction Philip was riding."

Bella walked to the water kettle. "Would you like hot tea or coffee?" Thankfully the water was still piping hot. "Boys, say hello to Josephine."

They looked up. "Hi, Aunt Josephine."

"Hello, boys. Tea, please." She eased into her chair. "I wonder if it's too cold for Hazel to come out and join us." Josephine took the cup of hot water from Bella and reached for the tea and tea strainer.

What had Marlow meant when he'd said he had business with her? They'd broken off all their business when he'd told her he didn't want to be saddled with someone else's kids. Bella looked to the door. "I hope she comes."

Josephine looked at Bella. It was obvious she wanted to ask who had been visiting, but politeness kept her from doing so. "Have you given any thought as to what we can stuff the pillows with?" she asked instead.

Bella grinned. She decided to push her worries away. "I was thinking beans."

"Like pinto beans?"

"Sure, why not?"

Hazel came through the door with a puff of snowy air. "It's so cold out there, I thought about not coming." She grinned. "But you two don't know how to have fun without me, so here I am." She hung up her coat and walked into the room. "What are you boys playing over there?"

"Checkers."

"Horsies."

"Which is it?" Hazel asked. She walked over to see for herself.

Josephine turned her attention back to Bella. "I guess you could use beans. We have lots of those and they aren't too expensive."

"What were you thinking of using?" Bella asked, taking the tea strainer from Josephine and dumping the spent leaves in the slop bucket.

"I hadn't given it any thought until I got here."

Hazel joined the conversation. "We could use rice, too."

"Did you know that rice will hold heat?" Bella asked. "Coffee or tea?" She directed the question to Hazel.

"Coffee. How do you heat the rice, and other than to eat it, why would you want to?" Hazel sat down across from Josephine. She placed her sewing box on the table and opened it up.

Bella poured hot coffee into one of her best mugs. She handed it to Hazel, then returned to start her own cup of tea. "Well, back home, they were putting it in a pan and warming it up. Then when it was nice and hot they'd pour it into the sleeve of a shirt, they'd tie off both open ends and then drape it around their neck or lean against it to make their back stop hurting."

"Who is *they*?" Hazel asked. She took a sip of the hot coffee and sighed. "That sure warms an old woman's bones right up."

Josephine tried not to laugh as she mimicked Hazel. "Yeah, who is *they*?"

Bella carried her cup of hot water to the table. "*They* are the ladies I worked with at the bakery."

"I wonder if I could wrap that around my feet at night. Sure would beat having a hot brick at the bottom of the bed. I can't tell you how many times I've kicked that thing in my sleep." Hazel looked around the kitchen. "You got any pie lying around here?"

Josephine laughed. "Have you known her not to have pie, or cookies, lying about?"

Bella grinned. "I made an apple pie this morning."

"Were you saving it for dinner?" Hazel asked.

"No, I made it for us this afternoon."

While she got the pie, Hazel and Josephine began working on their cushions and pillows. Bella slid a slice to each of them and then sat down again.

"I'm glad you talked us into doing this, Bella," Josephine said as she savored the sugary pie.

"Me, too," Bella admitted. She pulled out her fabric and began working on a pillow for the couch. It was a light green print with little leaves.

Both Josephine and Hazel worked on their cushions. They chatted back and forth. Bella smiled. Moving here and marrying Philip had been the best decision she'd ever made. Her gaze moved to the boys, who were happily playing with blocks.

Marlow's voice floated through her memory. Why was he here? She'd told him she was married, but he had asked her to marry him anyway. What was Philip going to say when he found out her ex-fiancé was in Dove Creek—and that he'd been out to see her?

Dread filled her.

Philip had been home for two days. Bella seemed quieter than normal. The house looked wonderful. While he was gone she'd made pillows and curtains for the window over the kitchen washtub. Maybe she simply needed some fresh air.

Now that he was rested, they could take a drive to Dove Creek. He could take the rocker and table that he'd made to sell at the general store. The boys were downstairs changing clothes. They'd managed to fall in the mud while feeding the pigs at the relay station.

"Bella, how would you like to ride into town? I could take the rocker and table to the general store and we could eat at the new boardinghouse." He took a sip of his coffee.

Bella's big eyes seemed to grow in her face. "I'd rather eat at the little diner, if it's all the same to you." She laid her dishcloth on the counter.

"We could do that."

Caleb and Mark came racing up the stairs.

"Boys, how would you like to ride into Dove Creek?"

Mark asked, "Can we get a peppermint stick each?"

"I don't want a peppermint stick. I want lemon drops," Caleb said and shoved his brother sideways.

"I tell you what. You boys help me load the table and chair into the wagon and we'll get both." He pushed up from the table.

The boys ran to get their coats. "Do you think we can stop at the livery, too?" Mark asked.

Philip went to put his coat on also. "Why?"

"Mr. Morris said I could sit on ol' Snowball next time we came to town."

Bella called from the kitchen, "While you men do that, I'll go to the dress shop."

Philip laughed. His small family seemed very happy with his idea of going to town. "We'll be ready to leave in about fifteen minutes, Bella. Do you think that will give you enough time?"

She nodded. "I'll put this food away and go put on a more suitable dress."

"That dress is fine," Philip told her. It was a light blue dress that brought out the blue in her eyes. He hated to admit it, but he'd missed Bella and the boys more than ever this trip. She'd greeted him with a smile and hot apple pie when he'd arrived home. He was getting used to such greetings.

"Thank you, but I'm still going to change," she told him and headed down the stairs.

Caleb watched her go. His young face had a worried expression on it. Did the boy know the reason for Bella's quietness?

"Can we go now?" Mark asked with his hand on the door.

"Sure can," Philip answered.

The little boys jerked the door open and ran down the porch stairs. Mark yelled, "Last one there is a rotten egg."

Caleb yelled back, "First one there has to eat it." He waited for Philip to step off the porch and then continued to walk with him.

"Anything exciting happen while I was gone?" Philip asked.

"Naw, we did the same ol' stuff. Aunt Bella won't let us do anything at Uncle Thomas's. We just stay here." Caleb kicked at a pebble.

"Is it just me or do you have something you want to get off your chest?" Philip asked, watching the boy from the corner of his eye.

Caleb looked to the barn. "Did Aunt Bella mention any visitors?" he asked in a low voice.

Philip stopped. "No. Did you have a visitor while I was gone?"

Mark came running back to them. "No fair, you didn't even try."

Caleb grinned. "You have to eat it."

"No, I don't. You cheated."

Did they even understand what they were saying?

Philip shook his head. "Mark, would you go make sure that Blaze has finished her breakfast? I think we'll let her pull the wagon today."

Excited to get to do something with the horses, the little boy took off running again. "All right!" he called over his shoulder.

"I'll go help him." Caleb started to make a run for it, but Philip caught him by his collar.

"What's this about visitors?" he asked.

"Promise not to tell Aunt Bella I told you? She wanted to tell you herself." Caleb looked down at the ground.

He'd been home two days and Bella hadn't said anything about a visitor and she'd sworn the boys to secrecy. Philip laid a hand on his shoulder. "No, don't tell me. If she wants to tell me, then she needs to be the one to do so. Go ahead and help Mark."

Relief washed over the boy's face. He ran to the barn and disappeared inside. Philip's legs felt like mud was caked to the bottom of his boots. He walked to the side of the barn and pulled the wagon around to the front. His mind chanted, *Bella has a secret. Bella has a secret. Bella has a secret.*

Ten minutes later, Bella came from the house. She carried a basket with her and her purse. Her blond hair shone in the sunlight. She wore it in a braid down her back. Bella had changed into a green dress with blue flowers. He still thought the blue one looked prettier on her, but he would never tell her that.

The trip to town had been quiet. Philip assumed it was because both he and Bella were thinking about the strange visitor. Of course, he had no idea what or who she was thinking about.

Her gentle voice pulled him from his thoughts. "Are we going to the general store first?"

"Yes, I thought we could drop off the furniture, then we'll drop you off at the dress shop and then me and the boys will go to the livery for a little while. Does that sound all right with you?" Philip pulled in front of the general store. He jumped from the wagon and then turned to help her down.

She smiled as he placed her on the ground. "That sounds like a good plan."

Philip moved to the back of the wagon to get the furniture. Bella walked to the front of the store and waited for him. Caleb helped him pull the table out and carry it to the door, where Bella stood holding it open. As they passed, the sweet scent of vanilla pulled at his senses.

He carried the table to the front counter, where the owner was finishing up an order. "Let's set it here and go get the rocking chair," Philip told Caleb.

The bell jingled over the door.

"Aunt Bella is carrying it in," Caleb announced.

Philip turned in time to see that Mark held the door open and Bella was carrying the rocking chair in front of her. He hurried to her side. "Honey, you should have let me get that."

Honey? Had he just called her "honey" in front of everyone? From the shocked expression on her face, he had. Philip took the rocker from her and walked back to the counter.

What was wrong with him? He knew his feelings for Bella were growing stronger than friendship, but what he didn't know was how to stop them. Philip told himself he was not meant to fall in love.

Chapter Twenty-Two

Bella stood in shock. He'd just called her "honey." Honey! She felt her face heating from the neck up. Bella looked down at Mark, who was grinning from ear to ear. She looked away.

Mark tugged at her dress. "Aunt Bella, can I call you 'honey,' too?"

She saw the teasing glint in his young eyes. Bella leaned down and whispered, "No, that's Philip's special name for me."

Mark nodded. "I like it."

Bella stood. Philip and the store owner spoke in soft tones. She decided to go look at the fabric. Mark and Caleb had wandered to the shelf that held toys.

Running her hands over the soft fabric, Bella dreamed of making shirts for the boys and dresses for herself. Calico colors filled the table. She loved the blues the best and thought Philip would look handsome in one shade in particular.

Why had he called her honey? He'd never used a term of endearment before. Her stomach fluttered. Heat filled her again at the thought. Bella walked to where he stood with the owner.

"Excuse me."

Philip turned to face her. She swallowed hard. "I've decided to walk to the dress shop. Do you mind keeping an eye on the boys?"

"Are you sure? I'm almost done here and can drive you over."

Bella backed away from him. "I'm sure."

"Well, all right. We'll come get you in a little while and we'll get a bite to eat before heading home." Philip ran his hand over the back of his neck.

She nodded, not trusting her voice. Bella turned and, with her head held high, walked outside. Once in the sunshine and out of the stuffy store, she inhaled deeply. There were so many thoughts and emotions running through her mind.

It was at that moment that Bella decided to face her romantic notions about Philip head-on. She told herself that he wasn't for her. He didn't want to fall in love.

At one time she'd thought she loved Marlow, but he'd betrayed that love and her distrust for men had been born. Philip had done nothing but treat her with kindness, but she still worried that one day he'd get tired and want to move on to something else. Something not as demanding as taking care of a wife and two children.

"I was expecting you in town sooner."

Bella didn't need to look at him to know that Marlow had joined her on the boardwalk. She continued walking. "Why should you?"

"Don't play games, Bella. You are curious about what business I have with you. I'm surprised it's taken you a number of days to come find out what I meant by that." He fell into step beside her.

"Go away, Marlow. I am in town with my family and did not come to see you." Bella tried to ignore him as she walked.

He sighed. "That's too bad. I guess I could go home and tell everyone where they can find Sam Jackson's murderer."

Bella stopped walking. For the second time in the same day, she felt shock race through her body and mind. "Sam is dead?"

"Yes. Your old boss was found dead in the bakery the day after you left. Someone hit him pretty hard with your rolling pin." He acted as if he was paying his respects for the dead.

His words began to sink through the sorrow she felt at the loss of a good friend. "Murderer? Are you implying that I murdered Sam?"

"No, the sheriff in Douglas City is."

She walked over to one of the benches in front of the drugstore and sank down onto the hard wood. "Why me?"

He sat down beside her. "Because it was your rolling pin that did the old guy in."

Bella scooted away from him. Her mind raced. Had she left her rolling pin at the bakery? It was possible. "I didn't kill him. He was my friend as well as my boss." She couldn't believe that Sam was truly gone.

She realized that Marlow was enjoying telling her about Sam. Bella searched his face. "Why are you really here, Marlow?"

"I told you. I came because I realized I'd made a mistake and wanted you back." He reached out and took a lock of her hair between his fingers. "I've missed you."

Bella pulled away from him. "I can't marry you, Marlow. I'm already married to Philip. You know that now, so why not just go home?"

He sighed. "You are wanted by the law, Bella. If I can find you, it won't be long before they find you, too. How is that new husband going to feel when he finds out he's married to a possible murderess? Do you think he'll stand by you? Or will he take the boys away from you and let the law do as they will with you?"

Fear wrapped its ugly fingers around Bella's heart. Would Philip believe her when she told him she hadn't killed Sam? Or would he do as Marlow suggested and abandon her to her own fate? And the boys? Would Philip take them from her?

Marlow leaned back on the bench and stretched his arm across the back. He played with the end of her braid at her back. "See? You don't know, do you?"

Bella wanted to say that Philip was her husband, that he loved her and would stand by her through good and bad. But she knew it wasn't true. He didn't love her and had no reason to stand by her side. "Going back with you won't save me from the hangman's noose," she stated wearily.

Marlow had some sort of plan, Bella knew it. But why? Why did he suddenly profess to care for her? What did he have to gain by offering her marriage?

"I'll see to it that you don't hang for murder." He twisted the braid until her head came back and she was forced to look up into his face. "As a high-powered lawyer, you know I can do it. Or I can send a bounty hunter after you and make sure that you are convicted and hung for murdering Sam. The choice is yours." He released her hair.

The callousness in his words and face scared her almost as much as the threat he'd just thrown down. "But why?"

He gently pulled her braid around and let it fall to her shoulder. "Because I love you. If you choose to go with me, we'll get married as soon as possible."

Bella shuddered. He didn't love her. Marlow had a reason for what he was doing, but she couldn't figure out what. She needed more time.

As if he read her mind, Marlow stood. "I'll give you until the end of the month to decide what you want to do." He stretched like a cat in the sun.

The month ended in a week. Bella stood and grabbed his arm. "Marlow, wait. I need more time than that. Like you said, I can't just outright tell Philip that I'm wanted for a murder I didn't do. He will take my nephews. I need to break it off with him, but not suddenly or he'll know something is wrong."

His smile scared her. Marlow thought he'd won. But what had he won?

"One month. We can't wait any longer than that. The sheriff and his men will eventually find you, too." His green eyes reminded her of a cat that had a mouse cornered.

Bella nodded. "One month."

Marlow patted her cheek. "I'll be watching you. Don't try to take off with the boys." He turned and walked away.

She lowered herself back down to the bench. How many people had seen them together? Bella had to tell Philip about Marlow, but how much did she have to tell him? Not everything. The boys were too important to her.

Bella lowered her head into her hands and wept. A few days ago her life had seemed almost perfect. She had a nice home, the boys were happy, she had friends and a family who had welcomed her as one of their own.

In just a few short moments Marlow had taken that away from her. The thought of leaving Philip forever tore a new rip in her heart. She'd grown to love him despite what her head told her. Now she was going to lose him forever and all because of a lie.

What was Marlow hiding from her? She knew he didn't love her, but he was determined to marry her. Why? Bella hoped to find out, before the one-month deadline was over.

The wagon bounced along as Philip drove to the livery. The boys sat beside him on the bench, finishing up their candy. All in all this trip into town had been a success. Mr. Jones bought both the table and chair and asked him to come back in a week to see if they'd sold. The store owner thought the pieces were of fine quality and would sell quickly. Philip hoped it was true.

Mark elbowed Caleb. "Look, that's Mr. Brooks."

Philip turned his head to look in the same direction as the boys. A tall man in a nice suit turned the corner by the bank. "Who is Mr. Brooks?"

Both boys pursed their lips together.

"The visitor?" Philip asked.

Both boys looked away.

"You told him about Aunt Bella's visitor?" Mark whispered to Caleb.

"No."

"Oh."

Philip knew he'd have to wait for Bella to tell him about this Mr. Brooks. He continued to drive to the livery. Had Bella agreed to come to town so that she could see him? Who was he? And why hadn't she already mentioned him?

Mr. Morris, the livery owner, came out to greet them when they pulled up to the barn. "Hello, boys. Mark, did you come to ride Snowball?"

"I did!" Mark jumped from the wagon and ran to the big man.

He nodded. "I thought so." His attention turned to Philip. "How are you today, Philip?"

"Good as rain," Philip answered. He pushed thoughts of Bella and Mr. Brooks from his mind. "You?"

"Doing pretty good." His gaze moved to Caleb, who leaned against Philip's shoulder. "What do you say, Caleb? Want to ride Snowball, too?"

The little boy nodded even though his face wasn't as animated with excitement as Mark's. He looked at Philip. "Are you going to stay, too?"

Philip sensed the boy's unease. He set the brake on the wagon. "I'd planned on it."

Caleb climbed down from the wagon. He stood by the wagon and waited for Philip to join him on the ground. His big blue eyes watched as Mark and the older gentleman walked into the livery.

Philip dropped a hand down onto Caleb's shoulder. "You know, Snowball is about sixteen years old. Mr. Morris let me ride her when I was a boy."

"I've never been on a horse before," Caleb said.

"Your pa didn't let you ride his?"

They began walking toward the barn. "No, he said we were too little."

"Do you think you are too little?" Philip asked. If the boy said yes, there was no way Philip was going to ask him to try it.

"Maybe."

Philip grinned down at him. "You don't have to ride Snowball today. She might be tired after Mark's ride."

Relief filled the little boy's face. His pace picked up and he said, "Mark loves horses. He'll probably ride her the whole time we are here."

An hour later, they left the livery. Caleb had watched Mark on the horse and had cheered him on. When Mr. Morris suggested Mark give Caleb a turn, Caleb had told him he wasn't ready to ride her today and to let Mark keep riding.

"I can't believe you didn't want a ride, Caleb. It was fun," Mark said as they entered the dress shop.

Bella sat in a chair by the door. She had a small bag in her hands and looked as if she'd been waiting for them. "What was fun?" she asked Mark.

"I got to ride Snowball. She's a big white horse. But Caleb didn't want to. I think he's scared of horses." Mark hugged her around the waist.

Caleb frowned. "I'm not scared of horses," he protested.

"Are, too."

Philip spoke. "Boys, let's not argue." He looked to Bella. "Ready to go find something to eat?"

"I'm famished," she answered with a big smile.

For a moment Philip wondered if the smile was forced. Her eyes didn't have their normal sparkle. "The diner is just up the street. We can leave the wagon here and walk." He opened the door and the boys ran outside.

Bella followed at a slower pace. "I don't mind walking." She followed the boys down the boardwalk.

Philip closed the door and quickly caught up to her. "Did you have a good time shopping? You didn't buy much."

She glanced at him. "I really didn't need anything. It's fun looking." Bella held up her bag. "I did find a hair comb—it didn't cost much."

He grinned at her. "Was there a dress you would have liked to have? The winter dance will be in a couple of days. If you need a new dress, I'm sure we have the money for it."

"That's very generous of you. It would be fun to have a new dress to wear." She looked down at the package in her hands. "I got the comb to wear to the dance, even though I wasn't sure if we'd be going."

Philip felt like a heel. Why hadn't he mentioned the dance sooner? He'd been so wrapped up in making furniture and teaching Caleb how to work with the wood that he'd forgotten about the dance until just now. "I'm sorry. I should have mentioned it earlier."

Her eyes looked a little brighter. "It's all right. You've been busy." Bella grinned. "Josephine said that she and Thomas will be going. She's already got a pretty red dress picked out."

The boys stopped in front of the diner and waited for them. Philip opened the door. "Then when we go back, you can get the one you want. I can't have my brother's wife looking better than mine at the dance."

A strange expression filled her eyes. Bella followed the boys inside. She remained quiet during their meal of meat loaf, mashed potatoes and fried okra. Philip couldn't help but wonder if he'd said the wrong thing when he'd teased that his wife should look better than his brother's. Or did Mr. Brooks have something to do with her silence?

Chapter Twenty-Three

Bella wanted to tell Philip about Marlow. She just didn't know how. They'd returned to the dress shop and she'd picked out a pretty pink party dress to wear to the winter dance, then they headed home.

She put the boys to bed in their new beds and then went to sit by the fireplace and wait for Philip to come in from putting away the horses and the things he'd purchased at the general store.

What would he say when he found out Marlow Brooks, her ex-fiancé, was in town? Bella rocked and waited. Her mind spun around the things Marlow had told her. Did the sheriff really think she'd murdered Sam? Was Marlow correct in saying that if Philip found out, he'd take the boys away from her? Could he even do such a thing legally?

Philip entered the house and hung up his coat. His gaze moved to where she was sitting. He'd continued to sleep upstairs on a pallet, while she'd moved downstairs with the boys. Normally, when she put them to bed, Bella retired also. "You're up late," he said, walking over to the cookie jar and pulling out a sugar cookie.

Bella stood and joined him in the kitchen area. "Would you like coffee with your cookie? I think there is enough in the pot for a cup."

"If it's already made, sure." He looked at the logs that they were still using for kitchen chairs. "Tomorrow I will start working on the kitchen chairs."

She poured his coffee. "That will be nice." Bella turned to hand it to him.

Philip had walked back into the sitting area and sat down in the rocking chair he favored. She followed. "I need to tell you something." Bella handed him the coffee and sat down.

"Sounds serious." He took a careful drink.

Bella shook her head. "Not really. But I think you should know that Marlow Brooks came by the other day and is staying in Dove Creek."

"Who is Marlow Brooks?"

"The man I was going to marry." She bowed her head. How much more should she tell him? Bella knew she'd never tell him that Marlow wanted her to go back with him. Or that she was suspected of murder.

He cradled the cup in his hands. "The one who broke off your engagement." It was a statement.

"Yes."

"Why is he here?" Philip asked.

Bella looked up. "He said he's sorry he called off the wedding and wants me back."

Philip tilted his head to the side. "Did you tell him we are married?"

"Of course. I told him to go home." Bella didn't want to tell him any more. If he continued to ask her questions, she knew she wouldn't lie.

"Is he going home?"

Bella stood. "When he's completed his business here, I'm sure he will." She didn't elaborate on the fact that Marlow's business was with her. Faking a yawn, she mumbled, "I just wanted you to hear it from me. I'm tired and heading downstairs now."

As she started to walk past him, Philip's hand shot out. "Bella, do you still care for him?"

Had she seen pain flicker through his eyes? Bella shook her head. "I don't love him anymore. I'm not sure I ever did."

He released her arm. "Thanks for telling me. Good night."

Bella walked from the room. She wanted to run, to hide her face from him and cry. Why did Marlow have to come to Dove Creek? Why now, when everything was going so well?

The next morning, Philip got up early and went to the barn. He'd had a rough night. His mind wouldn't shut down as thoughts of Bella and Marlow raced through it. He felt sure she hadn't told him everything.

What business did Marlow have in Dove Creek? How had he found her? Did the man truly realize that he loved her, after she was gone?

Philip fed and watered the horses, then began work on the chair he'd promised Bella he would start working on. She'd said she didn't love Marlow and probably never had. Did she mean it? Would Bella realize she'd rather be married to a man who loves her than one who didn't? And what about the boys? Was Marlow willing to take the boys along with her?

An empty ache gathered in his chest. Philip walked over to the water bucket and, using a dipper, took a long drink. He'd gotten used to having her around. She'd made the empty house into a home.

The barn door opened. Caleb entered with a big smile. "Aunt Bella said to tell you breakfast is ready." He came inside. "What are you working on?"

"Chairs for the kitchen table. What do you think of this one so far?" Philip liked that Caleb had taken an interest in his furniture-making.

Caleb picked up one of the legs. He looked down the length of the board. "It looks straight." He examined each finished piece. "It's going to be nice and sturdy."

Philip laughed. "Where did you hear the word *sturdy*?"

"Aunt Josephine told Aunt Bella that everything you make is nice and sturdy." He laid down the chair leg. "This will be, too."

"Well, thank you. We'd better get inside before Mark eats all our breakfast." Philip pulled the big barn door open and then followed Caleb out into the morning sunlight.

They walked across the yard to the house. Philip looked at the outside of it and was glad that he'd bought whitewash the day before to paint the outside. He followed Caleb into the house, where the aromas of sausage and fresh bread filled the warm air.

"Good morning." Bella smiled over her shoulder at him. Today her golden strands of hair were pulled back in a ponytail. She wore a brown house dress with a light blue apron covering the front of it.

He returned her greeting. "Good morning. I believe I could eat an elk this morning." Philip went to the washbasin and cleaned his hands.

"I could, too," Mark said from his place at the table.

While Bella set the table, Philip asked, "How would you like to help whitewash the house today?"

Her blue eyes met his. "Outside or in?"

She sat down and began filling the boys' plates.

"Today, outside. If you want to do the walls in here, too, we can do that tomorrow or the next day." Philip filled his own plate with sausage, eggs and two buttered biscuits.

Bella smiled at Mark. "I think that will be fun."

Caleb frowned. "How can painting be fun?" He started to take a bite out of the biscuit Bella had just placed on his plate.

Philip cleared his throat and the boy stopped his hand halfway to his mouth. He waited for Caleb to set the bread back down on his plate. "I'd better say the blessing."

Bella nodded and the boys lowered their heads.

After he said the prayer, Bella continued with their conversation. "We will be doing it as a family," Bella responded. "That will make it fun."

They all ate quietly for a few minutes. Philip chewed slowly, savoring every bite. Bella was the best cook in the territory as far as he was concerned. If she chose Marlow over him, he'd miss her cooking. And her easy smile. And the way her hair shimmered in the sunshine. He jerked his thoughts to a stop and focused on eating.

"Philip, are we going to Uncle Thomas's to help with the chores today?" Caleb picked at his eggs with a fork.

He nodded and swallowed. "Yes, as soon as we get done with breakfast. Why do you ask?"

"Well, if we do chores at the relay station and then come back and paint the house, when are we going to have time to build the chair?" Disappointment filled his face. Caleb already realized that the chair would have to wait.

Philip understood the little boy's unhappiness. He would rather be building than painting, too. "It may be a few days before we get back to that project."

Mark frowned as he looked from Caleb to Philip. He turned his attention back to his eggs and shoveled them into his mouth. Philip wondered what was bothering the little boy but didn't feel now was the time to ask.

"That's what I thought." Caleb began eating again, too.

Neither boy seemed happy with the prospect of painting the house. Should they let the boys go play while they painted? Philip's gaze met Bella's across the table. She shrugged her shoulders.

"Would you rather play while we paint the house?" Philip asked.

Bella spoke up. "No, they live here, too, and can help with the upkeep of the house." She smiled at him. "But it is really nice of you to give them a way out of the work."

Philip nodded. "Well, that settles it. We work on the house as a family." He chewed and thought, would they be a family much longer?

Bella laughed at the look on Philip's face. She'd just splashed him with paint. It had been an accident. At least she'd made it look that way.

"Oh, you think that's funny, do you?" He aimed his brush in her direction and then flicked his wrist. Paint sprayed from the brush and covered her pretty blue apron.

Mark cupped his hand into the paint and slung it at Caleb. The watery white paint hit Caleb on the side of the face and ran down his neck. He yelped and Mark laughed.

Caleb retaliated. Bella, thinking to stop the paint fight, stepped between the boys only to find herself covered in more paint as they both slung paint at each other but hit her instead. “Stop!”

Philip roared with amusement. “You started it.”

“Well, I’m putting a stop to it now. Besides, it was an accident that I got you with my paint.”

“Sure it was,” Philip countered. He looked at the finished wall. “Hey, believe it or not, we’re done.”

Bella looked at the freshly painted house. It had taken all day, but Philip was right, they were finished. “I can’t believe we finished it.”

He chuckled. “Me, either.”

The sun was almost down. Bella laid down her brush and wiped her hands on the apron. “Give me your brushes, boys.” She took the offered brushes and laid them beside hers.

Philip put the lid on the paint can and gathered up the brushes. “Caleb, you come with me to clean up these, and, Mark, you can help Bella start dinner.”

Bella smiled. “That means we get to work in the house, where it’s warmer.” She took Mark’s cold, wet hand in hers.

Philip and Caleb headed for the river. Mark watched them. His jaw hardened, but he didn’t say anything. Bella knew the little boy felt slighted. She really needed to talk to Philip about spending more time with Mark.

“What are we having for supper?” Mark asked. He led the way to the front porch.

Bella followed. “What would you like?”

"Something hot." Mark stopped at the door and pulled off his muddy boots.

"Well, I started a pot of soup at lunchtime. It should be ready by now." Bella had checked on it earlier and knew the soup was ready. She sat down on the steps to pull off her own boots. "Would you mind getting me a damp cloth so I can wash this paint off my face and hands?" she asked him.

"All right, Aunt Bella." Mark headed inside.

She smiled. The day had gone just as she'd hoped. They'd worked as a family and she'd almost forgotten about Marlow Brooks. But now that they were no longer working, Bella's thoughts returned to him. How was she going to find out if he was lying to her? And if he was, why?

Mark returned with a dripping wet cloth.

Bella took it with a sigh. "Thank you, Mark." She knew he'd trailed water from the back of the house to the front. After wringing out the cloth, she wiped her face.

Mark went back inside. Bella finished taking off her boots and followed him. He sat in her rocking chair and started rocking. She walked over to him and quickly scrubbed his face of paint, then she worked on his neck and hands.

By the time Philip and Caleb returned, Bella had dinner on the table and the floor wiped up of water. Mark played with his horse and the blocks by the fireplace.

Caleb joined his little brother. It was obvious that Philip and Caleb had used river water to wash the paint from their faces and necks.

After dinner, Bella pulled out her sewing. Philip sat down across from her and began reading from the

Bible. Caleb and Mark played by the fireplace. The fire crackled, creating a warm, cozy atmosphere.

If only it would stay this calm, Bella thought. She worked her needle through the fabric of Philip's torn shirt. The questions started flooding her mind again. How could she find out why Marlow was suddenly interested in marrying a murder suspect? And how could she do it so that Marlow wouldn't find out?

Could she trust Philip? If she told him what Marlow had told her, would he help her? Or would he take the boys and leave? If only she could trust him. But Bella couldn't. She'd trusted before and been rejected. She wouldn't do that again.

She couldn't.

Chapter Twenty-Four

Philip rode out of town feeling happier than he had in a long time. He'd asked around and discovered that Marlow Brooks had left. That alone had given him a sense of peace. He'd also stopped by the general store and not only had he sold the rocker and the table, but he also had orders for more. Tonight he'd talk to Bella about moving into town.

Plans of buying a building to work from filled him. Before he realized it, he was back at the relay station. He headed to the barn, where he was sure Thomas would be working.

He slid from his saddle and tied his horse to the hitching post beside the barn. Philip listened at the door until he heard Thomas humming inside, then he entered. It took a few seconds for his eyes to adjust, but he saw Thomas sitting on a barrel by the tack room.

"What brings you back my way?" Thomas asked with a wide grin. "Since you've gotten married, I don't see you alone much anymore," he teased.

Philip walked toward him. "Isn't that the truth? Caleb

is almost glued to my side most days." He leaned against a stall door.

Thomas stopped oiling the bridle he held across his lap and studied Philip. "You look as pleased as a mama hen with new chicks. What is going on?"

He couldn't hold it back any longer and blurted, "The rocker and table sold at the general store. Not only that, but I have orders for more. Mr. Jones says he believes I could start my own store and never run out of business." Philip took a deep breath. "What do you think?"

Thomas went back to oiling the leather. "I'm glad Mr. Jones bought the general store a couple of months ago. He's been doing a right nice job."

Frustrated, Philip asked, "What does that have to do with what I just told you?"

"Nothing. You asked what I thought. That's what I was thinking."

Thomas kept his head lowered. Philip suspected it was to keep him from seeing the teasing glint in his eyes and the smile on his face. "You know good and well what I meant."

"I think he's right. You probably could make a living selling your furniture. I've been telling you that all along." Thomas looked up and sure enough the smile and teasing look were there for Philip to see.

He nodded. "I'm beginning to think so, too. But if I move to town and start a business, what will you do out here?" Philip's concern was for Thomas. They'd started working the Pony Express station together. He hated to leave Thomas alone with all the work required to run it.

Thomas laid the bridle to the side and picked up another one. "I'll keep doing what I'm doing. If you quit riding, I'll quit also." He held up his hand to stop Philip from interrupting. "I'll stay on as the station manager until I find farmland. Then I'll ask the superintendent to find a replacement for me."

Philip let his brother's words settle in his mind. Thomas had already been thinking about what to do if he quit the Pony Express. "You knew."

His brother nodded. "Yep, you've been thinking and talking about your furniture for months. How does Bella feel about it?"

"I'm sure she'll be fine with moving to town." But he wasn't as sure as he sounded. Bella had begun to nest, as the old saying went. Would she really want to move to town? And the boys would be forced to accept change once more. Was it too much to ask of his new family?

Thomas stood and stretched out his back muscles. "Well, then I don't know what could possibly hold you back."

Now that Marlow had moved on, Philip felt the same way. But he needed to get home and talk to Bella. After that, he'd have to let the Pony Express superintendent know that he would no longer be an employee of the Pony Express.

The dinner bell rang out. Thomas slapped Philip on the back. "Would you like to stay for supper? I'm sure Josephine won't mind."

Philip knew Bella was making pot roast for supper at his house and he didn't want to miss it. "No, thanks. I told Bella I'd be home in time for supper. If I eat here, I'll be late getting home and she'll worry."

"Maybe next time." Thomas led the way out of the barn.

Philip untied his horse from the hitching post and

said, "Sure." He climbed into the saddle and then headed home.

Excitement coursed through his blood. So much was going to change, but he felt sure it would be for the best. Marlow Brooks was gone, and they would be moving to town and starting a new business. What could possibly go wrong?

The winter dance came and went, but Bella hadn't been able to enjoy it because of Marlow and his threats. Time was running out. Bella was no closer to figuring out a way to avoid leaving with him than she had been the day he'd threatened her. Maybe she should get advice from someone, Bella thought as she pulled the pot roast off the fire.

She lifted the lid and the aroma of meat, potatoes and carrots filled the room. But whom could she confide in? Josephine was Philip's sister-in-law, so there was a possibility she'd tell Thomas and then Thomas would tell Philip. No, she couldn't tell Josephine. There was always Hazel. But Hazel was as honest as the day was long and might feel obligated to tell Philip.

Her mind had made this trip around the bush before and Bella realized the path ended in the same place. There was no one she could share this burden with.

The sound of boots stomping on the porch told her Philip would soon be entering the house. Unlike her and the boys, he seldom removed his boots before entering.

"Bella! I'm back," he called as he entered.

She looked at the table and saw that it was set for supper. While her mind had been busy, her hands had completed the task. "Good. You are just in time to eat."

He looked around the house. "Are the boys downstairs?"

"No, Hazel took them to her house earlier. They should be back before too long." Bella poured a cup of coffee for him and a glass of water for herself, then sat down at the table.

He sat also but asked, "Should we wait for them?"

She shook her head. "I'm not sure when they will be back, and knowing Hazel, she's already fed them."

Philip nodded, then bowed his head for prayer.

Bella imitated his actions. She never tired of listening to him pray.

When he said, "Amen," his gaze met hers. "It's just as well that they aren't here. I have something to tell you."

She buttered their bread and handed him a chunk. "Something good happen in town?"

"Two things."

Bella waited for him to continue. His eyes were filled with excitement and his lips hadn't stopped smiling since he'd brought up the subject.

"First, Marlow Brooks has left town." He waited for her reaction.

She steeled her features, praying that they wouldn't give away her shock at the news. Where had he gone? Had he given up on her returning with him? Panic filled her. Was he already telling the sheriff where to find her? Attempting to sound calm, she said, "Well, that is good news."

"But my second news is even better." He leaned forward. "Both pieces of furniture have already sold at the store."

Bella tried to focus on that news instead of the dread that filled her heart. "That's wonderful."

His voice rose with excitement. "And Mr. Jones gave me orders for more pieces. He suggested I open my own furniture store. Of course, he plans on buying pieces from me to sell in his store also. He said that was the fastest money he's ever made."

The excitement in his voice was contagious. "I'm so happy for you. Didn't I tell you your work was excellent?"

He faked hurt feelings. "An 'I told you so' speech? That's the best you can do?"

She laughed at his expression and nodded. "Afraid so."

Philip chuckled. He took several bites of his food.

Bella felt uneasy. Philip had more to say and she could tell that he was trying to figure out how to say it. Several questions popped into her mind, but she waited for him to speak again.

Her own thoughts returned to Marlow and his sudden departure from Dove Creek. Bella had assumed he'd stay until she'd given him an answer. What was he up to?

Philip swallowed and then said, "On the way home, I stopped at the relay station and talked to Thomas." He waved his spoon about as he continued. "We discussed me quitting the Pony Express and moving to town."

Bella felt a moment of hurt that he'd talked to Thomas before her. She pushed down the feeling. They weren't really married and why wouldn't he talk to his brother? After all, his quitting the Pony Express would affect Thomas and the relay station. "I see, and what does he think?"

"He supports me in the decision. He and Josephine

are still looking for land to start a ranch on and he says he'll probably be quitting soon, too." He finished his food and leaned back in his chair.

She got up and refilled his coffee cup. "Would you like dessert?"

Philip shook his head. "No, why don't you sit down and tell me what you think about moving to town?" He reached for her hand after she'd sat back down.

Bella looked around her cozy home. They'd just settled in. The thought of moving into town both excited her and scared her. She allowed Philip to hold her hand. It soothed her frayed nerves and made her feel closer to him. "If you want to move, Philip, we'll move."

"What do you want?" he asked.

What did she want? A real marriage. One where she could talk openly with her husband. Tell him her fears. And know he'd be there for her when she was being threatened. But that wasn't an option. She looked into his excited blue eyes and smiled. "I want you to be happy. I want security for the boys. So if moving to town will guarantee those two things, then I want to move to town."

He patted her hand and then released it. "I want those things, too, and really feel like this is our opportunity to grab them." Philip walked to the sitting room and stood by the fire. "Just think, Bella. If we move to town, then the boys can go to school. Caleb can start as soon as we're settled."

If only it was true, but Bella felt as if she and the boys would be leaving soon. Marlow would come back for them or the law would. Either way, she'd be leaving Philip and Dove Creek. Her heart ached at the idea. When had she fallen in love with her husband? It had been so gradual that she hadn't fought it the way she should have.

Bella forced a smile and said, "Then let's move to town."

Chapter Twenty-Five

Philip knew Bella had reservations about moving. Her stance, the tenseness of her face and the sadness in her eyes spoke volumes. He crossed the room and hugged her close. "If you don't want to move, Bella, we can stay right here." Even though he didn't want to stay there, Philip realized he'd do so to make her happy.

She pulled out of his arms. "Oh, Philip, it's not that. I think it's a wonderful idea. I'm just feeling a little moody today." Bella offered him a sweet smile.

He leaned down and gently kissed her lips. What was it about this woman that brought out the protective side of him? And the warm fuzzies in his brain when he kissed her? She returned his kiss, turning the simple offer of comfort into something much more and something he didn't want to analyze.

Philip inhaled and then gently set her away from him. She smelled of vanilla and cinnamon. "Thank you for being so sweet. I'll do everything in my power to make you happy in town, Bella. You'll see we'll have a great life there."

The front door opened, sending cold air into the

room. He stepped away from Bella and turned to see who had walked into his home without knocking.

Hazel followed the boys inside. "Knock, knock. We're back."

Mark ran and hugged Bella around the waist. "Did we miss dessert?" he asked, looking up at her.

Philip laughed. "No, but you did miss dinner. Have you eaten?"

Hazel shut the door and hung up her coat. "Of course they've had dinner. What kind of great aunt do you think I am?"

Bella grinned. "Great aunt?"

Caleb wasn't about to be left out of the conversation. "Uh-huh. She can't just be an aunt like you and Aunt Josephine. She's too old."

"Caleb!"

Hazel laughed. "Don't get onto my sweet boy. He's right. So we decided I'd be great. That makes me even better than you and Josephine. Right, boys?" She walked to the kitchen and poured herself a cup of coffee.

"Right," both boys agreed. They followed Hazel to the kitchen like a couple of puppies. They climbed up on their logs and smiled happily at her.

Philip laughed. "You two are a mess."

Hazel added her agreement. "That's what happens when you go to a great aunt's house. You come home a mess."

He wondered how Hazel was going to feel about their moving to town. Philip's gaze sought out Bella's. Especially since she already knew Thomas and Josephine would soon be moving also. He decided now wasn't the time to tell her. "If you ladies will excuse me, I believe

I'll go check on the horses before it gets too late and unload the wagon."

Bella asked, "Do you have to do it now? I made fried pies earlier today."

He lowered his hand from his coat. "No, I don't have to, but I'd like to before it gets any colder."

She nodded. "All right, I'll save you a pie. You'll want something warm when you get back."

Hazel frowned. "Philip, do you think we're in for more snow?"

He pushed his arms through his coat sleeves and then buttoned it up. "Could be. Those clouds looked like it earlier today."

Caleb climbed down from his log and walked to Philip. "I can help you with the wagon."

Philip stooped down to his level and whispered, "I appreciate the offer, but I need you to stay in here and protect the women while I'm gone. Can you do that for me?"

At Caleb's serious nod, Philip stood. "I'll be back in a few minutes."

Caleb hurried back to the table with a wide grin.

Bella had just placed a plate full of moon-shaped fried pies on the table. Philip motioned for her to come to him. She looked to Hazel and the boys, and seeing they were busy talking and serving themselves, she did as he asked.

Philip took a step toward her and inhaled her sweet scent. He gently pulled her into a hug and whispered in her ear, "Don't say anything to Hazel about the move just yet." He buried his face in her hair for a second longer and then pulled back enough to look into her pretty face.

"All right," she whispered back, stepping out of his embrace.

Hazel laughed. "I thought you were in a surefire hurry to get to your chores," she teased.

"What can I say? I got distracted." Philip turned and opened the door. He glanced back to see Bella's face turn bright red.

He pulled the door shut behind him. *Philip Young, get ahold of yourself.* Bella really was becoming a distraction. He found himself thinking about her all the time and missing her when they were apart. Philip sighed. Yet another reason to move to town. With a new business, he'd be too busy to think about kissing his pretty wife again.

Later that evening, Bella sat on her bed brushing out her hair. So many things had pulled at her today that she felt emotionally exhausted. Philip's kiss and Marlow's disappearance were the two things that kept troubling her mind.

How many times would she ask herself what Marlow was doing? Had he pretended to leave town to torture her into doing his will? And why had Philip kissed her? Even worse, why had she kissed him back?

She heard the front door open upstairs and knew that Philip had returned from taking Hazel home. He hadn't been gone long. Had he only taken her partway home? Normally, he wouldn't be back this quick.

His footsteps above her head caused dust to fall from the ceiling. Bella sneezed. A few seconds later, she heard him coming down the stairs.

Philip walked slowly, as if he was unsure of himself. Was he hurt? Bella slipped from the bed and pulled on her dressing gown. She moved around the curtain and came face-to-face with Marlow.

A scream built in her throat, but then she remembered the boys were on the other side of the curtain. Bella dashed around him and motioned for him to go back up the stairs.

He grinned and followed her up.

In the kitchen she turned on him like a mother bear. "What are you doing sneaking around in my house?" she demanded, furious that he would have the gall to just come in.

"You weren't coming out." He leaned against the doorway between her and the boys downstairs.

"You can't stay here. Philip will be home any minute now." She couldn't imagine what her husband would think if he found her ex-fiancé standing in his kitchen and her in her nightgown.

"No, we have a little time to talk. Him and the old lady haven't been gone but a couple of minutes." He moved to the table and straddled one of the logs, sitting down.

Bella had no choice but to turn and face him. "Philip said you left town."

He sighed. "Well, with no real business in Dove Creek, doesn't it make sense that I mosey on? I mean after all, sooner or later folks would want to know why I was hanging around. What would you have me tell them?"

She couldn't begin to imagine what he would tell them. "Where are you staying?" Bella pulled her dressing gown tighter around her waist. She knew he couldn't see anything but also knew it wasn't proper for him to see her in her nightclothes.

"There's a house not too far from here. Looks like the owners are gone for the winter, so I moved in."

Revulsion filled her. "You just moved into someone's home?"

"Sure. There's not a neighbor for miles. Not the most comfortable place, but it will do me until you make up your mind what you're going to do." He traced the grain of the wood with his finger. "I was kind of hoping you'd already decided, but after watching the house over the last couple of days, I think you might be a bit too comfortable here."

Tears pricked the backs of her eyes. "I told you, this is going to take a little time."

He pushed the log back forcefully and it fell over and rolled across the floor. Marlow moved with the speed of a cat. He stood before her and growled into her face, "And I told you, we don't have a lot of time." He grabbed her around the waist and ground his mouth into hers. Just as quickly he released her and stormed outside.

Bella startled when she saw Caleb approach her. "Aunt Bella? Are you all right?" His big blue eyes showed his concern. The little boy's eyes then darted to the kitchen door.

She walked to the log and rolled it back to the table. Caleb helped her stand it back up. His eyes searched hers. "Was that Mr. Brooks?"

Bella swallowed. She wanted to lie but knew she couldn't. "Yes, he came to say goodbye."

"He kissed you," Caleb accused.

Her gaze darted to the closet. How much had he heard and seen? She motioned for him to sit down at the table.

Caleb did as she indicated.

She sat down beside him and sighed. "I know you don't understand. I really don't, either. But Philip would understand even less."

Caleb frowned. "Are we going to leave with Mr. Brooks?" His sad face tore at her heart. He shouldn't be worrying about things like this.

"No, I need to talk to Philip. I'm just praying he doesn't think badly of me when I do." An unbidden tear trickled down Bella's face.

He climbed down from the log and then hugged her around the waist. "Don't cry, Aunt Bella. Philip will know what to do."

She kissed the top of his head. "You're right. He will. But, Caleb, will you let me tell him when I'm ready?"

Caleb nodded against her side. "What if Mr. Brooks comes back?" He leaned back and looked up at her. "He scares me."

"I'm sorry, Caleb. I promise I will never let him hurt you or Mark." She hugged him tight once more. They heard a horse come into the front yard. "Go back to bed. I'll talk to Philip soon. You don't have anything to be afraid of."

He nodded and went back to the closet and down the stairs. Bella locked the kitchen door and then followed her nephew. She watched as he entered the bedroom he shared with Mark. Then she crept back up the stairs.

Philip came through the door and quietly closed it behind him. She slipped back down the stairs. Bella couldn't face him tonight. She had no idea what she was going to say when she did tell him about Marlow.

Instead of climbing back into her bed, Bella kneeled down beside it and silently prayed. She stayed on her knees for a long time, simply asking God to help her find a way to tell Philip about Marlow's threats.

The next morning, she woke early. Philip and Caleb were both gone. She opened the front door and heard hammering coming from the barn. Shutting the door, Bella decided to make oatmeal for breakfast with lots of butter and sugar.

She warmed the bread in a skillet over the fire. Still unsure how to approach Philip about Marlow's threats and demands, Bella prepared breakfast. At the last minute she decided to add a few strips of bacon to their morning meal.

Mark came up the stairs. The boy had a nose for bacon, she thought, smiling. He was so small and full of life. His hair stuck out in all directions. He looked around the room. "Where's Caleb and Philip?"

"In the barn working. Hungry?"

He ignored her question and stared at the door with a frown on his face. "Why didn't Caleb wake me up?"

"You'll have to ask him," Bella answered, setting the table with bowls and spoons. "Why don't you run and tell them breakfast is about ready?"

He walked to the door and pulled on his coat and boots. "I wish we could go to town today."

"Oh? Why?" Bella asked, setting glasses of milk on the table.

He looked up with a grin. "I want to ride Snowball again." Then Mark left.

Bella grinned. Mark would probably love living in town, where he could ride the white mare. Caleb would go to school and avoid working outside. It amazed her that one of her nephews loved animals and the other acted as if he feared them. They were as different as two brothers could be and still cared deeply for each other.

"I smell bacon," Philip said, coming through the door.

Caleb and Mark followed after taking their shoes off at the door. The three of them went to the washbasin to clean up, then returned to the table, where Philip quickly said grace.

Bella watched them eat and talk. She caught Philip watching her and smiled at him.

"Aunt Bella, can I have more bacon?" Mark asked.

She got up and walked to the skillet. "You sure can."

Bella felt a warmth at her back and turned to find Philip standing within inches of her.

He whispered, "Do you think we should tell the boys about our move?" His breath teased her bangs.

"I don't see why not."

He turned around and returned to the table. When she was seated, Philip said, "Boys, your aunt and I have something to tell you."

Caleb's head shot up and he looked at Bella. She knew he was thinking she'd told Philip about Marlow's nighttime visit.

Then he looked to Philip.

"What?" Mark asked with shiny lips.

Philip smiled at them. "We have decided to move to town."

Relief washed over Caleb's face. Bella wasn't sure if it was because he preferred town life, or if it was because Marlow wouldn't hurt any of them there. She looked to Mark. Sadness filled his face. Why would he be disappointed?

"What do you think?" Philip asked, also looking from one boy to the other.

Caleb answered, "I like it. Does this mean we get to build furniture in town and sell it like we did at the store?"

Philip nodded. "It does. We're going to go to town in a couple of days and see if we can find a house and a store."

Mark looked down at his plate. He didn't join the conversation, but Philip and Caleb didn't seem to notice. Bella's heart went out to her younger nephew. Things had already changed so much in his young life and now they were changing again.

Her life was about to change, too. There was no way she could stop it. Marlow had crossed a line when he'd come into their home, at night, uninvited. She just prayed Philip wouldn't be too angry with her when she told him everything.

Two days later, Philip saddled up three horses. Mark had proven he could ride a horse with very little assistance. Caleb could ride with Mark, Bella or Philip. The boy didn't seem to like the idea, but it would be much easier and faster if they all rode horses instead of taking the wagon.

He walked to the house to see if his small family was ready. Caleb sat at the table writing on a slate with chalk and Bella was packing a cheesecloth with sandwiches. She turned and smiled at him. His heart did a little dance.

Dark circles rested beneath her eyes. He worried she wasn't getting enough sleep, but every night when he came in from taking care of the livestock, she and the boys were already downstairs. Philip hoped she wasn't coming down with a cold or the flu.

"About ready?" he asked.

Bella placed the wrapped sandwiches into a flour sack that could be tied to her horse's saddle horn. "Just about."

Philip looked about. He didn't see Mark, so he told Caleb, "Go tell Mark we're about ready to go."

Caleb climbed down and walked to the front door. He pulled his coat off the hook, all the while keeping his eyes downcast.

Philip exchanged puzzled looks with Bella. "Where are you going?"

In a small voice, Caleb answered, "To the river to get Mark."

Bella's face faded to white. "The river?" she squeaked as if all air had just been shoved from her body.

"Uh-huh."

Philip ran from the house. What was Mark doing at the river? The boy had been quiet and reserved over the last few days, but they had just thought he was coming down with a cold. His heart beat in his chest as he ran. The silent prayer of *Please, Lord, please, Lord, please, Lord* ran through his mind as his boots slid on the wet ground.

He burst into the clearing beside the river. Frantic, Philip looked for the little boy. "Mark!"

He saw Bella crash through the woods. Her hair had come out of the combs she'd pulled it up into and flowed about her shoulders in disarray. "Mark!" she screamed.

Philip didn't want to, but he looked to the half-frozen river. Water flowed on the edges, but ice still covered the center. He searched for any sign of Mark. Then he saw what looked like a large hole off to one side. "Stay here," he ordered, sure that if he didn't Bella would try to follow him out onto the ice.

He found a thick place in the ice and then used his boots to glide across the ice to the hole. His heart sank when he saw blond hair floating to the top of the water in the hole. A stick with yarn tied to the top lay close to the hole.

Philip fell to his knees and grabbed Mark around the shoulders. He heaved the little boy's limp body out of the ice and water, all the while praying the ice wouldn't break further.

Mark's lips were blue. But his small chest still rose and fell. He carried him toward Bella. "Go to the house and heat up water, bricks, anything that you can find to warm him up," Philip called.

Bella spun and ran back toward the house.

It was all he could do to hold the child and walk across the ice at the same time. Once back on dry land, Philip laid him down on the ground and pounded on Mark's back. The little boy coughed up some water. Not sure what else to do, he picked the boy up. Fear and heartache propelled him back to the house. He ran as fast as he could and prayed the whole way.

Caleb was watching for him and held the door open. Philip carried Mark inside. Bella had piled quilts and blankets beside the fireplace. She had the fire blazing and was heating up a couple of bricks. He noticed she'd also placed dry rice and beans in a pot. Philip laid the little boy down on the quilts.

"Get him out of those clothes and boots." She looked to Caleb. "Help him." Then she turned back to the fire and stirred the rice and beans.

Philip and Caleb wrestled Mark out of his clothes. The little boy groaned his discomfort even though he never opened his eyes.

Bella ordered, "Tuck him between the bedding." She began pouring rice into a long shirt sleeve. When it was full, she tied off the top and then tucked it on one side of Mark, then put the covers back on top of him.

"Caleb, lie down by him and hug him close. You need to share your body's warmth with him." She turned back to the fireplace and the cooking rice and beans.

Philip stood helplessly by while Bella filled another sleeve. Caleb cried as he held his little brother close. She looked up at him. Tears streamed down her face as she worked.

His heart felt as if it was breaking. Philip refused to believe that Mark was going to die. He silently prayed over the little boy as they all worked together to warm up Mark.

Philip placed the bricks, wrapped in towels, around his feet and legs. Bella continued to warm up the sleeves of rice and beans while keeping him covered. And Caleb shared his body heat.

Fear thickened the tension in the room. Philip knew that Bella was thinking the same thing as him. Would they ever get Mark's little body warmed up?

Chapter Twenty-Six

Bella lay beside Mark. She rested a hand on his rising and falling chest. His face color had returned to normal. She thanked the Lord above.

Caleb slept beside his little brother.

Philip rocked in the chair by the fire. He held the Bible in his lap and read.

Exhaustion weighed on her. She closed her eyes and listened to the little boys sleeping. Both of them snored softly. Thankfully Mark hadn't developed a rattling in his chest.

Philip had told her that Mark had thrown up quite a bit of water while he was running home with him. She guessed that the jarring had forced the water from his lungs. Forcing herself to sit up, Bella walked to the kitchen.

She heard the rocking chair creak and Philip's stocking feet following her. In a low voice, she asked him, "Are you hungry?"

"No, but you must be."

Bella dug inside the flour sack and pulled out the

wrapped sandwiches she'd placed in there earlier. "A little," she admitted.

He walked to the coffeepot and poured them both a cup. Philip motioned for her to sit and then handed her the coffee. "Why don't you get some sleep after you eat? I'll keep an eye on the boys."

She shook her head. "I don't think I could sleep downstairs away from him."

"I understand. I think that boy took ten years off my life today." He sat down and watched her bite into the sandwich.

Bella had to agree with him. Until she'd met Caleb and Mark she'd had no idea how much care they took. She swallowed. "Philip, I'm not sure if this is the time, but I need to tell you something."

He leaned forward. "Sounds serious."

"It is."

She pushed the hair out of her face. "Well, first off you have to know that those two little boys mean the world to me."

"I know that. They do to me, too."

After today Bella was sure that Philip loved her nephews. He'd worried and fretted over Mark as if he was his own child. "I know and I'm grateful." She really was.

He reached out and took her hand. "What has you so scared, Bella? You've been on edge for days."

Bella took a deep breath and released it. "Marlow Brooks hasn't left town. He was here a few nights ago."

Confusion laced Philip's face. "When?"

"When you took Hazel home. We had already gone to bed and I thought you came home early. Only it wasn't you in the house, it was him. He threatened me and scared Caleb."

His eyes flared with anger. "How did he threaten you?"

She looked to the boys. "It's kind of a long story." They were still sleeping.

"We have all night."

Bella had to ask the question that was burning in her mind. "Why are you so angry?"

"Because a man has threatened you and scared Caleb. Why wouldn't I be angry?" he snapped.

"I need to know if it's because we are your property or do you care about us?" she persisted.

Philip raked his hand through his hair. "Of course I care about you and I have never thought of you as property."

Bella sighed. "I'm sorry, *property* is the wrong word. Let me rephrase my question. Do you love the boys?" She had to know that if she was hanged for murder that Philip would love and care for Caleb and Mark.

His blue eyes searched hers. "I do love the boys. They are my family now." Philip looked to where the boys slept.

There was no longer any doubt in her mind that he loved Mark and Caleb. His love for them shone in his eyes. He hadn't included her, but that was all right. They'd agreed this was a friendship within a marriage, but it still hurt a little.

When he faced her once more, Bella continued. "Promise that no matter what happens, you will take care of the boys until they are at least eighteen years old. Promise me."

Confusion furrowed his brow. "I promise. Now, what is this all about?"

She inhaled deeply once more and began. "When Marlow first arrived here, he said he still wanted to marry me." Bella paused to get her thoughts in order.

"You told me that."

"Yes, but what I didn't tell you was that he had business to discuss with me. But when Thomas and Josephine arrived, he left. It seemed odd to me, but not in a threatening way. I had already told him to go home and had hoped that he had done as I'd asked."

Philip leaned back and crossed his arms over his chest. "But instead you met him in town."

A harshness had entered his voice. Bella hurried to reassure him. "Yes, but not on purpose. When I was walking to the dress shop, he stopped me. He claims that the day I left, my old boss, Sam, was struck with my rolling pin. The sheriff says he was murdered, and since the rolling pin is mine, they are looking for me."

His arms dropped and he reached for her hand. "What else did he say, Bella?" Concern filled his voice, making it easier to continue.

"He says that if I will go back with him, he'll make sure that I don't hang for murder." The words caught in her throat. The fear of hanging ripped through her once more.

"How does he intend to do that?"

Bella met his gaze. "Marlow Brooks is a well-respected attorney. He plans on marrying me to prove to them that there is no way I'd kill anyone."

Philip shook his head. "You're already married to me."

"Yes, but he wants me to divorce you." Tears rolled

down her cheeks unbidden. Her heart broke every time she thought of life without Philip.

His hand tightened around hers and his jaw worked. "Why didn't you tell me this sooner?"

"I was trying to buy time. Think of a way to prove he is lying about Sam and the law." She didn't want to tell him that Marlow had said Philip would think she was capable of murder and take the boys away from her. "Marlow wouldn't help me if there wasn't something he would gain. He claims to love me, but it's not true."

Philip released her hand. "How do you know it's not true?"

"On the day I told him that we would be raising Caleb and Mark, he told me to put them in an orphanage or to get out of his life. He said he didn't love me, but with his stature in the community he needed a pretty wife. I fit the bill. To him I was pretty and could cook. The perfect little wife." Her voice cracked. "I saw him for the monster that he is then and I saw it again the other night."

Philip wanted to pull her into his arms and protect her from the man who could put such fear in her eyes. Instead he continued to hold her hand and ask questions. "Were you just going to take the boys and leave?"

Blue, tear-filled eyes looked at him. "I don't know. Marlow says the sheriff is looking for me and I need to make a decision fast. If the sheriff finds me before I marry him, Marlow says he won't help me."

"Why didn't you ask me to help you? I don't understand. Do you not trust me?" It hurt to think that she wouldn't come to him. It hurt even more to think she might have just left and never said goodbye. Could she do that if they were married?

Bella's tears flowed freely down her face now. "Philip, aren't you worried that the law thinks I murdered someone?"

"No. I don't believe you murdered anyone. You are one of the kindest women I've ever met. I don't believe you are capable of murder."

Her shoulders slumped at his words and sobs tore from her throat. "Why did I believe him? He said you would turn me over to the sheriff here. That you'd take the boys away from me."

Philip could stand it no longer. He stood and pulled her to her feet. Wrapping her in his arms, he held her. Her tears wet the front of his shirt and still he held her.

How could a man break a woman so badly? And why had Brooks done it? What did he have to gain by hurting her like this? Philip rubbed Bella's back until the sobs subsided.

She stepped out of his embrace. "I'm so sorry. I should have trusted you." Bella pulled a handkerchief from inside her sleeve. She sat back down.

Philip also sat down. "Bella, I agree with you. Brooks wants something you have. Any idea what it could be?"

"No. I've been trying to figure out what it could be, but I have nothing other than my nephews and you. And he wants to take you away from me."

When she looked at him, Philip saw the pain in her eyes at the thought of losing him. He also saw a deep love there. Yet she was willing to give him up if it meant saving her own life and keeping the boys.

"Bella, how did Marlow know where to find you?"

"I suppose he went to Denver, where my sister lived, and asked her lawyers if I'd left a forwarding address."

"Did you?"

She frowned. "Kind of. I told them I was heading to Dove Creek and would send an address once I was settled."

The more she talked, the more confused he became. "I thought you said your brother-in-law and sister had left debts and didn't have any money or property left."

"I did." She picked up her coffee and took a drink.

Philip sighed. "So why did you tell them where you were going?"

This time Bella sighed. "Mr. Jenkins said that the boys' toys were tied up with the rest of the estate, but as soon as everything was settled, he was sure he could send the boys their personal belongings and possibly a keepsake from their parents."

He grinned. "That's it. If we write to your Mr. Jenkins, he'll probably tell us that the estates have been settled."

At her quizzical expression Philip pressed on. "When Josephine came here, she was running from her greedy uncle and his gambling partner. To make a long story short, the reason they were looking for her was because her father had discovered gold and they wanted it. See?"

"So you think my sister and her husband left something for the boys? Why else would Marlow come searching for us? But what about saying Sam was murdered and the law thinks I killed him?"

Philip stood up and began pacing the room. "It's probably a lie. A means to get you away from me. If you had married him, he'd just tell you it was all a mistake or that he'd taken care of it. As your new husband

and the boys' guardian, he'd have access to whatever resources have been left to you."

"What you are saying makes sense, but is it true?"

He grinned at her. "Bella, your husband isn't without his own resources."

Bella wanted to smile back at him but felt too drained to do so. "What kind of resources?"

"The Pony Express. With my network of friends, we can find out how much of what Brooks is telling us is true." He kneeled down beside her. "How much time did you tell Brooks you needed?"

"A month."

"And how much of that time has passed?"

"A little more than a week."

Impulsively he kissed her quickly on the lips and then stood. "That gives us plenty of time. In the morning I'm having Brooks arrested for breaking into my house and scaring my wife and kids almost to death."

"He's staying in someone's house who is gone for the winter. But I don't know the name. Will he be able to get out of jail fast?" Worry lined her voice.

Philip shook his head. "No. If he's staying in someone's home, the sheriff might have to hold him until the owner comes back." He grinned at her. "Trust me, the sheriff will help us detain him for a long time."

Her eyes lit. He assumed it was because with Marlow in jail, he couldn't threaten or hurt the boys anymore. "But what about poor Sam?"

"The sheriff can look into that, too. But I have a feeling that's all a lie just to get you to go with Marlow." Philip picked up his coffee.

Bella yawned. Her eyes drooped and her shoulders slumped.

Now he understood why she hadn't been sleeping. Anger burned deeply in Philip, but he was trying hard not to show it. He walked over and took Bella's hand in his. She looked up at him, the shadows under her eyes even more prominent. Philip pulled her to her feet. "Go lie down by the boys. You need rest. I'll stay up and keep an eye on Mark."

She didn't argue and simply turned away, but then Bella wheeled back to face him. "Thank you, Philip."

He nodded. "You're welcome, honey."

Bella grinned. "That's the second time you've called me that."

Philip chuckled. He wasn't deeply in love with this woman, but he did love her. It was a realization that had hit him earlier when he'd learned that she'd been threatened. Philip became aware he was staring and answered her. "It won't be the last, either. Go get some sleep."

Loving a little bit was all right. He just had to guard his heart and not fall deeply in love. Was that possible? Now that he'd admitted that he loved her, could he keep himself from falling so deeply in love that should something happen to her he'd survive? Or had his father passed on that weakness to him?

Chapter Twenty-Seven

Bella woke to the sound of boys giggling. Mark was sitting up playing horses with his brother. His cheeks had a rosy glow. Both boys had dressed and their hair had been combed.

"Mark's better this morning, Aunt Bella."

She looked about but saw no sign of Philip and sat up. "I see that. Do you feel sick or anything, Mark?"

"No. Philip said he should tan my hide but is too happy that I'm not sick to do such a thing." He grinned. "I've never had my hide tanned. Have you, Aunt Bella?"

Bella frowned. "No, but I can guarantee you it probably isn't a pleasant experience. So I'd wipe that grin off my face if I were you, young man."

Mark's smile faded. "I'm sorry, Aunt Bella. Philip said I scared you real bad. I didn't mean to."

"I know you didn't." She pulled him into a quick hug. "But if you ever do anything like that again, I'll do worse than tan your hide."

She stood up and started folding their blankets and quilts.

"Philip saved me," Mark told her.

The awe in his voice touched her heart. "Yes, he did. Where is he, anyway?" She wondered if he had left her and the boys alone. Bella refused to believe that he had deserted them because of what she'd told him, even though it was what she feared.

"I'm here." He stepped through the closet door and grinned at her. "I was beginning to think you might sleep all day."

Her gaze moved to the kitchen window. Sunshine flooded the kitchen. "I guess I did sleep longer than most days."

Caleb hugged her around the waist. "It's all right. You helped save Mark, too."

"So did you." She smiled at him. Bella thought about scolding him for not telling them sooner where Mark had gone, but she decided the little boy had suffered enough watching his little brother recover from the cold ice and water.

A knock sounded on the front door. Philip motioned for Bella to step back. He opened the door.

Bella sighed when she heard him say, "Well, hello, Josephine. Come on in."

Josephine stepped inside. She carried a basket. Her gaze jumped from Philip to Bella. "Is everyone all right? Thomas said you didn't come over this morning to help with chores and I didn't get my bread." She smiled to take the sharpness out of her voice.

Philip looked past Josephine into the yard. "Did Thomas come with you?"

"Of course. He's putting the horses away." Josephine frowned. "What's going on here?"

Bella looked to Philip. He answered, "Bella can tell you all about it. I'm going to see what Thomas is up to out there." He turned and looked at the boys. "Either of you want to come?"

"I do," Caleb answered, hurrying to put his boots on.

Mark shook his head. He crawled up in the rocking chair with his horse. "Aunt Bella, can I have a cookie?"

Josephine's eyes narrowed. "Are you sick, Mark?" She walked over and put her hand to his forehead, then looked at Bella. "He feels all right."

Philip and Caleb shut the door behind them when they left. Bella smiled. "He's fine. Probably just tired."

Mark nodded. He set the chair to rocking and pretended his wooden horse was galloping on the arm.

"And no, you may not have a cookie. I have to fix breakfast first." She headed to the kitchen with Josephine following close behind.

"Breakfast? Don't you mean lunch?" She plopped the basket on the table. "And tell me about what? I bet you thought I'd forgotten, didn't you?"

Bella laughed. She was glad to see her friend and even happier to finally be able to tell her about the previous day and the shenanigans of Marlow Brooks. While she cooked, Josephine helped. Bella retold the story of Mark almost drowning, and then when it came time to tell Josephine that Marlow said she was wanted by the law, Bella stopped speaking.

Josephine set plates and silverware on the table and then turned to face Bella. "How come I have the feeling you aren't telling me everything? You can tell me anything."

Bella swallowed hard. "Really? What if I told you that I'm wanted for murder?"

"Did you kill someone?" Josephine placed her hands on her hips and waited.

She shook her head. "No, but my ex-fiancé, Marlow, says that the sheriff is looking for me because they think I killed my boss at the bakery."

Josephine walked over to her, put her arm around her shoulders and hugged her. "If you said you didn't do it, you didn't do it."

"Thank you for believing me." She wrapped her arm around Josephine's waist and hugged her back.

"We're sisters." She leaned her head against Bella's. "I'll always believe in you and I'll always believe you. Nothing can take that away from us."

Bella missed her sister but was thankful that the Lord had seen fit to give her a new one.

Chapter Twenty-Eight

That night, Philip moved his family back to the relay station. He wanted them safe and knew that he'd need to do chores and ride the Pony Express trail. The thought of Marlow Brooks breaking in on Bella and the boys again worried him.

Thankfully Josephine and Thomas didn't mind them all moving back. Josephine even teased that with Bella around, they'd never go hungry for fresh bread. The boys were happy to sleep in the bedroom with Bella and Philip again. They all four slept on the floor.

The next morning, Philip hitched up the wagon and he and Bella headed to town. Caleb and Mark stayed behind with Thomas and Josephine. Both boys were excited because a rider was going to pass through and they loved watching them come and go.

Their first stop was the sheriff's office, where Bella told the sheriff all the things that Marlow had said and done since he'd arrived in town. She also told him that Marlow had bragged about breaking into someone's home and living there while they were away.

"But I'm not sure where the house is. All I know is

that there aren't any neighbors for miles around," she explained.

He smiled at her. "You know enough. There is only one farm like that. It's the Miller place." The floor creaked as he stood. "They are an older couple who have started going to their daughter's place during the winter. I'll go out now and get our man."

Bella stood also. "Will he be free soon?"

Philip and the sheriff exchanged grins. "Mrs. Young, I can hang on to him until spring. I have it on good authority that's when the Millers will be heading home."

She sighed but then caught her breath. "Will I have to see him?"

"No, ma'am. He's squatting on someone else's property. That's nothing to do with you." He opened the door for them to leave. The sheriff held out his hand to Philip. "Thank you for bringing this to my attention. I'll keep you posted."

Philip shook his hand and nodded. "Appreciate it."

Just as they stepped out onto the boardwalk, the sheriff asked, "You folks going to be in town long?"

"Most of the day," Philip answered. He placed his hand on the small of Bella's back. She seemed to be trembling.

The sheriff untied his horse from the hitching post. "Then I'll be seeing you in a while."

They watched the sheriff ride out of town. Bella shuddered. "I'd hate to be Marlow today."

Philip laughed. "Now that that is done, are you ready to go to the bank and see if there are any buildings in town to buy or rent?"

She nodded. "Are we going to be able to afford a house and a business?"

Using the palm of his hand, Philip guided her to the bank. "I guess we'll find out." He'd had the same thought but hoped his savings would be enough to at least put a down payment on something and then carry a loan with the bank.

Bella led the way inside the bank. There didn't appear to be any customers. The teller cages were located at the back and a small office was off to the left.

The banker stepped out and grinned. "Philip Young, what are you doing in the bank with such a pretty lady?"

Philip laughed and clasped hands with Mr. Peters, the one and only banker in town. "Good to see you, Mr. Peters. This pretty lady is my wife, Bella Young. We thought we'd come by and see if you had any property for sale."

"Come on into my office." He indicated they each take a seat in front of the big oak desk. Before shutting the door, he called out, "Mrs. Crabtree, make sure I'm not disturbed."

Philip heard a young voice answer, "Yes, sir."

Mr. Peters shut the door and walked around the desk. He sat down and leaned back in his chair. "What kind of property are you folks looking for?"

"Business."

He studied Philip for several long moments. "You giving up on the Pony Express?"

Philip nodded. "Yes, figure it's time I settle down and start my own business."

The banker leaned forward and began to go through stacks of papers on his desk. "What kind of business?"

"Making furniture." Philip pulled up one leg and laid his booted foot over his knee.

Mr. Peters nodded. "I heard the telegraph lines were

going to put the Pony Express out of business. I'd hoped that wasn't the case." He pulled out a couple of sheets and laid them in front of Philip.

"Me, too." Philip left the papers where the banker had laid them. His fingers itched to reach for them, but he didn't want to seem too eager.

"What do you think of this business idea, Mrs. Young?"

Bella sat up a little taller. "I think my husband has real talent when it comes to wood and making furniture." She smiled broadly at Philip.

Mr. Peters laughed. "Spoken like a true newlywed." He pulled out another sheet of paper. "I have three properties you might be interested in." He pushed the papers closer to Philip. "Look at those and let me know if they might be something you are looking for."

Philip did as he was asked. They were all a little more expensive than what he had saved. He recognized the locations of each of them. Two of them were close to the church, school and parsonage. The other one was closer to the new restaurant. "Would you mind showing them to us?" he asked.

"I'll do you one better and let you have the keys. You and the missus can go look at them to your heart's desire." He turned behind him, where a board with pegs had several keys hanging on it.

Bella leaned over to look at the papers in his hands. The soft scent of cinnamon drifted up into his nostrils. "Mr. Peters, the two that are close together, are they both business buildings?"

He turned back around and handed Philip the keys. "No, one is for business. The other is a small house that, as the family grows, can be added onto."

She turned her head up and looked at Philip. "That might not be too bad."

Mr. Peters reached across the desk and tapped the other paper, drawing their attention. "That property is two stories. The upper portion has living quarters; the bottom was meant to house a business. So you might like that one also."

Philip stood. "We'll go look. Are you in a hurry for us to get back? After we look, we'll go grab lunch and talk about the properties."

He came around the desk and opened the door. "No hurry at all. Take your time." Mr. Peters looked out into the empty lobby. "As you can see, we aren't that busy today." He walked with them to the door.

"Thank you." Philip opened the door for Bella, who smiled at the banker and stepped out into the sunshine. He followed her down the steps and onto the boardwalk. "Which do you want to go see first?"

"The one by the restaurant is closest, but if we go to the one by the church first, we can eat after we look at the one by the restaurant."

Her reasoning made sense. "Sounds good to me." They walked down half a block and then over two more. The town of Dove Creek was small.

Bella pulled her coat tighter around her body. She stepped carefully around the patches of ice and snow, reminding Philip that it was still wintertime. He should have considered her before suggesting they walk to the various buildings.

"Are you cold?"

She smiled. "A little, but I'm also enjoying being out in the sunshine. So I'm all right."

They arrived at the business building first. Philip

liked that it sat on a corner lot. The parsonage, church and school filled the lot directly across from the business building. "I like the location," he said, opening the door and then stepping back for her to enter first.

It wasn't very big. Philip tried to picture in his mind what it would look like.

Bella nodded. "This would work. You could have your counter and register over there. The furniture could sit here and here." She pointed at each spot as if she could see it in her mind's eye. "I would set up a wall here and make that your work space." She turned to look at him. "What do you think?"

He thought she was beautiful. Everything about Bella made him happy today. He couldn't say that, so instead he said, "I think it will work. You'll probably need to help me see your vision if we get this place. How about we check out the house now?"

She practically danced out of the building. For the first time in a while, Bella seemed happy. Philip enjoyed spending time alone with her—he didn't want to admit it, but Philip wanted to be with Bella forever. And the love he felt was growing. He tried to ignore it but feared it was too late.

Bella looked around the house. It was much nicer than where they lived now. The hardwood floors shone with fresh polish. The walls were a soft cream color. The kitchen was a room by itself on the left. The sitting room was on the right and the bedrooms were more toward the back.

"Would you want to live here?" Philip asked, looking out a window.

"It's very bright and sunny in here." Bella walked

to the kitchen. "Oh, look. A real stove." She touched the black metal.

Philip smiled. "I bet you could make wonderful bread with that."

"Maybe." Bella didn't want to show her excitement at having a real stove. Cooking over an open flame wasn't the easiest, but she was used to it and her meals came out just fine that way.

The two bedrooms were simple rooms. Bella decided the boys would use the one with no windows. That way she could be sure they were safe at night. "It's a nice house, but let's not make any quick decisions until we see the last one."

He nodded. "Agreed. Are you ready to go to the last one?"

"Yes. We might like it even better, since we can live in the top half and run the business from the bottom." Bella walked out the door and onto the wide porch. She could picture herself sitting in a rocker, enjoying the quietness of evening.

Philip talked about the business as they walked. "I liked your idea of blocking off part of the store to create an area for building. I wonder if we can do that at this next building."

"I don't see why not," Bella answered. Her feet were starting to get cold and the wind seemed to have picked up since they were in the house.

"I do believe it's getting colder," Philip said as he entered the big two-story building. "This place looks huge."

Bella agreed. She hurried inside to get out of the wind. The downstairs had one large entry room and then three more rooms that created a circle. "I've never seen a house like this." The stairs wound from the top floor to the bottom right beside the doorway.

Philip walked around the large area. "Well, there is lots of space. I could use one of those rooms to build in. And this main area as a store." He looked in the last room. "But what would I use this one for?"

Bella grinned. "You can always use it for a bedroom. We could shut it off and no one would be the wiser."

He bobbed his head. "Yes, I could. Or make it into a guest room."

"Oh, I know. You could rent it out to an employee when you get so busy you have to build all the time and they could run the store." She started up the stairs. "Let's go check out the house part of this building."

"Right behind you." Philip followed her up the stairs.

Bella came to a small landing. She looked around and saw that there was a door to the right of the stairs. "This is different." She walked to the doorway and opened it.

To her delight, it opened into a sitting room. Stepping inside, she felt sunshine from all directions. Windows filled the room. "This is wonderful, Philip. Look at all this natural light."

Philip grinned. "It's amazing what you find wonderful."

Bella turned. "You don't like it?"

"I don't know. All we've seen is a large room with lots of windows." He walked past her to the kitchen. "Uh-oh."

She hurried after him. "What?"

He stood in the center of a huge room. The largest cookstove she'd ever seen stood against the back wall. Built-in cabinets filled one wall. A sideboard ran across the wall under the cabinets. A door led to what

Bella could only assume was a pantry. "Oh" was all she could think to say.

Philip grabbed her hand and pulled her out of the most wonderful kitchen she'd ever seen. "Let's check the bedrooms."

Bella wasn't nearly as impressed with the bedrooms as she was the kitchen. One of the bedrooms had windows much like the sitting area and the room was filled with light. The other had only one window. Both had tall, freestanding closets. Of the two, Bella preferred the one with the windows. She looked to Philip. "This place is really something."

"Yep, and it's also the most expensive of the three." His stomach growled.

She giggled. "Maybe we should go eat and discuss the three places."

They returned downstairs. Philip locked the door. The wind had picked up and now tore at his hat and her hair combs. They hurried across the street to the new restaurant.

Once seated, Philip asked, "So, which one did you like best?"

Bella smiled. She wasn't going to let him off that easy. This was his business and he needed to decide which one he liked best. After all, if they found out that Marlow wasn't lying and she was wanted for murder, Philip and the boys would be the only ones living in the house.

The thought of being separated from Philip and the boys saddened her. Even though she'd tried to convince herself that Marlow was lying, she still feared the possibility of being arrested for a murder she didn't commit.

Chapter Twenty-Nine

Philip knew that Bella would love to have the last house. The kitchen was every woman's dream. And that stove. Her eyes had lit up like candles on a Christmas tree.

She countered his question by bouncing it back to him. "Which one do you like best? After all, it is your business."

"Well, I liked the first two best, but moneywise, buying them together will cost as much as buying the big house." He looked over the menu.

"Yes, but if we got the two, you would have separation from work and home. That might be nice." Bella laid down her menu.

Philip set his to the side, deciding he'd have the roast beef sandwich with potatoes. "But you really like the big house, don't you?"

"I do, but the porch on the first house was very nice. I could picture myself having a hot cup of tea out there in the mornings." She grinned at him.

"You aren't going to make this easy on me, are you?"

The waitress came by and took their orders. When

she'd returned to the kitchen, Bella answered. "Philip, you need to get the house you like best. I may not be here. If you get what I want and you don't like it, well, that would be horrible for you." Worry lined her face.

What did she mean she may not be here? Did she still believe she was wanted for murder? "Bella, I really don't believe you will be going anywhere."

"Still, you are the one who needs a good place for your store. I liked both houses, so either one will work for me." She laid her napkin on her lap.

Philip waited until the waitress had served their food and then responded. "If you are sure you don't mind the smaller house, I think we should get that one and the building beside it for the furniture store."

Bella nodded. "I think that's a good choice." The smile she offered was genuine, but so was the worry in her eyes.

Philip knew she was concerned about Brooks and his lies. The thought of her not living in the cozy little house troubled him more than he cared to admit. He blessed their food and silently prayed that they'd have answers soon.

Bella stepped out of the bank, happy for Philip. All the paperwork was complete on their new home and his furniture store. They would soon be able to move into the little house and he would start his business afterward. Everything was falling into place, for him.

She smiled at him. Then saw the sheriff coming up the boardwalk behind him. Her heart began pounding fast. Had he found Marlow? Was the man in jail? So many questions ran through her mind.

The sheriff tipped his hat to her. "Good afternoon, folks. Do you have a minute?"

Philip smiled broadly. "Sure do."

"Then let's step to the side of the building and out of this wind." The sheriff led the way into a narrow alley.

Philip took Bella's elbow and leaned over to whisper in her ear. "I believe he caught our man."

"I hope so," she whispered back.

When the sheriff stopped, he turned and grinned at them. "I did get our man." He directed his gaze to Bella. "You will be happy to know that the good attorney is as snug as a bug in a rug at the jailhouse."

"Did he put up a fight?" Philip asked.

The sheriff laughed. "Naw, he's not much of a fighter. But he sure wasn't happy to be found squatting on another man's property. Kept saying he had rights."

Philip chuckled. "Good. Now can we find out if Bella is wanted for murder?"

"That's next on my agenda." He turned to look at Bella. "Ma'am, would you write to those lawyers in Denver and find out how things are going with your sister's estate? After what you and Philip have told me, I think Philip is right and that Mr. Brooks knows more then he's told you."

Bella nodded. "Yes, sir."

"Good. In the meantime, I'll draft my own letter and send it to the sheriff. We'll get to the bottom of this in no time." He pulled up his collar. "Well, I think that about sums it all up. You let me know when you hear from the lawyers and I'll let you know when I hear from the sheriff." He started to walk away, but Bella stopped him.

"Sheriff?"

He turned to face her. "Yes, ma'am?"

Bella swallowed hard. "How come you aren't arresting me, too?"

The big man walked back toward her. "What do you mean?"

"Well, I've been accused of murdering someone. Aren't you supposed to arrest suspected murderers?" Bella felt Philip's hand tighten on her elbow.

The sheriff tilted his hat back on his head. "Well, ma'am, no one has accused you. Brooks didn't mention it to me when I was arresting him. So, if it's all the same to you, I'll wait and see what the sheriff of Douglas City has to say about it."

Bella smiled at him. "Thank you."

He chuckled and winked at her. "My pleasure, ma'am."

Once he was out of earshot, Philip whistled low. "Woman, are you trying to get locked up?" He turned her to face him.

"No, but I needed to know if he'd suddenly change his mind and come arrest me. I didn't want the boys to see it if he did." She looked Philip in the eyes. "It's not a memory I want them to have."

He released her arms. "No, I reckon it isn't." Philip ran a gloved finger down the side of her face. "You really are something."

Bella laughed to cover up the nervousness she felt at being so close to him. "Thanks. So are you."

At that, Philip laughed also. He grabbed her hand and pulled her out of the alley. "Come on, let's go tell everyone our good news."

They hurried to the wagon. "Do you mind if I stop at the lumber mill and pick up some wood and nails?" he asked, helping her up to the seat.

"No, not if you don't mind dropping me off at the general store first. I'd like to get a bag of flour and some salt."

The wagon tilted slightly as Philip climbed on. "That sounds like a fair bargain to me."

Within a few minutes, Bella was entering the store. She smiled at the thought that she would soon be able to go to the store whenever she liked. The smells of spices and leather filled her senses.

"Hello, Mrs. Young. What can I help you find?" Mr. Jones asked.

"Would you mind weighing out ten pounds of flour and a cup of salt for me?"

"I'd be happy to." He walked to the dry goods section of the store. "Is that all you need?"

"Yes, thank you. While you do that, I'll look around, if that's all right." She walked to the fabric table. The boys could use new shirts. Since they were going to be living in town, they'd need nicer clothes for church and school.

Bella continued walking about the store. It had a toy section for children. Her heart ached for her nephews, who had left their toys in Denver. Why hadn't her brother-in-law taken better care of their finances? It wasn't like him or her sister to be so careless.

She sighed and walked to the counter, where Mr. Jones was checking in merchandise. There was a big bag of flour and a smaller bag of salt in a box on the counter.

"Did you find anything else you needed?" he asked, looking up from his list.

"No, but I do need a couple of sheets of writing paper

and an envelope, please." Bella smiled at him, hoping he'd have what she'd just asked for.

Mr. Jones reached under the counter and pulled out the items. "I keep those items behind the counter." He counted out two sheets and one envelope and handed them to her. "Do you need a quill and ink also?"

Bella nodded. "Yes, please." She watched as he added those items to the box.

"I'll add them to Philip's tab." He jotted the totals down in a ledger.

"Thank you."

The bell over the door jingled. Bella was happy to see Philip coming through the door. He smiled at her and Mr. Jones.

"Are you about ready, Bella?"

"I am. That was good timing." She started to get the box from the counter, but Philip stopped her.

"I'll get that." He crossed the room and picked up the box. "Did you put this on our tab?"

Mr. Jones answered, "We sure did. How are you today, Philip?"

"Great. We just purchased the properties on Maple Street across from the church."

Bella didn't miss the fact that he no longer said "I did." He was now saying "we did." And he'd referred to his tab as their tab. Her heart swelled. Whether Philip knew it or not, they had moved from being friends to being a couple.

Philip grinned at Thomas. "Well, I did it."

Thomas looked up from the hammer he was trying to fix. "Did what?"

"Quit the Pony Express and bought property in Dove

Creek for my store." He couldn't contain the smile on his face.

Thomas grinned up at him. "That's good news." He laid down the hammer. "What happened with the sheriff?"

"He found Brooks and arrested him for squatting on private property. He's also going to write to the sheriff in Douglas City and see if Brooks told Bella the truth about her old boss."

"Sounds like you two have it all taken care of." Thomas walked toward the front of the barn. Philip followed.

"Just about. Bella is inside with Josephine and the boys, she's writing a letter to send with the Pony Express. She's hoping her sister's lawyers will know who sent Marlow after her or what they had told him that would have sent him looking for her on his own." He closed one side of the barn doors while Thomas closed the other.

Once that was done, they headed toward the house. "I'm going to miss you around here," Thomas said.

"Don't kid yourself. We'll be coming out for visits. Bella and Josephine have become very close," Philip answered.

Thomas rubbed his boots on the porch rug. "Well, I wouldn't be so sure of that." He opened the door.

"What's that supposed to mean?" Philip asked, wiping his boots and following.

"Just that we've found the ranch we're going to buy. We'll be going to the bank next week and signing the papers on it."

Josephine giggled as they entered. "We've been

dying to tell you two, but so much has been going on that we haven't had the chance." She hugged Mark close.

The little boy struggled to get away from her. "Aunt Josephine, you are squishing me," he protested.

It was obvious from his laughter that Josephine wasn't hurting the little boy. Caleb joined in the fun by trying to help his little brother escape. Everyone laughed.

Philip and Bella spent the rest of the afternoon enjoying Thomas and Josephine's company. They intended to stay with the Pony Express at least for a month or two longer, as winter wasn't the best time to jump into the ranching business. The current owner assured them that in the spring they would have plenty to do.

Since Brooks was in jail they felt free to go back to their place, so later that afternoon, Philip took his family home. He still needed to tell Hazel they were moving to town. How was she going to take the news that both he and Thomas would be moving away?

Caleb pulled him from his thoughts. "Will I get to go to school when we move to town?"

"Yep. And I want you to study really hard."

The little boy looked up at him. "How come?"

Philip looked to Bella, who was cleaning the kitchen. "If it's all right with your aunt, I'd like to legally adopt you and Mark."

The boys had been building with the blocks and farm that Hazel had given them. Mark stopped and asked, "How come?"

Bella stopped her work and waited for the answer along with the boys.

"For two reasons. First, I want you both to know how much I care for you, and also because I want to name the furniture store 'Young and Sons Furniture.'" Philip held his breath, waiting for Bella's reaction. Would she let him adopt the boys? Or would she be too afraid he planned to take them from her?

Bella nodded her blessing. "I think that is a wonderful name for a furniture store." She knew that Philip thought Marlow was lying about Sam, but she couldn't just pretend it wasn't a possibility that Marlow could be telling the truth. Someone could have murdered him and the sheriff of Douglas City might be searching for her. Even if she didn't hang for the crime, Bella knew that she could be arrested and held in jail until they found the real murderer.

Mark walked over to Philip and leaned on his knee. "What's adoption?"

Philip laid his hand on the little boy's shoulder. "Adoption means that I want to raise you and your brother as my little boys. It means I love you."

Tears filled Bella's eyes. Mark climbed up into Philip's lap and hugged him around the neck. "I love you, too, Philip."

Bella watched her older nephew. "What do you think, Caleb? Do you want Philip to adopt you?"

Caleb looked at her. "I don't know."

Hurt filled Philip's eyes. He set Mark back on the floor and turned to Caleb. "I don't have to adopt you, Caleb."

"But if you don't adopt me, you won't love me." He gulped, fighting back tears.

Philip walked over to the little boy and stooped down. "I already love you, Caleb. Nothing will ever stop me from loving and taking care of you."

Bella walked over to them and sat down on the floor beside Caleb. "Why don't you want Philip to adopt you, sweetie?" She brushed the hair from his forehead.

"I love Ma and Pa."

She pulled him onto her lap and into her arms. "I love and miss them, too. Philip's loving you and wanting to adopt you will never take your love away that you feel for your parents." Bella felt as if her heart was breaking for the confusion that the little boy was feeling.

Philip eased to the floor with them and wrapped both Bella and Caleb in his arms. His hug felt warm and comforting. She lay her head on top of Caleb's. Not to be left out, Mark joined them. Philip pulled the little boy down on the floor with them.

Bella held her nephews close. How could she explain to them that loving her and Philip wouldn't take away from the love they had for their parents? She kissed the top of Caleb's head. "Boys, I want you to know that no matter what happens, we will always love and care for you. Your ma and pa would want you to be happy."

Caleb's watery blue eyes looked into hers. "But I don't want to forget them, Aunt Bella."

"You will never forget them, Caleb. They will always be in your heart. Sometimes God calls people away to heaven. It hurts our hearts because we miss them, but that doesn't mean that we shouldn't allow other people into our hearts."

"How come?" Mark asked, pushing until he was closer to her.

Bella smiled. "Because love isn't something that you can control. God is love and He made us like Him. Like Him, we can love lots of people in our lives and it's good."

Caleb ducked his head. "But it hurts when they move to heaven."

She nodded. "Yes, it does."

"Will you ever move to heaven?" Mark asked, laying his head on her shoulder.

Bella felt Philip ease away. "I will. And when I do, I want you to find another person to pour all your love into." Missing Philip's embrace, Bella hugged the two little boys even tighter.

"Like Philip?" Caleb asked.

Philip froze in place.

"Yep, like Philip." She tickled both little boys until they jumped up and ran away.

Philip had scooted back. He'd pulled his legs up and sat with his arms on his knees. Caleb ran to him and jumped. Philip was quick to catch him.

"I love you, Philip. If you still want to adopt me, you can."

He held the little boy tightly in his arms. "Thank you, Caleb. I love you, too."

Mark joined in the fun and soon all three of them were wrestling on the floor. Bella moved to get out of their way. She returned to the kitchen and wiped off the table.

Watching them play and wrestle, Bella silently thanked the Lord for bringing Philip into their lives. She didn't know what her future held, but she was thankful that Philip would take care of Mark and Caleb.

Chapter Thirty

Philip rode over to Hazel's the next morning to tell her that they were moving to town. He dreaded it and had put it off long enough. He swung down from his horse and stomped up the stairs.

She and her dog met him at the door. "'Bout time you came and checked on me. Come on in here and have some breakfast."

"Well, good morning to you, too." He wiped his boots off and followed her inside.

She walked to the kitchen and he followed. "I made a pot of oatmeal, but my eyes were bigger than my stomach, so there is plenty to share." Hazel dished up two bowls and carried them to the table, where butter and sugar already sat.

Philip sat down and waited for her to get fresh coffee for both of them. When she was finished bustling around, Hazel joined him at the table. She asked him to say grace, which he did.

"So, what have you been up to? I thought for sure you'd have come to check on me sooner. 'Course, with a new family I suppose you've been busy."

Philip added sugar to his oatmeal. "We had a scare a few days ago with Mark. That boy went to the river again, only this time Johnny wasn't there to save him. I thought he was a goner for sure, but thankfully the Lord heard our prayers and that boy didn't even get a sniffle."

Hazel laughed. "At that age, they bounce back much quicker than, say, an old lady like me." She waved her spoon at him. "Those boys are going to keep you busy for a long time. Then when your own young'uns start arriving, you are going to be busier than a mama bear with two cubs."

He nodded. "I'm sure you are right."

"Know I am." She spooned in a mouthful of oatmeal and then washed it down with hot coffee.

While she ate, Philip told her about Marlow Brooks and the trouble he'd been causing Bella. She nodded and grunted in all the right places.

"I knew that something was bothering our girl. Just couldn't put my finger on it. Thought maybe she was with child." She looked at him expectantly.

Philip laughed to cover his nervousness of talking about delicate stuff with her. "Nothing like that."

She took both their empty bowls to the washbasin and dipped them into the water to soak. "Would you like a refill?"

"No, thanks. But I do have one more thing to discuss with you."

Hazel refilled her coffee and sat back down. "Something serious?" She eyed him over the top of her cup.

"Well, with all that's been going on with Brooks and the telegraph lines, Bella and I decided it was time to make some changes." He paused and drained the last of his coffee.

Hazel huffed. "Get on with it, boy, I ain't getting any younger."

"I quit the Pony Express last week and bought a place in town so that I can open Young and Sons Furniture store." He waited for her to explode, either with anger or happiness. With Hazel he never knew which he'd get.

Silence filled the room. She pursed her lips for several long seconds, then said, "That's good for you and Bella."

"Rumor has it that the Pony Express won't be able to compete with the telegraph lines. Even Thomas and Josephine will be moving onto their ranch in a little while."

She swallowed hard and nodded. "Yep, I figured that would happen sooner or later."

"Hazel, Bella and I have discussed it and we'd like for you to move with us. The house is only two bedrooms, but we're going to expand it and the first extra room we build will be yours." He watched her face, still not sure what to expect.

Hazel rocked the cup in between her palms. "That's really sweet of you both, but my home is here."

"But you're all alone here," Philip protested. "In town, life will be so much better."

She pushed her chair back and walked to the washbasin. "Aw, Philip. I'm not all alone. Johnny visits from time to time. I can't leave my home." Hazel washed a bowl before turning to look at him. "I hope you'll come out for visits."

He stood and walked over to her. She'd taken such good care of him and Thomas when they'd first moved to the relay station. Hazel felt like a mother to him. He pulled her into his embrace and simply hugged her.

Bella was right. God did want him to love. Without even realizing it, he'd been loving. He loved Hazel, Josephine, the boys and Bella.

Only, his love for Bella ran deep. The thought and realization struck deep in his heart. Philip released Hazel. "Thank you for breakfast. I'd best be getting back." He started walking toward the door.

"Tell Bella if she needs help packing to let me know."

He opened the door. "I will, and thanks again." Philip hurriedly shut the door. He had to get away someplace alone.

The river babbled a greeting as he jumped from his horse. When had Bella worked her way so deeply into his heart? *Lord, how did You let this happen? I told You I couldn't love like this. Look what this kind of love did to my pa. If anything should happen to her, will I be weak and leave the boys the way he did?* Philip sat on a fallen log and continued to pray silently. *Please, help me to push her away.*

Even as the prayer formed, Philip knew it was too late. He'd never be able to push Bella away. He loved her.

Taking several calming breaths, Philip decided to be still and listen for the Lord's still, small voice. After thirty minutes of listening, Philip realized that he wasn't his father. As strange as it seemed, he'd always believed that he could be weak and kill himself if he loved deeply and lost the one he loved the most.

Then it dawned on him. The one he loved the most was God, and God would never leave him. If Bella was to be called home first, God would still be with him.

Philip climbed back onto his horse. It was time to go home, time to tell Bella that he loved her and wanted a real marriage. The question was, did she love him, too? Or would she reject his love and still demand that they just remain friends?

Bella looked about. They really didn't have a lot for her to pack up. She'd thought to maybe start the packing but had now realized there was no rush. Her gaze kept moving to the door.

Philip had been gone for a long time. Had Hazel taken their news hard? Would she want to come live with them? Bella wished that he'd hurry home so that she'd have some answers.

She tucked the letter into its envelope and sighed. If only her future was more secure, Bella could look forward to her new life in town. But right now all she felt was fear of the unknown.

Watching Philip with the boys the night before reassured her that the boys would be safe and cared for, no matter what happened to her. Her gaze moved to the kitchen window. Sun filtered through it, promising a beautiful day.

Bella walked to the front door and opened it. She heard sounds of laughter and shouting that told her that the boys were downstairs playing in their room and she grinned. If she wanted a few minutes of silence, she'd have to go outside. Pulling her coat off the nail, Bella quickly put it on and closed the door behind her.

She heard the sound of horses long before she saw either of them. Philip rode in hard on her left just as Thomas slid to a stop in front of the porch.

Thomas jumped from his horse with a wide smile on his face. He waved an envelope as he climbed the porch stairs. "Special delivery for one Bella Young.

Well, it says 'Bella Wilson,' but we all know it's you." He laughed.

Philip leaped from his horse. He thundered up the steps much like Thomas had done moments earlier. "Give it to her." He shoved his brother.

Thomas handed the letter to Bella. She flipped it over and read the address aloud. "'From the law office of Jeremiah Jenkins.'"

She looked up at Philip. "What do you think it says?"

He grinned. "You won't know, honey, until you open it."

Honey. He'd called her "honey" again. Her heart soared every time he used the endearment. She stared into his eyes until Thomas cleared his throat.

"Oh!" Bella flipped it over and tore into the envelope. She pulled out the paper inside and read aloud.

"'Dear Miss Wilson, it is our pleasure to inform you that a substantial amount of money has been discovered in trust funds for Caleb Rhodes and Mark Rhodes. According to the Rhodes' will, the funds are to be put in your care and used to help raise the children. Please contact us soon so that we may transfer the funds to a bank of your choice.

Sincerely,

Jeremiah Jenkins'"

Thomas whistled low when she finished reading. "Substantial. That means a lot. Right?" He looked to Bella and then to Philip.

"Yes. It would seem that my sister and her husband took care of the boys financially before their deaths," Bella answered. She looked to Philip. "I need to get a letter back to them as soon as possible. Can we have them put the money in your account at the bank?"

"Yes, or we could open an account in the boys' names and make it so that you can handle that money," he offered.

Bella smiled. "No, we'll put it in your bank. After all, you did tell the boys you were going to adopt them. So you might as well take care of their money, too."

Philip nodded. "We'll make sure that you can sign for their money, as well."

"Well, I guess I should get back to Josephine," Thomas said. "She wasn't feeling too good this morning and will want to know what the letter said." He climbed back on his horse.

"What's wrong with Josephine?" Bella asked.

Thomas grinned. "Just an upset stomach this morning. She's had it for several mornings now, but it usually passes pretty fast."

"Oh, all right." Bella grinned back at him, pretty sure that she knew what ailed her friend. "Thomas, when does the next rider come through?"

He leaned on the saddle horn. "I'm expecting one tomorrow morning. Why?"

"Can you wait just a second and I'll answer Mr. Jenkins's letter? I already have an envelope addressed," Bella said.

"Sure. But you know, it won't go in the manila but inside the rider's pocket, that envelope is locked and will remain so until it reaches its next destination." He climbed down from his horse and rejoined them on the porch.

"I know." She hurried inside to write a quick note back to the lawyers with information on where to send the money. Through the door she could hear Philip and Thomas talking.

"Well, that explains why Marlow wanted to marry Bella so fast. He must have talked to the lawyers before coming out here," Philip said. He leaned against the porch post by the door.

"Yep, makes sense. Get rid of you, marry her and have control over the boys' inheritance," Thomas agreed. "But what about his claim that she murdered her boss?"

"I really think it was just a form of blackmail to get her to go with him. You know, scare her into thinking he was her only rescuer," Philip growled.

Bella sealed the envelope and carried the letter outside to Thomas. "Thanks for bringing me their letter and for taking care of this."

He smiled. "We'll get it to them as quick as possible." Thomas tucked the letter into his front shirt pocket and then got back on his horse.

Philip waved as his brother rode away. He turned to her. "Well, now we know why Marlow was in such a hurry to marry you."

She nodded. "He just wanted the boys' money." Bella watched Philip's face go from happy to thoughtful. "Is something wrong?"

He shook his head. "No, I'd best follow Thomas and see if I can help with the chores." Philip climbed back onto his horse and rode off.

What was that about? She watched him go and sighed, then turned back to the house. When he'd first ridden up, she'd thought he was happy. Since he'd seemed pleased, Bella could only assume that he'd told Hazel about the move and she'd agreed to go with them.

Bella called downstairs, "Caleb, bring Mark up. I want to talk to you boys."

The sound of running feet on the stairs told her they'd heard her summons. She waited for them at the top.

Caleb came out first. "Whatcha want to talk about, Aunt Bella?"

"I was wondering if you boys would like to help me hitch up the wagon and pack a few things to move to town."

Mark danced around. "I'll hitch up the wagon for ya."

"Wait a second, Mark." Caleb rubbed his chin. He looked up at her. "Aunt Bella, shouldn't we pack first? Then load the wagon?"

He reminded her so much of Philip when he rubbed his chin like that. She laughed. "I guess you are right."

"Aww." Mark dropped his shoulder and huffed.

Bella reached down and tickled him. "The sooner we pack, the sooner we can hitch up the wagon and head to town."

"I'll get our clothes." Mark dashed down the stairs.

Caleb shook his head. "What do you want me to pack, Aunt Bella?"

"Well, if you would round up the bedding, that would help."

He nodded, then followed his brother downstairs.

Bella smiled as she hurried to the kitchen and pulled out several wooden boxes. She began packing dishes and using tea towels to cushion between them. Wouldn't Philip be surprised when he got home? They'd be all packed up and ready to go.

Chapter Thirty-One

He was a coward. Philip knew he should have already headed home. But when Bella had said Marlow had wanted her just to get to the boys' money, he thought she would think the same of him if he declared his love now. For the last three hours, he'd been trying to figure out how to tell her how he felt and her not think it was because of Caleb and Mark's newly acquired wealth.

The sound of a wagon pulled his attention from the leather bridle he was oiling. He walked out of the barn. Thomas was coming from the pigpen. Both stopped when they saw Bella and the boys pulling into the yard.

Josephine sat on the front porch rocking. She stood and waved to Bella. "Is it moving day?" Josephine called.

Bella laughed. "It's a start. We had a lot more stuff than I realized."

Philip walked to the wagon. "Honey? What are you doing?"

She grinned down at him. "Well, I figured that since we have the house in town, we might as well move into it."

He rubbed his chin. “What about the animals?”

Thomas stepped up beside him. “We can move those over here.”

“Did you want to continue today? It would be really late when we get to town.” Philip couldn’t believe she was in such a hurry to get moved. He wondered if it had something to do with what the sheriff might find out.

“No, but I figured we could maybe spend the night here at the relay station and head out first thing in the morning.” She held up a bag. “But if it’s too much trouble for us to stay here, I packed us an overnight bag. We can go back to our house and leave the wagon here with Josephine and Thomas. By doing so, we’ll get to town faster tomorrow.” Bella looked pleased with herself.

Thomas laughed. “She’s thought of everything. I’m sure there is no problem with you spending the night here.”

Josephine walked toward them. Her face still looked pale from her morning sickness. “Of course you can spend the night.”

The boys had already jumped down from the wagon. “Uncle Thomas, can I go see the pigs?” Mark asked.

“Stay out of the pen,” Thomas answered.

Caleb chased after his brother. “I’ll watch him,” he called back.

The adults laughed when Thomas called after him, “Yeah, but who’s going to watch you?”

The next couple of days were spent moving to town. Mark and Caleb liked their room and were excited to help Philip set up the store.

Over the next two weeks, Bella set up housekeeping in town. Philip couldn’t believe how quickly time passed. Every day that went by, he thought about telling Bella how much he loved her, but he couldn't make himself do so. He never wanted her to think that he'd changed his mind about their marriage of convenience because of the boys' money.

Bella seemed to adapt to town life quickly. The ladies from the church had come by to welcome her and invite her to their Bible study. Another set arrived the next day to invite her to join their quilting bee.

He had to admit it was nicer having lumber delivered to the store than having to haul it out to the farm. However, Philip missed seeing Thomas every day and riding the Pony Express trail.

Caleb had started school that morning. He'd been so excited that he'd almost forgotten his boxed lunch. Mark wanted to go also but was told he was still too young.

The bell jingled over the door. Philip stepped out from behind the wall he and Thomas had built to separate the store from his workshop. Bella and Mark stood inside.

She held up a picnic basket. "Hope you are hungry."

"For your cooking, always," he answered, motioning for them to come back to the workshop.

Bella walked toward him. The sweet scent of sugar and cinnamon drifted with her. When she came even with him, Philip leaned in and took a sniff of her.

"Something smells wonderful," he said.

She slapped at him. "Stop that."

Mark giggled. "It's the sweet rolls." He clapped a hand over his mouth.

Bella narrowed her eyes at the little boy. "You rascal. That was supposed to be a surprise."

"I'm sorry, Aunt Bella. I was just so excited." He looked down at the toes of his boots.

Philip rubbed the boy's hair. "No harm done. The smell gave them away."

The doorbell jingled again.

The sheriff walked in. "Howdy, folks. I hope I'm not disturbing your lunch."

"Not at all, Sheriff. What can I do for you today?" Philip glanced at the chairs, tables and small boxes he'd created, thinking the sheriff might be looking to buy new furniture.

"Nothing today. I'm here on official business," he answered.

Bella's face turned white. "Have you heard something?" she asked, gripping the basket with white knuckles.

He took off his hat and twisted the brim. "I have bad news."

Philip grabbed the closest chair and carried it to where she stood. "Here, sit down." He took the basket from her hands and handed it to Mark. "Son, take this to the workshop and wait for us. We'll be back in just a few minutes."

Mark did as he was told. When he was out of the room, Philip asked the lawman, "What news?"

"Well, part of what Brooks said was truth. I'm sorry, ma'am, but Sam Jackson is dead."

She gasped and covered her mouth. Philip placed a hand on her shoulder. "Are you here to arrest me?"

"Oh, no, ma'am. Sam died at home in his sleep. He wasn't murdered. The Douglas City doctor says his heart simply gave out. I came by to tell you the sad news about your friend, not to scare the life out of you. So sorry." He looked wearily from Philip to Bella.

She sagged. "So it's over. He lied."

"Yes, ma'am. He lied about the murder." He twisted his hat in his hands.

Bella jumped up and ran to him. She hugged him around the waist. "Thank you so much."

The sheriff's shocked look shot to Philip. Philip laughed. "Sheriff, that's the best news we've gotten, ever."

Bella released him. "I'm sorry. I am just so happy. Thank you, thank you." She moved to Philip's side and put an arm around his waist.

The sheriff put his hat back on. "My pleasure. You folks have a good day."

Bella turned and gave Philip a hug. She looked up at him and laughed. "I'm free, Philip. Free to tell you how much I love you, and even though you don't feel the same way, it's all right." She laid her head against his chest.

She couldn't help but think Philip probably thought her terrible, but Bella didn't care. She'd wanted to tell him how she felt since the day Mark had almost drowned. Her love for him was so great she could endure him not loving her back.

Philip pulled her back and looked into her face. "You love me?"

Bella swallowed hard. "I do, more than I can express. I'm sorry, I know we said we'd only be friends, but I love you more than any friend I've ever had." Bella watched his face. The last thing she expected from him was joyous laughter.

He cupped his hands around her face. "Honey, I love you, too. I've wanted to tell you for a long time that I prayed to God, and I realized a few things, making it possible for me to understand that everyone deals with grief differently. Honey, I'm free to love you, too." Then Philip kissed her.

He kissed her like a husband who'd been out of town for far too long. Bella savored his closeness. Her heart sang that they loved each other and now could express that love.

"Aunt Bella, I'm hungry. Can you kiss Philip later?" Mark asked.

She pulled away from Philip and laughed. "Well, if you insist." Bella glanced down at her nephew.

"I do," he answered, then turned toward the workshop.

Philip growled, "He really is a little rascal, isn't he?"

Bella laughed.

Philip pulled her to him for one more sweet kiss.

Her heart pounded in her chest with joy and love. When he released her, Bella praised the Lord that she'd been the woman who had answered the mail-order-bride advertisement that brought them together.

Epilogue

Two months later, Bella and Philip stood in front of their family. Her heart beat rapidly in her chest. They had an announcement to make. One that gave her great joy.

Philip smiled at his family. "Bella and I are expecting our first child."

Rebecca and Seth were the first to reach them and give hugs. Thomas and Josephine were next.

Thomas smiled from ear to ear. "Our kids are only going to be a few months apart." He was pushed to the side by the rest of their brothers and sister.

After all the hugs were given, Seth called everyone to order. "That's wonderful news, Philip and Bella. Our family is growing by leaps and bounds."

Bella looked around. Rebecca was expecting her and Seth's first child together. Josephine was also expecting, and now her. She felt Philip looking at her and turned to smile at him. His family was now her family and she loved them all.

Seth pressed on and asked, "Andrew, do you and Emma have anything you'd like to share?"

Bella smiled. She was happy for Emma and Andrew. They had decided to move out to the relay station and live in Josephine and Thomas's house. Philip had told her that he'd talked to Andrew about taking over his job as station manager and Andrew had accepted. Bella was glad that Andrew and Emma would be living near Hazel. She was sure they would grow to love Hazel as much as Thomas, Josephine and Philip did.

To her surprise, Andrew and Emma stood. It seemed kind of a funny thing to do just to tell the family they were moving.

Andrew cleared his throat and looked at Emma. "I think I'll let Emma tell you."

Mark looked up. "Tell us what?"

"That we're going to have a baby, too." Emma beamed.

Once more the festivities began. Since they were sitting closest to Emma and Andrew, Bella and Philip each congratulated them.

Philip grabbed Bella's hand and pulled her into the kitchen, where he wrapped her in his arms. He held her close for several long moments before releasing her enough to still hold her but let her have room to look up at him.

"What was that for?" Bella asked.

He smiled at her. "I'm sorry that Andrew and Emma stole your moment to shine."

Bella laughed. "They did no such thing. I'm happy for them."

Philip kissed her quickly on the lips. "Have I told you how happy I am that you and the boys were my special delivery package?"

"Yes, but I can live my whole life hearing you say it again and again."

Philip pulled her close and whispered in her ear. "I love you, Bella Young. You were a special delivery from the Pony Express, but more important, from God above. I am a blessed man."

She rested her head on his chest and listened to his steady heartbeat. Bella knew she was the one who was blessed. "I love you, too." These were the moments she loved. The moments she'd been waiting for all her life.

* * * * *

Dear Reader,

Writing Philip's story was fun. Bella and the boys were just the special delivery he needed to make his life interesting. Years ago my husband, James, came up with the idea of sending a mail-order bride on the Pony Express. I liked the general idea and tweaked it a little for Philip's story. I hope you enjoyed meeting Philip and Bella and the boys as much as I did. Feel free to connect with me on Facebook and Twitter. Also, if you'd like to receive my newsletter, email me at rhondagibson65@hotmail.com. I love connecting with my readers. You may also write to me at: Rhonda Gibson, PO Box 835, Kirtland, NM 87417.

Warmly,
Rhonda Gibson

COMING NEXT MONTH FROM
Love Inspired® Historical

Available April 4, 2017

THE RANCHER'S SURPRISE TRIPLETS
Lone Star Cowboy League: Multiple Blessings
by Linda Ford

After stumbling on triplet orphans abandoned at the county fair, rancher Bo Stillwater's not sure what to do with them. But when he leaves them in the care of the town doctor's lovely spinster daughter, Louisa Clark, he finds he can't stay away—from her or the babies.

COWBOY HOMECOMING
Four Stones Ranch • by Louise M. Gouge

When cowboy Tolley Northam returns home, he's determined to finally win his father's approval. Perhaps a marriage to family friend Laurie Eberly will help him earn it. But when Laurie discovers *why* he began pursuing her, can he convince her that she holds his heart?

UNDERCOVER SHERIFF
by Barbara Phinney

After a woman, a child and Zane Robinson's small-town-sheriff twin all go missing, the woman's friend Rachel Smith has a plan to find them. But for it to work, Zane must pose as his brother and draw out anyone involved in their disappearance.

FAMILY OF CONVENIENCE
by Victoria W. Austin

In need of a father for her unborn child, mail-order bride Millie Steele agrees to a marriage in name only with single father Adam Beale. But as she grows to love her new children—and falls for their handsome dad—can their convenient family become real?

When local rancher Bo Stillwater finds abandoned triplet babies at the county fair, the first person he turns to is doctor's daughter Louisa Clark. But as they open their hearts to the children, they might discover unexpectedly tender feelings for one another taking root.

Read on for a sneak preview of
THE RANCHER'S SURPRISE TRIPLETS,
the touching beginning of the series
LONE STAR COWBOY LEAGUE: MULTIPLE BLESSINGS.

"Doc? I need to see the doctor."

Father had been called away. Whatever the need, she would have to take care of it. She opened the door and stared at Bo in surprise until crying drew her attention to the cart beside him.

"Babies? What are you doing with babies?" All three crying and looking purely miserable.

"I think they're sick. They need to see the doctor."

"Bring them in. Father is away but I'll look at them."

"They need a doctor." He leaned to one side to glance into the house as if to make sure she wasn't hiding her father. "When will he be back?"

"I'll look at them," she repeated. "I've been my father's assistant for years. I'm perfectly capable of checking a baby. Bring them in." She threw back the door so he could push the cart inside. She bent over to look more closely at the babies. "We don't see triplets often." She read their names on their shirts. "Hello, Jasper, Eli and Theo."

They were fevered and fussy. Theo reached his arms toward her. She lifted him and cradled him to her shoulder. "There,

LIHEXP0317

there, little man. We'll fix you up in no time."

Jasper, seeing his brother getting comfort, reached out his arms, too.

Louisa grabbed a kitchen chair and sat, putting Theo on one knee and lifting Jasper to the other. The babies were an armload. At first glance they appeared to be in good health. But they were fevered. She needed to speak to the mother about their age and how long they'd been sick.

Eli's wails increased at being left alone.

"Can you pick him up?" she asked Bo, hiding a smile at his hesitation. Had he never held a baby? At first he seemed uncertain what to do, but Eli knew and leaned his head against Bo's chest. Bo relaxed and held the baby comfortably enough. Louisa grinned openly as the baby's cries softened. "He's glad for someone to hold him. Where are the parents?"

"Well, that's the thing. I don't know."

"You don't know where the parents are?"

He shook his head. "I don't even know *who* they are."

"Then why do you have the babies?"

For an answer, he handed her a note and she read it. "They're abandoned?" She pulled each baby close as shock shuddered through her. He explained how he'd found them in the pie tent.

"I must find their mother before she disappears." Bo looked at Louisa, his eyes wide with appeal, the silvery color darkened with concern for these little ones. "I need to go but how are you going to manage?"

She wondered the same thing. But she would not let him think she couldn't do it. "I'll be okay. Put Eli down. I'll take care of them."

LIHEXP0317